DISTURBIN

DISTURBING GROUND

Priscilla Masters

Chivers Press • **Thorndike Press**
Bath, England **Waterville, Maine USA**

This Large Print edition is published by Chivers Press, England, and by Thorndike Press, USA.

Published in 2003 in the U.K. by arrangement with Allison & Busby.

Published in 2003 in the U.S. by arrangement with Allison & Busby Limited.

U.K. Hardcover   ISBN 0–7540–8805–7 (Chivers Large Print)
U.K. Softcover   ISBN 0–7540–8806–5 (Camden Large Print)
U.S. Softcover   ISBN 0–7862–4745–2 (General Series Edition)

The text of this Large Print edition is unabridged.
Other aspects of the book may vary from the original edition.

Set in 16 pt. New Times Roman.

Printed in Great Britain on acid-free paper.

British Library Cataloguing in Publication Data available

Library of Congress Cataloging-in-Publication Data

Masters, Priscilla.
    Disturbing ground / Priscilla Masters.
      p.   cm.
    ISBN 0–7862–4745–2 (lg. print : sc : alk. paper)
    1. Women physicians—Fiction. 2. Wales—Fiction. 3. Large type books. I. Title.
PR6063.A833 D5 2003
823'.914—dc21   2002028920

Dedicated to all my friends in South Wales, my family and all my pals at S4C, especially Catrin and Pat. Also to my ultimate heroes—the Scarlets—especially Rupert. I did promise I'd put you in a book one day!

And for those of you that have trouble with the Welsh 'll', simply put your tongue on the roof of your mouth and blow through the back of your teeth. Have fun!

Who in the rainbow can draw the line where the violet ends and the orange tint begins? Distinctly we see the difference of the color, but where exactly does the first one visibly enter in to the other? So with sanity and insanity. In pronounced cases there is no question about them. But in some cases, in various degrees supposedly less pronounced, to draw the line of demarkation few will undertake.

HERMAN MELVILLE (1819–91)

Saturday August 3rd 2002

'You foul, sick-minded HAG.'

She put her hands over her ears. But the voice seeped through her fingers.

'Your mind is sick, diseased. You think things, imagine events. But who will believe you? Everyone knows you are mad. Mad.'

She backed into the corner, whining softly, trying to blot out the words. But it was no use. They were inside her head.

'I know what happened . . . I have the . . .' She wanted to say a word but the voice interrupted her.

'You have nothing.' It was angry. 'You know nothing.' The voice was taunting her—as it always did. 'You don't even know if I am real, do you?'

She was silent. So was the voice. Hoping it had stopped and not just paused she lowered her hands.

It was a mistake. The voice had been waiting to repeat the sneer. 'Who do you think will ever believe anything you say?'

She wanted to protest—to say Esther was her friend. Esther believed her but she dared say nothing. To argue with the voice was to make it angry.

And as it was she was frightened. Very frightened.

1

The voice was merciless. He could always do this—concentrate on her worst fear. 'Have you any idea what it must feel like to have water close over your head?'

She nodded.

'Not to be able to breathe, Bianca?'

'Leave me. Leave me.' She was screaming now.

But the voice continued, relentlessly. 'To feel the water trickle inside your nose, inside your mouth. And from there to fill your lungs, slowly.'

'Please.' Terror was suffocating her.

'Please!' she begged again.

There was no pity. 'Imagine, Bianca, what it must feel like to struggle to breathe.'

She whimpered.

'Tell me. Are you very afraid of water?'

'Very.' Maybe if she agreed with the voice it would stop. If she took her hands away from her ears now she would hear—blessed silence.

Tentatively she moved her fingers down a millimetre. A centimetre . . . Two.

It found her. 'What if all you could see above your head were dark dark waters? And however hard you tried you could never reach the air again, never fill your lungs with anything but filthy, coal-soaked water. Yet that's what you deserve, Bianca. And it is what will happen to you. Because you are quite mad.'

There was no point pleading with the voice.

She had tried it before. Hundreds of times. He never never shut up but always stood on the edge of her mind, waiting to catch her with his cruel words.

She would do anything to make him stop— forever. She tried to beg again for mercy.

Knowing there would be none.

In a sudden flash of lucidity she knew there was only one way to silence the voice. If she was dead it would stop.

She moved. He moved.

And soon the voice was silent.

CHAPTER ONE

Monday August 5th. 10am.

Megan had stopped listening to her patient.

'So you see, doctor. The pain is like hot needles driving through every joint of my body causing me pain like I've never suffered before. I can't get no relief . . . I can't get no sleep. I can't even get comfy at night.'

Part of Megan's mind sifted through facts. Rheumatoid arthritis. Painful, common, virtually untreatable, incurable.

But her eyes drifted towards the window with the rest of her mind.

Even sliced by vertical blinds she knew that outside it was a perfect day. Blue sky, clouds as soft, white and fleecy as the wool on the back of a newly born lamb, birds singing. A yellow sun that shone. Not aggressively enough to burn the skin but sufficient to warm and illuminate the grass to a vivid, Disney green, swaying to a soft breeze. The colours outside were bright enough to make the rows of slate roofs gleam like polished steel and the coal tips behind a wonderful shade of purple. Illuminated by the sun, even Llancloudy displayed colour enough to satisfy the most demanding palette—the colours of Van Gogh, Gauguin, Klee. It was that sort of day. Perfect.

Until it became imperfect. Then the colours would revert to duller tints, sludge browns, slate grey, dark, dingy greens and plenty of black. Sombre, Dylan Thomas's Bible Black. Or maybe they would simply appear to change. Maybe events affected her later perceptions of the changing colours and the reds, blues, yellows and whites had been simply illusion.

As Gwendoline Owen's voice droned on, Megan's wandering attention was snatched by a foreign movement outside. Difficult to decipher through the narrow lines of stiffened linen. But once her attention had been grabbed it was held prisoner. Unlike Gwen Owen's mind which was absorbed with detailed description of her ailment.

'So I took the tablets what you gave me on a prescription, doctor, but they made me repeat my food something awful. I don't know what was worse, doctor, the burning in my stomach or the agony in my joints. For certain I was no better off.' There was more than a hint of accusation, of disgruntlement in both her tone and her words which Megan pushed to the back of her mind. She had rejected the wealthier practices of Cardiff and Swansea, choosing to return, as a native, to her home ground. Why, she sometimes asked herself? And the answer was always the same. Because here she was

needed.

Even by Gwendoline Owen.

Megan focused on the movement outside.

They had built their surgery on the sunny side of the valley, the west side—sunny in the morning at least. Sometimes. Llancloudy was prone to mists—the church in the clouds. By afternoon the sun would have swung around to the West and the surgery would be thrown into shade. Megan was looking through the window at this opposite side of the road, at the dark side.

The purpose built surgery was by the side of the main road that led to nowhere—to the end of the valley and stopped, thwarted by the height of the mountains. Here, halfway down, outside the doctors' surgery, the valley swelled enough to accommodate a small roundabout ringed by a terrace of miners' cottages and beyond that a flat grassy knoll used as a recreation area with a central hollow which formed a pool. It was an old pit pool, once marking a stop for the steam trains that chugged up and down the valley taking their precious cargo of black gold out into the wide world to win wars, fuel trains, power ships, turn engines. Over the years the waters had been polluted with coal dust which had settled on the bottom. The valleys might have been prettied up in recent years. The council might have named the pool Llancloudy Pool but the locals knew better. The old miners who

7

coughed up forty years of accumulated coal dust peered into its sooty, watery depths and reflected. Then they had renamed it Slaggy Pool. And it was towards Slaggy Pool that a crowd of people was gathering.

Megan stood up, approached the window and sharply drew the blinds aside.

Gwendoline Owen continued, seemingly oblivious.

'I was left with a really big quandary. What am I to do? I asked Gwilym. Do I take the tablets and suffer with my stomach? Or do I put up with that awful burning in my joints? And do you know what he said to me?'

Megan was vaguely aware of a brief pause before Gwendoline rattled on again.

'Go and see the doctor.' She left a short, pregnant silence before continuing. *'So here I am, Doctor Banesto. Here I am.'*

At last she stopped. 'Is everything all right, doctor?'

There were two people standing on the edge of the water, staring and pointing downwards. Three people now. More approaching. All staring, shouting, pointing. They'd found something in the Slaggy Pool. Afterwards Megan would ask herself the same question over and over again. Why had she assumed the discovery was of significance? It could have been anything. An old bicycle. A fridge dumped. A pram. Anything. People often tipped things in there. More than once

8

she had witnessed the Council JCB hauling some rusting object out of the pool. So why had she made that jump and assumed the discovery was of an object so unwelcome?

Foreknowledge? Premonition?

Rubbish. They didn't exist. Not in her scientific, medical world. These were explanations manufactured for people who failed to understand reality. It was only later when she freeze-framed each individual shot and matched the sounds to the action that she began to understand how very sensitive human beings are to the abnormal. And she knew what she had instinctively picked up. There had been an excitement subtly mixed with revulsion in the way people were staring at the water's surface. A shrinking back combined with curiosity. There had been one sharp scream. Quickly checked. Some sudden gesture of horror followed by a rejection, a turning away. And she had picked it up.

At last Gwendoline Owen stopped speaking, her sharp ferrety eyes boring indignant holes into the doctor's back. Only then when she failed to will the doctor to respond did she finally relinquish her few minutes of exclusive consultation time, rise stiffly to her feet and join Megan at the window. And now that the doctor had swept back the blinds completely, even with her typical invalid's self absorption, Gwendoline registered that there was something very strange about this morning.

She was already selecting her words ready to gossip at the Co-op on her way back home.

'The doctor wasn't listening in the first instance. Staring out the window, she was. No doubt thinkin' about . . .' And the gossips would sagely nod their comprehension. They knew exactly what the doctor would be thinking about. 'And then halfway through when I was explaining to her about my arthritis she just got up and pulled the blinds right back. All the way.'

And because it was now obvious—even to her—that Megan was oblivious to anything inside the surgery, Gwendoline Owen stood at her side and took her first real look out of the window.

The crowd was thickening around the pool and pressed so close together Megan could no longer see any glimpse of the surface of the water. There were so many people they spilled out onto the road, careless of the passing traffic which was slowing as it reached the border of the pool. A car swerved to avoid a child. The driver expressed his anger with a sharp blast on his horn. And still the people hurried along the road towards the pool. Twenty, thirty. Megan stood, riveted to the spot, her hands spread along the sill, her eyes glued to the backs of the people nearest the water. Someone must have summoned the emergency services. A police car slid into view, bossily proclaiming its status with a screaming

10

siren and flashing blue light which shifted the pedestrians. As though it were a tableau Megan carried on watching as two burly, uniformed policemen elbowed their way through the crowd, shoving people out of the way. And even though the window was only open an inch to allow the entry of the faintest whisper of summer breezes, Megan knew the people had finally hushed.

By her side Gwendoline Owen broke the silence.

'What on earth is going on out there then, doctor?'

'I don't know.' *She only knew already that it was something that would change the primary colours of the day from those on a child's palette to the terrible insane depths of Gericault.* Her eyes flicked to the picture on her wall and back outside.

Gwendoline Owen's sharp, small eyes burned with inquisitiveness as she peered through the glass. 'Don't you think you should offer your services, doctor?'

But Megan could see no justification. She didn't know what was happening.

'I don't know, Mrs Owen. I don't know.'

'Perhaps you should just see. Maybe someone's been hurt.'

It was more than that. But even so Megan opened the window wide and called across the street. 'Hello. Can I help?'

No one took any notice. Probably no one

11

had heard. Their attention was all directed to the front.

One of the policemen had vanished into the crowd. The other was moving traffic on with brisk arm movements. Gwen Owen's eyes were aflame with morbid fascination. 'What do you think it is, doctor?'

Megan shrugged. 'I don't . . .'

'Well it looks to me as though . . .'

Say it.

Say it.

The crowd dropped back. Words drifted in through the open window.

'It's a person.'

'Alive?'

'Don't be daft.'

'It's a woman.'

'Looks like she fell in and drowned.'

Someone echoed the words. 'Drowned, she did.'

Gwen turned away from the window for no more than a second. 'Well,' she said with relish. 'What do you think of that? Someone's dropped themselves into the Slaggy Pool.' She twisted back to stare out of the window. 'I've always said it was an accident waiting to happen. And now it has. A miracle that it wasn't a child.' And with the Valley's love of just retribution falling on the heads of sinners she added righteously, 'Someone drunk, I wouldn't be surprised.'

Megan could think of nothing to say.

12

And in a village sealed in by mountains and with only one road in—or out—Gwen Owen's next sentence was predictable. 'I wonder who it is.'

She shifted slightly towards the door, patently anxious to join the growing crowd of voyeurs and find out for herself. And again she prompted Megan, 'Per'aps you should go over, doctor. Offer your services. Just in case . . .'

Megan closed her eyes briefly. *Did people believe she had magical powers? That she could raise the dead? This was not a person who had tumbled in seconds or even minutes ago. If it was a person—a woman—they were dragging from the Slaggy Pool—that person was dead. Dead beyond resuscitation.*

*   *   *

But habits die hard. She had a responsibility both towards the living and the dead of this place. Megan moved towards the door. She should show willing at least.

She opened the door and moved down the corridor towards the reception area, Gwen Owen stomping heavily behind her. Ten yards from the counter she realised they were coming for her anyway. One of the policemen was already talking to the receptionist. As she reached the counter he spoke to her. 'Excuse me, doctor. Megan.'

13

Police Constable Alun Williams who years ago used to kiss her behind the bike sheds at the Comprehensive School when they'd both been sixth formers. Since then she'd slogged her way through medical school and a gruelling GP training scheme scanning the slums of Cardiff docks and he had remained here to become a Police Constable.

He was waiting for her reply. He always had been good looking. The best that the Welsh could possibly offer. A forward lock on the school rugby pitch. A huge, strong frame that complemented the leggy seventeen-year-old she had been. He had been the hero of every single game, the only reason she had stood, shivering, at the touchline of countless school league rugby games. She, the swot, honoured by his attention.

*   *   *

And she saw in his honest face that he remembered something of their old relationship as he smiled down at her. 'Doctor,' he began again. Awkwardly. And again, 'Megan. Someone's . . . You wouldn't come and have a look, would you?'

'Of course.'

He might still make her blush but he had lost the power to make her heart miss beats.

She returned to her surgery just long enough to pick her stethoscope from the desk, apologise in the corridor to Gwendoline Owen and invite her to wait or make another appointment even though she knew the old gossip would be unable to resist following her out. Despite the arthritis she was already snapping at her heels like an impatient terrier, her bright, inquisitive little eyes anxious to miss nothing. Calmly Megan Banesto followed Alun Williams out into the sunshine of that imperfect day.

CHAPTER TWO

Moments later she was staring down at the dripping, sodden mess that had been one of her patients and forming incongruous thoughts. It had been a strange name, Bianca, for a woman who had probably never left Wales. Almost certainly neither she nor her parents had ever visited Italy. But then so much more than simply her name had been odd about Bianca Rhys.

$$*\qquad*\qquad*$$

And it had ended in this.

Megan took in the rim of people, nosily watching. Always a few to explain as though the others were blind—or stupid.

'It's the doctor. Come to see her.'

Alun Williams was watching her expectantly. So—pointless as she knew the action to be—she knelt beside Bianca in the damp grass and unbuttoned the dress. A familiar one. Tangerine flowered crimplene missing a belt and a couple of buttons, now streaked with coal-water, sticking to the thin body, a vague aroma of sweat still clinging to it. Immersion in the Slaggy Pool had hardly diminished the scent of cigarettes and body odour. Megan put her stethoscope over the spot which should echo a heart beat. Not for at least a day it hadn't. She knew the signs. Washer-woman hands, the beginnings of putrefaction, bloating and discoloration. And she made other observations too, broken fingernails solid with black dirt. Having fallen in, had she tried to escape the Slaggy Pool?

Someone stepped forward. The other policeman. Not Alun. It was difficult to hear what he said with the earpieces of the stethoscope both in. She removed them and he repeated his question.

'I said, doctor,' A stagey, carefully mouthed shout, 'can you pronounce life extinct?'

Megan nodded and stood up.

'We'd better get the police surgeon over then and the SOCOs to take a couple of pictures.' She knew Nigel Jenkins less well. He had been a couple of years behind her at school. A slow ponderous character with pale, freckled skin, sandy hair and eyelashes. 'We

16

can move her then, you see, once you've done that.'

Megan faced him. 'Yes. She's dead. For at least twelve hours I'd say.'

Surely they should at least cover the body from curious eyes? Megan glanced downwards. Hers were open. Sightless.

She closed the lids and they stayed shut.

*   *   *

Alun Williams stepped forward. 'Megan?' She swivelled round. Tall herself, she only reached his shoulder. It was a good, reassuring feeling, this solid Welsh manliness, as typical of a race as Guido had been typically Italian, short, snake-hipped, olive skinned with white, white teeth. Alun's face was more red than olive. He stood more than six feet four. And she knew he'd lost his front teeth in a rugby scrum while still at school. The two incisors must be implants or on a plate.

'Megan,' he said again and she studied him properly. He must have helped drag Bianca from the water and slide her onto the bank. His uniform was wet, the trouser legs dripping, a dark tide mark just below the knee.

'When possible . . .' He spoke woodenly, 'we like to get them pronounced dead at the scene. Then they can be taken straight to the morgue. Saves a lot of trouble later. Red tape. Easier on the relatives.'

She nodded, knowing Bianca had only the one relative. A daughter. And she would be relieved that the embarrassment that had been her mother was removed so expediently from the scene.

Megan glanced around, trying to ignore the audience of gossiping people.

'Well, there's a thing.'

'Always said that pool should be fenced off.'

Gwendoline Owen in full and hearty voice. *'I always thought she'd come to a peculiar end.'*

'What do you think happened?'

'She must have slipped and fallen in.'

But the grass was dry except the spot where the body lay. The only mud had been created by the water streaming from Bianca's clothes. There had been only a little light rain in the last couple of weeks. And she had seen Bianca herself on Friday when the grass surrounding the pool would also have been damp but not slippery. Megan was already trying to piece together the facts.

But what was the alternative to an accidental slip?

'So what then?' she asked Alun. 'After the police surgeon's done his work?'

'We'll get her taken down to the mortuary, inform the Coroner. There'll have to be a postmortemm, of course, but I daresay it'll only find out what we already know.'

They both looked down at the figure. Small, dark rivulets still trickled back towards the

18

pool like the delta of an Indian river, meandering and slow.

Take her up tenderly. Lift her with care. Phrases of a poem her grandfather used to read to her drifted unbidden but appropriately through her mind.

'You know who it is, of course, Megan?'

She smiled at him. 'The minute I saw her hair.'

It had been yet another strange aspect of Bianca. The pink hair. She must have been seduced by the picture of chestnut locks on the front of a box of hair dye. Forgetting, of course, that hair prematurely whitened, would turn pink rather than chestnut—or plum—or any of the other descriptions on the side of the box. And she wouldn't have either read or understood the caveats. So Bianca Rhys had further drawn attention to her strangeness by topping that odd head with even odder pink hair.

Megan kept her eyes trained on Bianca's face and felt a bleak cloud of sadness. So Bianca's eccentric life was over in this dark, village setting. There would be no more requests for late night visits to check some manifestation of paranoia, plugs that ticked, radios that listened, water tanks that whispered threats. Or stories that sounded more like science fiction than clinical emergencies. No more paranoid accusations against neighbours or tales of poisoned food.

19

No more injections of Largactil or Haloperidol in an attempt to quieten the voices that ordered, threatened, whispered or confided.

Megan smiled. For her it meant no more hanging around for the duty social worker to sign the Section 29 form of the Mental Health Act to commit her patient, always against her will, to a psychiatric institution for her own and the public's safety. Megan should have felt relief. Instead she felt only sadness. Because, like her ex-husband, Bianca would never exasperate her again. And even irritation can be preferable to a void.

Alun Williams ventured an opinion. 'Looks like she's drowned herself.'

Megan smiled at him too. His character always had been advertised by his appearance. Stolid, solid. Predictable, sensible. Unimaginative. Obvious.

She wished she had less imagination. That her mind didn't constantly ask questions. How could it have happened? How exactly? An accidental trip? Arms flung out. Choking surprise.

'I would have thought it unlikely,' she said. 'She had a horror of falling into water. Hated trips to the seaside and that sort of thing.'

Had it been deliberate? Had Bianca been a suicide risk? Maybe the questions were already flitting through her mind like flies up and down a sunny window because due to her dual role—patient's GP and first medic on the

20

scene—she would be asked this particular question by the Coroner.

'Was Bianca Rhys a suicide risk?'

And her answer?

She had never thought so. Not suicide. Not something so planned and structured because Bianca's mind was incapable of being either. But who could really know? She never had been able to assess Bianca's mental state with any degree of confidence. Partly because the workings of her mind had been so tortuous, so different and unpredictable and partly because her mental state had made her emotionally labile, shifting through anger, curiosity, terror and ecstasy all within the whirlwind space of a fleeting moment. And, once discarded, the old emotion was not only dropped but forgotten. Completely. Bianca would have moved on to another state of mind. Like the lands at the top of Enid Blyton's Faraway Tree, once abandoned they were out of reach.

Even standing on the edge of the Slaggy Pool on that warm August morning, Megan acknowledged that this was the first time she had ever felt quite comfortable in Bianca's presence. The schizophrenic's unpredictability had made even her own doctor wary of her, during each consultation preparing for the paranoia that would one day, inevitably, turn patient against the doctor who had tried her hardest to help her. And now, for the first time able to ignore Bianca's threatening mental state, she was able to observe her physical condition without distraction. She hadn't realised how thin and wasted her patient had become. Little more than a collection of sticks in a bag of skin. *Fashioned so slenderly.* Again Hood's poem put her thoughts into words, the motionless form of Bianca providing only one movement, the water still streaming back into the pond from her clothes, her hair and her skin, as though her very body had been saturated with the filthy water. Megan pulled away a frond of pondweed from between her lips and tidied back a strand of hair, at the same time recalling one of many peculiar conversations she had had with her patient. 'I dye it chestnut,' she had confided to her doctor, 'so that people will realise.'

'Realise what?' But Bianca's answer had been no answer but the usual mixture of half truth and half fantasy. 'I only hope the birds won't think of nesting in it,' she had said with a broad wink. 'Chestnuts is such a big tree.'

*   *   *

Megan looked down again at the huddled body and wondered whether it had been delusion that had finally pushed Bianca over the brink. Or whether despite the supervision of her medication she had somehow managed to hoard it and overdose on the tranquillisers before tumbling into the pool.

22

                    *   *   *

Alun Williams was speaking into his two way
radio, leaving her alone for the moment. The
other uniformed policeman was trying to shoo
the crowd away with friendly banter. 'All right
now you lot. You've had your gawk. Now go
home. Leave the doctor to do her examination
and let the poor lady rest in peace now. Leave
her her dignity. There's a good lot.'

A few of the crowd did shamefacedly obey
but their places at the ringside were soon
replaced with others who had been attracted
by gossip that spread fast up and down these
narrow valleys with their cramped streets of
terraced houses.

Megan hung around, not liking to leave
even though her role here was finished. She
ran her eyes around the watchers, recognised a
few familiar faces and reflected. Bianca had
never had so much attention in life.
Anticipating embarrassment, people usually
gave her a wide berth, tolerating her, even
defending her to outsiders but she'd been
difficult. She'd been known to approach folk in
the street and accuse them of all sorts of
crimes—stealing was the favourite. *Was it you
took my dress from off the washing line?'* Often
tagging on, *'Knickers and all. Quite nice white
ones. With lace on.'* Or, *'Money is missing from
my bag. And I have the feeling . . .'* Small

                            23

wonder people were so uncomfortable in the presence of mental illness. *We translate their weird ramblings into truth. Then half believe it. Only ever half. We never give them the whole credit.*

*   *   *

Megan glanced across the road at the surgery. She ought to go back. But it would look callous to abandon the scene. Alun was still rapping out messages into his two way radio. And Jenkins had returned to the car for something. There was only her to mount guard and wait for the police surgeon and the scenes of crimes officer to trail up from Bridgend. Her gaze fell again on the pink hair. As she bent to touch it she recalled that although the colour must have been a hairdresser's nightmare, Bianca's hair had always been well cut. She must have had the attention of someone else with professional skill besides her medical team, a reasonably competent hairdresser, however hard it was to believe. Strands of it, sopping wet, some of the coal dust speckling the pink in a bizarre, punk pattern. Now Megan was touched with curiosity she had never experienced when Bianca was alive. Who had cut her hair? One of the equally strange people she hung around with? The dispossessed, the mad. The 'care in the community' bunch. Someone handy with a pair

24

of scissors? The hairdresser who attended the Parc mental hospital to which Bianca had been consigned during her more psychotic events? Now she may never know. And before she had not asked. Every consultation had been dealt with as quickly as possible; not prolonged by irrelevant chatter about hairdressers.

*　　　*　　　*

Alun was back. He put a friendly hand on her shoulder. 'Thanks, Megan,' he said. 'I've radioed in and told them.' He scanned the pool. 'Must have slipped in and drowned herself. It's a bit muddy round the edge. I've often thought it was lucky a child didn't fall in. Per'aps we should think about having fencing put round.'

Meggie nodded. 'Maybe,' she said indifferently without pointing out that the rim of the pool would not have been muddy until the dripping body had been pulled from it.

'It's terrible how it often takes a tragedy to get things done—especially by the council.' His blue eyes met hers. 'Mind you, she was such a funny old stick. Caused us no end of trouble.'

'Really?'

'Always callin' us out she was, sayin' someone was breakin' in, stealin', that the next door neighbour had killed someone and hidden the body down the mine, that she knew things about people tellin' lies, that the TV

25

aerial on the top of the house was takin' messages from aliens. It went on and on. Accusations all the time. And I expect she was the same with you?'

Megan merely smiled. It was no use him fishing around for medical detail. By the laws of confidentiality she could not divulge even what had been the commonest of knowledge. That Bianca Rhys had been a paranoid schizophrenic. In layman's parlance, *nutty as a fruit cake.*

Alun tried again. 'Got a daughter, hasn't she?'

'That's right. Carole Symmonds.'

'Then I'd better send someone up there right away.' He looked troubled. 'One of the WPCs. I wouldn't want her to find out about this . . .' His head jerked back towards the sodden heap of clothing. *Strange how we can acknowledge the clothes containing a dead person easier than the corpse itself.* ' . . . through one of these people.' He scanned the ring of people constantly shifting around the pool. Thinning now.

The crowd was, at last, beginning to disperse. *Short work to travel up to the head of the valley to Carole Symmond's door.*

'I'd better get back.' Her feet turned towards the red brick health centre. 'There's nothing more I can do here. Shall I get you a blanket to cover her?'

Alun nodded. 'Thanks.'

26

He stared down at his shoes. 'You knew her well?'

Everyone knew her well. Everyone in this claustrophobic village that masqueraded as a town.

'She was a patient of mine.'

It was pointless to obey the Medical Defence Union's directive for confidentiality. She and her two partners were the only GP group serving the valley. Bianca had to be one of their patients.

It was too obvious a fact to be a secret.

'Can you think of a reason why she might have . . . ?'

Knowing Alun's missing words were, 'committed suicide' or more likely 'topped herself', Megan shrugged. Who knew what motives these people could dredge from their aberrant minds to justify a mortal dive into a filthy pond. It could be anything. An escape from an alien invasion; a search for the lost city of Atlantis; swimming with brilliantly coloured fish; hiding from a tiger; a conviction they could dive without oxygen; a lack of recognition that ponds were not paths; a desire to escape the ever-bidding voices of schizophrenia. The list was infinite.

'I can't say,' she said simply. 'I'm sorry, Alun. I can't. You might try speaking to Doctor Wainwright, the consultant psychiatrist. She was a patient of his.' *And even disclosing that tit-bit had crossed the hidden line of secrecy.*

27

'Was she due some . . . medication?'

The straight answer was no. Megan had given her her monthly injection only three days ago, Friday. Bianca's mental state should have been stabilised temporarily. 'I'd have to look at my records,' she said, adding regretfully, 'you know we can't divulge.'

Alun put a hand on her shoulder then. 'But she's dead now, Megan. There isn't any point in keeping secrets about her. It'll all have to come out at the inquest.'

'Even dead she has her rights. As do her family,' she said uncomfortably. 'I can't simply give you all her medical . . .'

His hand was on her arm again. 'I know that, Meggie. Sorry. I'm sorry for asking.'

She smiled at his use of her pet name again. He always had been swift to apologise when he believed himself in the wrong. But if he was convinced he was right it was a different story. Not the penitent. Something else. Some steeliness that she had witnessed on more than one occasion. 'It's OK.'

'And the coroner will probably want you to . . .'

'Give a statement? Attend the inquest? It's OK, Alun,' she said again. 'I do understand.'

Afterwards she felt she should have done more than simply lend a blanket. But it was all she could do—at that time. Lend a blanket, return to her morning surgery. And to her irritation, as she crossed the road Gwendoline

28

Owen detached herself from the crowd and followed her back into the health centre. 'I realised our consultation wasn't quite finished, Doctor,' she said, 'but I didn't mind waiting.' Her bright eyes glistened with curiosity. 'I wonder what happened. What do you think, Doctor?'

'I can't say.' Megan knew she sounded excessively brisk. She gave her patient a brief smile. 'Look, Mrs Owen. I'm sure you can appreciate. Time's short. I'm very behind in my work. I have to get out on my visits. Why don't you make another appointment.'

It was deferring the problem. But for today she had had enough.

'That's all right by me,' Gwen Owen said, obviously piqued. 'But I still don't know what to do. Do I take the tablets for the pain and suffer with my stomach? Or do I . . . ?'

Suddenly Megan felt depressed at the self centred attitude of the chronically sick. 'I'll change your prescription for the pain killers.'

CHAPTER THREE

Megan had two partners. And when she arrived for evening surgery on that balmy evening they were both standing in the reception area, talking. Not hard to guess what about.

At least it wasn't about her this time.

Phil Walsh spoke first. 'Trouble this morning?'

'Bianca. They found her drowned in the Slaggy Pool.'

'Nasty.' He put a friendly hand on her shoulder. 'But it's funny how many of these elderly schizos come to a sudden and violent end. I was reading an article the other day about it. Apparently they fall victim to assaults, accidents. Prevalence much much higher than the general public. Still upsetting for you though.'

'Yes.'

'Andy' was her other partner. They called him Andy. Staff and patients alike. Because his real name was unpronounceable to Welsh tongues. So they didn't even try. And calling him 'Andy' seemed to make him one of them. He was a handsome, turbanned Sikh with flashing dark eyes and white teeth. A hardworking partner.

'So. Rhys finally topped herself. Not a surprise.'

'We don't know she was trying to drown herself. She might have slipped in accidentally.'

'Oh come on, Megan,' Phil Walsh interrupted with a touch of impatience. 'She had a self destruct button. She was always slicing through her arms with razor blades. You must have seen the scars.'

30

'Yes. Couldn't miss them,' Andy agreed.

Megan picked up her box of notes from the receptionists' counter. 'Self harming was one of things she did, I agree. If she'd accidentally hit an artery and bled to death I wouldn't have been a bit surprised. But this . . .' She abandoned the sentence.

'She had a great habit of swallowing all her pills at once too,' Andy said. 'That's why the psychiatric nurse went in every day to check her.'

Phil Walsh interrupted. 'Did she check her this morning?'

'I doubt it,' Megan said drily. 'She'd been in the water for some hours when I saw her.'

Phil persisted. 'So why didn't Pauline Carver report the fact that she was missing?'

'Because as usual Bianca had fallen out with her. Asked her to leave the tablets with a neighbour, Doris Baker, who in turn administered them to Bianca. It made things terribly difficult. But then Bianca was not the easiest of patients.'

'She was such a nutcase,' Andy said, still smiling, 'nothing should surprise us about her.'

'Nothing except this,' Megan said slowly. 'She was absolutely terrified of water. You know that, Andy, she was your patient before you fell out. She wouldn't go near any body of water—the river, ponds. Absolutely refused to even visit the seaside.'

'Sensible woman,' Andy muttered.

31

'Yes but it wasn't because of the trippers. It was because she really was frightened,' Megan persisted. 'She wouldn't take a bath. And you would have thought Pauline Carver was trying to murder her one day when she tried to get her under the shower. Bianca ran out of the house screaming she was being drowned, she was. She was absolutely starkers too. And it was in the middle of winter. Freezing night.'

Phil lifted his eyebrows. 'Streaking through the streets of Llancloudy?'

All three of them laughed but Megan soon sobered up. 'No—really. Keeping her relatively hygienic was very very difficult. I'm surprised at her going up to the pool—let alone being close enough to slip in.'

And both her partners nodded their agreement.

Phil Walsh wrinkled his nose. 'I can remember the smell after a consultation,' he said. 'It was so disgusting I had to open the windows and use half a tin of air freshener before I could see another patient.'

'But she *must* have slipped in the pool,' Andy said. 'What other explanation could there be?'

'I don't know.' Megan spoke reluctantly. 'Except that she wouldn't have been able to swim. Not that it's deep enough anyway. She must have felt herself slip and panicked. Just like a child falling in shallow water. They *could* get out but they don't.'

32

She closed her eyes for a second.

'You all right?'

Sirwan was watching her, concern furrowing his forehead. 'Yes, yes. I'm fine, Andy.' She tried to laugh it off then realised both were watching her with the same concern. They needed some explanation. 'It's a poem. *The Bridge of Sighs*. By Thomas Hood. It was my grandfather's favourite. About a woman who drowned herself. Keeps running through my head.' She laughed again. 'Doing my head in, as they say.'

Andy gave her one of his warm smiles. 'It's been a shock for you, seeing her dragged from the water, having to identify her. When you knew her so well.'

'I didn't enjoy it,' she replied stiffly.

Phil Walsh grinned. 'You've had a tough time recently. Come round for supper one night with me and Angharad.'

Megan flushed. 'I'd love to. Thanks.' She and Angharad had been at medical school together—and then survived their house jobs—before twin sons had cut short Angharad's medical career.

'Good.' He was still watching her carefully. 'Got any holiday planned?'

What was the point? What was the fun of going anywhere—alone? Most of her friends were married, had husbands to holiday with. She had only one single friend—at the moment. It was a time of adjustment, this newly single status. Of

33

course there were always Singles Holidays. She winced.

'I'll get away later on in the year. At the moment I'm still sorting out the new place.'

'Ah yes. And how are you settling in?'

'I'm just about getting straight—apart from getting the shower adjusted so it doesn't either scald me or try and turn me into a human ice block.'

Andy grinned at her. 'Had the same problem myself,' he said, 'but I do know a good plumber.'

And so the conversation veered away.

*   *   *

It was on the next day that the Coroner's office contacted her.

'We understand you were attendant on the recovery of the body of Bianca Rhys from Llancloudy Pool on Monday morning?'

'That's right.'

'And you were also the deceased's doctor?'

'Yes.'

'The postmortem will be this afternoon. Is there anything you feel the Coroner ought to know about the deceased? Anything relevant?'

'She was a schizophrenic receiving medication.'

'One of the . . .' She could hear the assistant leafing through documents, 'antipsychotics?'

'Yes.'

34

'Would they have made her drowsy?'

'Very possibly.'

'And her condition was well controlled?'

'Reasonably,' Megan answered cautiously.

'You hadn't been concerned about her mental or physical condition in the last fortnight?'

'Not especially.'

'Well—we'll see what the postmortem turns up but I would think the pathologist will be quite happy with an open verdict considering her mental state. Balance of mind—and all that.'

'So no open inquest?'

'Should suit the relatives. She's just got the one daughter. That's right, isn't it?'

It crossed her mind then that she should visit Carole Symmonds.

It proved unnecessary.

*　　　*　　　*

Carole Symmonds barged into her surgery on the following day. She was a hugely overweight woman in her thirties with short, bleached blonde hair which was badly cut and stuck out in all directions. Whoever had cut her mother's hair had not extended the privilege to the daughter.

Carole plonked herself down in the protesting chair and dabbed her eyes with a tissue. 'I heard you found her, doctor. I just wanted to know.'

Megan already knew what she was going to ask.

'Did she suffer?'

It was always easier to lie. Easier on the doctor, easier on the relatives.

But it wasn't always the truth.

'I'm sorry. I just don't know,' she said.

'That damned bloody pool.' Carole Symmonds had found something to vent her anger on. 'Ought to be filled in. It's a bloody miracle some child didn't fall in. As it was . . .' The bitterness was making her voice harsh. 'I suppose the council won't act in response to some old nutcase topping herself in it.'

And for the second time in two days Megan found herself taking an opposing stance to the suicide verdict. 'We don't know she intended suicide.'

'No—nobody knows and nobody bloody well cares either. Perhaps it was just an accident. Quite honestly,' Carole gave a harsh laugh. 'I don't suppose we'll ever know what my mother was intendin'. Mind you. It's probable she didn't know what she was intendin'. Off her bloody rocker she was no matter what tablets and injections you gave her. They never made her sane. Just easier to control.'

Megan felt admonished, nakedly exposed. Bianca's daughter was right. The medication had not normalised her mother's mental state

36

but had made her less of a social and medical nuisance. To divert Carole's focus she inserted a question of her own. 'Was she in the habit of frequenting the Slaggy Pool?'

A touch of humour brushed Carole's lardy face. 'At least they're doin' Mum the courtesy of callin' it Llancloudy Pool in the papers. Sounds nicer than that old filthy pond.'

Megan winced as words of the poem flicked again into her mind.

Dreadfully staring Thro' muddy impurity . . .

'No. She never went up there. You know what she was like about water. Well—of all the places she hated Slaggy Pool the most. I think it was the blackness of the water. Hated the place, she did. You know where she liked to hang around, doctor. Outside the Co-op, runnin' through the videos in the video shop, beggin' batter bits from the chippie. I always knew where I could find her—in one of those three places. She never went up to the Rec or the pool. I used to say to her, sometimes—on a nice fine day—*Why don't you go and occupy them seats by the swings* and she'd look at me as though I was the crazy one.' She laughed then mopped her eyes, her face twisted with grief that was softened by humour.

'So what do you think took her up there on that day?' Megan paused to think. 'That night,' she corrected.

'Well—when are we talkin' about?'

'I saw her on Friday, in my evening surgery,

37

to give her an injection. I didn't see her again until . . .' The next time she had seen her patient, Bianca had been stone cold. More than a few hours dead.

'Doris Baker said she gave her her tablets on Saturday morning. The police came to see me Monday late morning. About eleven. They said they thought she'd been in the water some time. No one seems to have seen her from when she swallowed her tablets on Saturday to when she turned up in the Slaggy Pool drowned on Monday. I asked at the video shop and the chippie and at the Co-op and they all said they didn't see her all weekend. Mrs Baker said she didn't see her on Sunday but Esther took the tablets from her and said she'd give them to Mam when she got in. She tried again on Monday and just got hold of Esther again. She was goin' to ring you Monday after your surgery to say it looked like Mam had gone missin'. Then someone told her it was too late.'

'When did Esther Magellan say she'd last seen your mother?' Esther and Bianca had shared a house.

Carole rolled her eyes towards the ceiling. 'You know that old fruit cake. She couldn't remember *when* she'd last seen Mam. And the more we asked her the more hassled she got so in the end we had to leave her be.' Carole Symmonds stood up. 'Look—while I'm here I wonder if you'd give me something to help me

38

sleep. I keep thinking, you see. Goin' over and over it in my mind. I keep seein' her fallin'. You know Mam.' Her dark eyes held a terrible hurt. 'She must have been terrified. She couldn't stand water. For the life of me I'll never know why she went up there. And it must have been in the dark. 'Cos no one saw her go.' She gave a deep, long, why me, sigh that Megan knew she would never be able to answer satisfactorily. Indeed. Why her? The stigma of having a mother so afflicted, so embarrassing, such a responsibility. Always to worry about her 'Mam'. And now. Megan tapped a few keys on the computer and printed out a prescription for sleeping tablets. 'Look,' she said awkwardly. 'Most of these drugs are habit-forming. Be careful. Just use them to tide you over the first week or two. Treat them with caution, Carole.'

She watched her leave with a feeling of disquieted sadness.

CHAPTER FOUR

So now the gossips of Llancloudy had something else to talk about. Something other than the scandal of the doctor's husband running off to Cardiff. And rumour had it that he was not with . . .

Megan put her hands over her ears.

39

Sometimes she could swear she too could hear the whispering, insinuating voices, the malicious, salacious shock at the turn this clean living valleys girl had ended up. When she walked into a shop, a pub, even the surgery, conversation stopped, people would turn to look and the voices breathed just behind her shoulder, murmuring inside her ear.

Gossips had had a field day ever since she had returned from her holiday four years ago with a new husband in tow. That was when they had first turned their attention on to her. *'Went on holiday, she did. To Italy. Met a man there. A foreigner. Married him! Quickly.'* The words had been full of meaning, the implication harping back to the old phrase— that those who married in haste repented at leisure. The chatterers had stilled for the briefest of honeymoon periods before the gossips had sat back to await the arrival of an 'early' baby. None had appeared. But they had still waited. And eventually they had been fed the richest and most satisfying of diets.

'And have you heard the latest. Left her he did—for a . . .'

'No,' the listener would rejoin, right on cue with plenty of shocked horror.

'Ye-es. Ah well—that's what happens when you marry a foreigner. Quickly. Don't really know 'em, do you? Not like someone from here.'

40

They were right. There was safety in marrying a boy from the valleys. Predictability too. You knew his stock. Whereas outsiders . . .

Work had proved a great distraction from personal life, money worries, traumatic events and the grossest public humiliation. Forget it all in a plethora of visits and consultations, prescriptions to be signed, letters to be composed, clinical meetings and medical lunches.

Lunch. Three days after Bianca's body had been found, Megan was queuing up in the local sandwich bar. Maybe it was the heat of the day or the scent of freshly baking bread mingling with herbs, basil, oregano, parsley. It was probably the combination of all factors which evoked acutely painful memories. She and Guido had been married happily—at first. But their marital contentment had lasted less than two years before disintegrating until there was no trace of happiness left. Initially the whispers had been soft and insidious; their marital discord was carefully concealed from the outside world, almost hidden even from the probing ears and the prying eyes of the gossips of Llancloudy who dredged the town for juicy titbits. But like water breaching a hole in a sea wall the force of tittle tattle had gained momentum and the damage inflicted huge.

*   *   *

41

The low point had been a dull, December day when she had finished her surgery unexpectedly early and decided to surprise him with an offer of a peace-restoring lunch out. She had taken no notice of a strange car parked along the road, nor even of the curtains still drawn late in the morning. But when she had unlocked the front door she had known something was strange. And walking into a candlelit lounge to see her husband bent over another man, both of them stark naked, she had flipped.

Even now a waft of some scented candles was enough to make her vomit. The gossips had been wrong. Guido's interest in women had been superficial only. Flirtation to smokescreen his real predilection.

The same day he had gone from her life. But now Megan screwed up her face and allowed herself to recall the early, happy days. During their first two years, on balmy afternoons like this, she had often queued up to buy two sets of sandwiches, a couple of cakes, some flavoured, bottled water and they would meet halfway between the health centre and his restaurant—a point marked by a small chapel and a sunny graveyard. Quiet and peaceful, reminding her of Rupert Brookes and long-ago deaths, nothing too near or too painful, nothing she could be held even remotely responsible for, but as distant as the far off memory of drums beating soldiers to war.

*   *   *

The graves almost all dated from the first half
of the last century—well before this bright
beginning of the millennium. Most of the
stones in this ancient place had lost even their
mourners now. And because the deaths had
been long ago, she and Guido could amuse
themselves reading out loud the inscriptions.
Er Cof. Yn annwyl. Cariad. The Welsh phrases
sounding so much more poignant than their
English equivalents, In memory of . . . Dearest,
Beloved, the stones marking all ages—from
the elderly happy releases to tragic and
multiple deaths of children, early, untimely
and plentiful. Doctor-like she would wonder
what they died of? Infectious diseases,
accidents, genetic disorders, congenital
malformation, malnutrition? The South Wales
mining valleys had witnessed some of the most
terrible, grinding poverty between the two
wars. Tales abounded of the Means Test men,
of the miners' strikes and the vast families
spilling out of tiny homes.

'What sort, love?'

She came to with a start accompanied by a
thrust of panic. She was thirty-one years old.
Young, she corrected. But already she was
beginning to live in the past. She stared at
the assistant in the sandwich bar, patiently

43

regarding her, waiting for her to make up her mind. And she almost felt a confused and pitiful old lady. She ran her eyes along the counter. She and Guido had always had the same sandwiches—egg and cress. Despite the restaurant he had been an almost vegetarian, rarely, guiltily, tucking into huge, bloody fillet steaks before solemnly declaring it had been horrible, disgusting, and he never would indulge again. Until the next time. Meggie caught her breath at the sudden vision of Guido making solemn promises—to love, cherish and obey.

And she had believed him.

'Bacon and egg,' she said firmly, 'and a chocolate covered flapjack and a diet coke.'

Everything must be different. *Everything*. She glanced behind her at the growing, impatient queue.

'One pound eighty five, please, love.'

Meggie handed over two pound coins, waited for the change to rattle into her palm, picked up the plastic carrier bag of lunch and moved outside into the street. The valleys were all this shape, long and narrow. There was only really room for one main street. The others climbed either side in steep terraces. The gardens were slanted too. Coal dust dark, with soil so impregnated with good Welsh coal you could almost believe you could burn it on a fire. But the mud could be a threat too. It was prone to slipping in heavy rain as the slag

44

heap had on that terrible day in Aberfan. The land in these valleys shifted because some of the hills were not real hills but dumps of waste soil, slag heaps deceitfully grown over with grass that never grew as true lush vegetation but always looked half starved of nutrients; pale, poor scrub.

*   *   *

Even the streets were deceitful, the houses built on the catacombs of the ancient mine workings that burrowed beneath most of South Wales. Many of the buildings bore their cracks like the battle scars of a sword slash. The Coal Board would compensate. It was a common enough phrase. And people today were anxious to forget all about the old days and put them behind them. The mines were shut, the tips overgrown or flattened into playing fields, the hollows filled with dark water and renamed—as Llancloudy Pool had been.

*   *   *

A couple of the mines had been opened as museums. *Lest we forget* sorts of places, *Pwll Glo*. Black Gold. Kids were taken down on school trips to teach them about their heritage. But all that people imagined about 'the valleys' was different now. And the kids wanted to forget it all. Every bit of it. The male voice

45

choirs, the chapel, the mines, the dirt, the hardship. All was gone except the real mountains. Nothing could shift those. 'Not even a Conservative Government'. It was the standing joke during Maggie's time. Those mountains and this graveyard remained unchanged. One a sign of stubborn constancy, the other a reminder of mortality. Not that she needed one in her job.

*   *   *

The fleeting thought conjured up the picture of that still dripping body being dragged from the small pond. Meggie frowned, her fingers looped around the handle of the plastic carrier bag tightening. It had been a strange way to die—even for a mad woman. Had no one seen her approach the pool, sensed her intent—if intent there had been. Had no one heard a splash—and wondered—or seen her struggle? Had there been no witnesses?

Megan walked slowly, struggling still with the question of intent. Bianca's mind had been occasionally threatening, frequently downright peculiar. Always unfathomable, invariably illogical.

So why was she, Bianca's doctor, who had seen so many manifestations of her patient's sick mind, disturbed by the fact that she was unable to understand Bianca's final illogical act?

46

*　　　*　　　*

As she continued down the main street she pondered this point and like leafing through the pages of a reference book she found the answer.

Folk in the Welsh Valleys were prone to gossip. Call it a trait of the Welsh. Or maybe it was something to do with the geographical narrowness of the valleys, of the limitation of an area so sealed in by mountains that there was only one road in. And that too was the road out. But, chin up, defiantly Megan had returned from Italy with Guido in tow fully aware that she would be the subject of this gossip. She already knew every row or kiss, quarrel or hug would be the focus of much attention. Maybe the locals had sensed that all was not perfectly right with Guido long before she had, not blinded by romantic love as she had been but guided to trouble by their antennae. But even very early on, soon after their marriage, their sideways glances had been laden with malice. They had wanted her to look foolish. Most of her class chums from the comprehensive had married and had families quickly and had watched her very public exit to Medical School with a tinge of envy. The valleys loved their successes. But they watched them too for signs of it 'going to their heads'. And when Megan had dumped

Alun it had been seen as a sign that she had been too ready to shed her roots. This was considered a bad thing. Her return as a qualified doctor had puzzled them. Why here, she could almost hear them question. She could have gone anywhere—the world. *Why come back?* The answer that they could not work out for themselves was that she loved the valleys. She belonged here. And she wanted to give something back to its inhabitants. Bringing Guido to Llancloudy had alienated her from the locals—as she had known it would. Her early ecstatic happiness had made them shake their heads. *And wait.*

Only Bianca, hesitating one day, after a long, pointless and difficult consultation, had pressed her hand, looked at her with penetrating sincerity and wished her happiness. Staring back into the powdered face with its brilliant red lipstick curved into a clown's smile, Megan had been touched beyond belief.

Now she remembered that day vividly. No one, not even her parents who now refused to even mention Guido's name, had really, truly, wished her luck from the bottom of their hearts. For that she owed Bianca.

She paused outside the gateway to the Bethesda chapel then pushed open the gate. It was a small building of grey stone with brown paintwork and arched windows. A modest building, like most of the Welsh chapels, remnants of the old country. There were still plenty of those, the rows of terraced miners' cottages, derelict mine workings, slag heaps and chapels with Biblical names: Bethesda, Hebron, Carmel, Tabernacle. The geographical narrowness was unavoidable. But today there was a forward looking hope and vibrancy that had been absent from the Wales of her childhood. It lifted her heart as she pushed open the gate.

*   *   *

She suddenly realised she was very happy and very hungry.

A cloud that seemed to have sprung from nowhere blacked out the sun temporarily but she refused to let it influence her intention and rediscovered direction. She would eat here again. Alone. Guido's final humiliating indiscretion would not prevent her doing things she enjoyed—just because she had once done them with him.

But the elements conspired against her. The cloud burst. Heavy rain splashed onto her arms and face. The darkness now seemed to encompass the entire sky. She was forced to shelter inside the doorway.

No reading tombstones today.

The food tasted good. Salty, smoked bacon, a hard boiled egg. Fresh brown bread. Meggie realised how much even the small enjoyment of eating had diminished in the last eight months. Since Christmas time. Guido's seasonal indulgence had been the last straw.

She must stop thinking about him. She had a new life now. One without him. A new home. She was still young-ish. But it was hard to keep her head up. It had been a public humiliation. She, the pinup of the sixth form, dumped in favour of a man. The whispering had started within hours, the gossips conducted like a WI choir by Gwendoline Owen. Everyone quickly knew each small detail.

And now they had a diversion. Bianca Rhys found drowned in a pond little larger than a child's paddling pool. Megan chewed her sandwich thoughtfully and pictured Alun wading in to recover the body. His trousers had only been wet to the knees. Even if Bianca had fallen in she could have stood up and climbed out. Megan frowned. So it was not like the Hood poem, *In she plunged boldly—no matter how coldly?* Neither had it been the accidental drowning of Clementine, *Hit her foot against a splinter. Fell into the foaming brine.*

She smiled. Even with the most poetic imagination the Slaggy Pool could hardly be described as 'foaming brine'.

*   *   *

She finished her sandwich and opened the bag

50

containing her flapjack just as her mobile phone rang.

She fished around for it in her bag. 'Hello?' She was never at her best responding to it when the number display read Anonymous. She liked to know to whom she would be talking and always answered with a cautious, 'Hello?'

'Doctor Banesto?'

'Yes.' The voice was unknown.

'Franklin Jones-Watson here.'

The name meant nothing to her. 'Yes?'

'We haven't met before . . .' A soft, educated, Cardiff voice. 'I'm the pathologist here at The Princess of Wales Hospital. I've just finished the postmortem on a patient I believe was yours who drowned earlier this week. The police said you were first on the scene.'

It was as though a stone had been thrown into the deep, dark waters; ripples forming on its surface. 'We are talking about Bianca Rhys, are we?'

'Yes. I understand from the Coroner's Office that she had a bit of a medical history.'

'She was a schizophrenic.'

A pause.

Her turn to ask a question. 'How long did you think she'd been in the water for?'

'Hard to say. About twelve hours, I think.'

'But I'd have thought her body would have . . .'

'Floated? It was near the surface but according to the police the dress was caught in an old pushchair that had been dumped. And there was some stone thing in the pocket.'

'Her body was weighted?'

'Well—yes. No—not really the stone wasn't that heavy.'

'You're telling me you think she might have drowned herself? Deliberately?'

'Hard to say.'

'I've sent some serum for barbiturates. Hit her head nasty on something in the bottom of the pool too.'

Megan felt a tightening of the muscle at the back of her neck. 'She had a head injury?'

'Done at round about the point of death.'

'But you're not suspicious about it?'

'Good gracious me no. No . . . No I don't think so. I mean you never know with these people what they're going to do next. Talk about unpredictable. Gets hard for us to work it out. How can we ever know what is in the mind of someone who is psychotic?'

'So you're saying . . . ?'

'Balance of mind was disturbed. I can call it accidental death. Easier for the relatives, you know. No need to call it suicide. She might have collected the piece of stone out of interest or as a talisman, or even because she thought it was the currency of Llancloudy.' He laughed. 'Who can know? Anyway. Poor woman. Died quickly. Dry drowning. Not a drop in the lungs at all.'

'She didn't even draw breath?'

'No. Usual vagal inhibition. Shock really.'

Megan didn't know whether to be relieved Bianca hadn't drowned or concerned as she said goodbye to the pathologist. She put her phone back in her bag, gathered up her things and returned to her car.

And so through tacit agreement between GP and pathologist the verdict was passed.

The coroner would not argue.

Schizophrenics can be so tantalising, sliding in and out of the truth. Fantasising with the assurance of sane fact, yet terrified of water. And yet Bianca's most irrational delusion had turned out to be rational after all.

CHAPTER FIVE

Touch her not scornfully
  Think of her mournfully

The words of the poem were still echoing round her mind as she returned to the surgery that afternoon. Bianca's death was still provoking her curiosity so instead of walking straight into her consulting room for her evening surgery, Megan went upstairs to the practice library, selected a pathology book from the shelf, found the chapter on 'dry drownings' and started reading.

'15–20% of all drownings are so called 'dry' in that there is no deep inhalation of fluid. Many of these deaths are very sudden and show no evidence of a significant struggle by the victim. The precise mechanism of death remains speculative. One proposal is that the sudden inrush of fluid into the mouth and throat results in laryngospasm with consequent asphyxia.'

Megan closed the book with a feeling of bleakness. So that was how Bianca Rhys had died. Simple asphyxia.

It fitted.

Her terror at finding herself falling into the filthy pool would have been enough to cause paralysing fear, laryngospasm and death. She would not have dared draw breath.

Only one aspect of Bianca's death did not fit quite so neatly.

What had she been doing up there in the first place?

According to her daughter the pond had been one of the places Bianca had avoided like the proverbial plague. She would not have strolled around it on a sunny afternoon. Let alone on a damp evening. Megan sat very still for a while. It could not have been on a sunny afternoon anyway. Not Sunday. Someone would have seen her. Throughout the day there were always people milling around the place—walking dogs, sitting, gossiping— whatever the weather. And Sunday had been fine. Like the well in Biblical times, the Slaggy

54

Pool had become something of a meeting place, even if it sprouted with urban rubbish—abandoned pushchairs and old Tesco's trolleys—and its grounds were simply a small well trodden patch of grass with two, tiny, non-productive flower beds. Vandals never allowed the council plants to grow. They dug them up and transplanted them to their own gardens or simply urinated all over them after a night out, poisoning the flowers.

So Bianca had fallen in the pool under cover of darkness. On Sunday night, according to the forensic evidence. Megan sat with her chin cupped in her hand and tried to picture this scenario too—and again ran into a problem. Bianca's paranoia had been deep rooted enough to ensure that she rarely left her house after dark. And it wasn't solely the result of psychotic imaginings. The strange figure, with her vivid pink hair, thin enough to have posed for one of Lowry's stick women was a bizarre enough sight. But hunched up, muttering to herself and moving in jerky steps had made her an obvious target for the drunken gangs of mouthy youths which walked the streets of Llancloudy. Once she had been physically attacked—a bottle thrown in her face leaving her with a scar which pulled up the corner of her right eye to add to her bizarre appearance. She was too instantly recognisable as different. To be different is to be noticed. And to be noticed can, in some circumstances, be dangerous.

So it was unlikely she would have wandered near the pool and after dark unless she had a specific reason for going. The trouble was a 'reason' to Bianca might be just about anything. The voices might have ordered her to go there, or she might have believed the pond was filled with money or the gateway to another world. It was even possible that 'the voices' had made her more frightened of staying in the house with Esther than leaving it. Or she might simply have become confused and wandered to the pool without knowing where she was. Maybe the best thing would be to speak to Esther Magellan and the next door neighbour.

Megan smiled, closed the pathology book and wished her mind would stop asking unanswerable questions. The police would surely have followed up these lines of enquiry. It wasn't really any of her business. Her responsibility towards Bianca had finished. She headed back down the stairs and threaded through the packed waiting room.

But as she worked her way through the evening surgery only half her mind was concentrating on her patients. The other half was dipping in and out of Bianca's mind, as though she should not yet abandon her patient. It was almost as though Bianca had some access to her mind and was claiming unfinished business. It was probably because she could not quite banish Bianca from her thoughts that she was not surprised when, at the end of the surgery, the receptionist buzzed through to say that Carole Symmonds had rung, wanting to speak to her. Feeling as though subconsciously she had been waiting for the call Megan took the message and closed her door. She did not want the receptionists eavesdropping.

Carole answered on the first ring. She must have been sitting over the phone. She launched straight in.

'The police have told me about the postmortem.' She sniffed and Megan was acutely aware of the depth of Carole's grief for her mother. She was touched.

At the same time she was wondering exactly what the police had told Carole.

'They told me my mother didn't suffer,' she started. 'That she died before she hit the water. She didn't really drown.'

'Ye-e-s?'

'But I've been thinking, doctor, and there's some things I don't understand.' She sniffed again and Megan knew she was crying.

'Go on,' she prompted.

'Mam wouldn't have *drowned* herself. You know what she was like about water. She couldn't have done it. I've told them about Mam hatin' water and then they suggested she'd accidentally fallen in and what with bein' frightened and her clothes catching on the rubbish in the pond . . .' She stopped. Megan heard a few more sniffs before Carole started again. 'I've got an idea, doctor, of what might have happened and I sort of wondered whether you thought it was possible.' Carole hesitated and Megan sensed her embarrassment. 'Go on,' she prompted again.

'Well—you know what Mam's voices were like. Sometimes they told her to do daft things. And even though she didn't want to she couldn't argue so she'd do anything to try and make them shut up. She told me once they screamed in her ear. Other times they'd whisper. Sometimes they'd sing. Other times they'd hum, tuneless like, like those monks chanting. She *had* to give in to them. The policeman said they found something a bit strange in her pocket. A bit of a statue—or something. If they said to get it—I mean— Mam did collect things.'

'Collect' was a polite word for frank kleptomania. Bianca had been charged with shoplifting on numerous occasions; the empty video cases she was so fond of touching, sweets and other items from the long suffering Co-op. Usually objects she could have no possible use for, babies' nappies, bars of slimmers' chocolate, bags of anything—potatoes, dog food, bird nuts, guinea pig straw—stuffing it all in an ancient brown vinyl shopping bag. The shop owners took her to court, attempted to ban her from their store. But she sneaked in

58

and filled her pockets. She always got off on the same defence so what really was the point? It merely clogged up court time. But although the shop keepers were not unsympathetic to Bianca's diagnosis they were true to the notices pinned up in the front of their shops. They prosecuted every time. And what struck Megan now was that the defence plea which had been trotted out as often as a seaside donkey was exactly the same phrase as was being used now to explain her death. 'Balance of mind disturbed . . .' It was not only an apt phrase to account for aberrant behaviour in a schizophrenic but a very useful phrase which could be used to explain any occurrence, including now her death.

Megan swallowed a smile. 'Yes—she did *collect* things. You're right.'

Carole laughed. 'Empty beer cans, bottle tops, video cases. You name it, doctor. She collected them all. You know what her house was like. And the piles of newspapers. Well—it was ridiculous. Boxes of them. Some dating back to the 1960s. Her place was a fire hazard. And a health hazard. I told her so. So I suppose I shouldn't be that surprised that she had a stone in her pocket.' She paused to breathe in and exhale in a long sigh. 'But it still feels all wrong, see?'

Megan did see, only too clearly. The trouble was she could not picture any other way it could have happened. Bianca's death *must* have been an accident. No one would have wanted to murder her, not in such a hit and miss, cold blooded, calculated way as to first of all lure her to the Slaggy Pool, risking being seen, hit her on the head and push her in. Particularly when she could have paddled out of a three foot pond. But on the other hand the drowning bore none of the hallmarks of a random mugging, apart from the 'head injury'. Megan found herself nodding vigorously in agreement with Bianca's daughter and was relieved she could not be seen.

It did not do to plant doubts in the minds of grieving relatives. Grief alone was enough without asking questions no one would be able to answer. So she gave a non-committal, 'Ye-e-es,' realised she was not being much help or support and waited for Carole to continue.

But Carole was answering her own questions. 'She must have wandered up there and fallen. Just chance she had the bit of stone in her pocket. There's no other way it could have happened.' She still sounded dubious and she had not finished.

'There's another funny thing, Doctor. No one saw her on the Saturday. Not all day. And that's really peculiar—don't you think?'

'Ye-e-s.'

'I've asked around. She wasn't at any of her usual haunts.'

'Did you speak to Esther Magellan?'

Carole's laugh was explosive. 'You know

60

what she's like. Still expects Mam to walk in. It hasn't sunk in at all that she's not comin' back.'

'But did you ask her about the weekend?'

'She doesn't know what day of the week it is, let alone when she last saw Mam.'

'Well, what about Doris Baker?'

'She gave Mam her medication Saturday morning and never saw her again. She says she put it out Sunday but Mam wasn't around. Monday when she saw the tablets were still there she was going to ring the police but then she heard the news and they rang her instead.'

'So you don't really know whether your Mum was home over the weekend or not.'

'Not for sure. But you know Mam. Hung around the shops for her entertainment. She went there every day. That's why they noticed that she wasn't there Saturday or Sunday. I spoke to the girls at the Co-op. They hadn't seen her. I asked at the chippie and I went in the video club. Not one of them had seen her. Not all day Saturday and not on the Sunday either.'

But she had not died until Sunday night. After dark.

'She could have stayed in the house all day.'

'She didn't used to do that.' Surprisingly Carole laughed. 'She didn't do that even if the weather was awful. Used to say stayin' in all day with Esther drove her mad.'

Megan found herself joining Carole's daughter and laughing too with wry humour.

61

But when they both stopped Carole's voice was still troubled. 'And I can't see her going up to that pool after dark. You knew my mam, Doctor Banesto. She *never* went out at night. Barricaded herself and Esther in as though they were under siege. She wouldn't even let *me* in after dark. So why did she go out?'

Megan had met all this before, this pondering over questions that never would be explained. Sometimes it was a necessary part of the grief process. *Why had they gone out? Why hadn't they worn a seat belt? Why had they had that one last drink? Why had they made that final, fatal mistake?* At other times it delayed recovering from grief because it was a pointless, round and round and round again thought process, which led nowhere but back to the beginning. *Why?*

So she fed Bianca's daughter with the empty truth that they would probably never have answers to these questions and Carole Symmonds wound up the conversation. 'Ah well, doctor. I just wanted to go over these few things that have been bothering me, to thank you again for all you did for my mam. She thought the world of you, you know.' Another sniff. 'The funeral's set for next Thursday. Two o'clock at the church.'

'I'll be there, Carole.' It was the final courtesy that could be paid to her ex-patient, one that would be noted and approved in Llancloudy. Funerals were important to the

62

valleys folk.

'She wanted to be buried but she didn't want a tombstone, you see. Didn't like 'em. Said she worried what we'd put on it.'

Megan smiled at the strange request, at the same time almost sympathising with Bianca's suddenly sharp perception. Not wanting a stone of her own must surely be the final anomaly of Bianca's life and death. As she put the phone down she was still smiling. Why should she be surprised at the unusual circumstances of Bianca's death and interment when everything about the woman had been unexpected, unexplained.

She suddenly realised how much she would miss her, leaning against the door of the video shop, falling in every time it was opened, smoking revolting-looking rollups made from a kit housed in a tobacco tin which she replenished not only with Rizlas and shop-bought tobacco but dog ends rescued from the gutter and gifts from the generous valleys folk, or wandering around the Spar or the Co-op with a huge trolley empty except for a battered red leather purse. Megan felt a wave of sadness. Bianca had gone and behind her she had left people memories they could smile at. She would be remembered. She took her bag from the desk drawer. It was time to go home. She stood up, preparing to leave the surgery. But her eyes were caught—and held.

The walls of her surgery were washed in

pale pink with only one picture—a print of a portrait by Gericault. Megan crossed the room and stood in front of it. She knew the title but today, now, it seemed subtly pertinent.

Madwoman afflicted with envy.

She had always loved the painting because it intrigued her. Was it really envy that peered out from the woman's eyes? Not blunt envy as we would understand it but a distortion of the emotion.

'She thought the world of you.'

As she stared at the print her eyes lost focus so it was not Gericault's inhabitant of a French lunatic asylum but Bianca who stared down at her from the pink walls. Wall merged into hair and she stared down at her as though she hated her. Megan was transfixed—as though she had never seen either the painting or her ex-patient properly before. And deep behind the brushwork she seemed to find a frightening dimension of insanity. The expression in the old woman's eyes was a distortion of human emotion. And distorted who knew what it really meant? *'She thought the world of you . . .'*

Megan stared at the painting for a further minute or two. Then she moved, snapped the light off and left the room behind her empty— apart from the mad woman, still staring down from the pale pink walls.

She hurried out of the surgery. It was late. Almost seven thirty. A balmy, golden evening.

64

Time to go home. The receptionists were waiting to lock up. The cleaners had finished. But Megan was pulled back, suddenly aware that she was letting Bianca down. How little she had really known about her patient. She had understood her illness but there were glaring gaps in her life that Megan knew nothing about. And again the Hood poem was supplying the words.

Who was her father? Who was her mother?
Had she a sister? Had she a brother?

Resolutely she turned back, startling the receptionist shuffling the last of the notes back onto the shelves.

'Have we still got Bianca Rhys's notes, Hazel?'

'They were just about to be sent back to the Health Authority, Megan. Did you want to have a look at them before they go? I'll put them in your room ready for tomorrow, if you like.'

But Megan shook her head. 'No, tonight. Don't worry. I'll lock up.'

Hazel looked surprised but she shrugged and seconds later was handing Megan the notes and a cup of tea. 'If you're going to read the latest bestseller,' she said, 'you'd better have something to whet your whistle.'

Megan took the tea, waited for Hazel to close the door behind her and shook the notes out onto the desk. They were a thick set, two beige, Lloyd George envelopes sellotaped

65

together. And apart from the GPs' cryptic consultations they were full of letters from family doctor to psychiatrist, psychiatrist back to family doctor, community psychiatric nurse to family doctor and to psychiatrist.

Bianca had been christened plain Bianca Owen. Born 1945 at the Brynhafod Maternity Hospital to one Catherine Owen and her husband Gethin—a normal daughter. There were early documentations of the 'usual childhood ailments': mumps, German measles and whooping cough. There was a greenstick fracture of the left radius aged fourteen and an admission to hospital aged fifteen with abdominal pain which had resolved spontaneously leading to her discharge two days later without treatment. Then, when she was sixteen years old, strange things began to happen to Bianca Owen. She began to imagine the girls at school were calling her names. Nothing strange in that—except that she claimed they also got into her bedroom at night, still calling her names, shouting in her ear and preventing her from sleeping. At first her parents had believed that her victimisation at school was giving her nightmares and had complained to the teachers. When all the accusations had been hotly denied and not before the police had been hauled in to talk to her schoolmates' parents, her frantic parents had brought her to the family doctor, Megan's predecessor's predecessor, a Doctor Parry-

Jones. He had talked to Bianca and reassured her parents.

But events had become more and more bizarre. Bianca had stopped washing. She had attacked her mother causing a penetrating eye injury. Two months later she had accused her father of sexual abuse and Doctor Parry-Jones had referred her to the psychiatrist at Bridgend. Numerous letters had been exchanged between GP and consultant psychiatrist. The case against her father had been dropped. Bianca had been admitted to the local mental hospital under section 29 of the mental health act for a long term stay and when she had finally been allowed out her life-long medication had been started. From now until her death she must have an injection of Modecate once a month 'to control symptoms of acute paranoic schizophrenia'.

*   *   *

Megan read on, moving through the years. There had been admissions at regular intervals, various claims of witnessing events, people talking to her. Plenty of callouts to her predecessors for plugs that ticked, wires that hummed, a rat that hid under the sink. The imagination of a schizophrenic was boundless. Unshackled to reality, they were capable of reading threats into the most banal, everyday occurences. Each admission to the institute

67

was followed by quiescent periods and it was during one of these in 1968 that Bianca had changed her name to Rhys by marrying a Thomas Rhys. A few quiet years had followed until 1973 when she had started throwing accusations at her husband. He was a killer, she had claimed, a serial killer who 'interfered with little children'. Despite a diagnosis which put any of her statements into doubt, the police had again been called in. After months of investigations during which the psychiatrist firmly lobbed his opinions into the field of battle, the case against Thomas Rhys was finally dropped. A brief stay at the Parc mental hospital followed. And now the psychologist's letters read like a modern day thriller. Bianca had filled in plenty of details. Children tortured, old people left to starve, chained against walls, a boy, buried in a graveyard, still alive. A serial killer who buried his victims beneath the old mine workings, trains that ran into rusting sidings, driven by a screaming skeleton. The stories were horrific, endless, and graphic. Even the psychologist had professed shock at the horror of it all.

Bianca's medication had been increased. There were letters between GP and hospital about drowsiness, side effects, confusion. Somehow in the middle of all this Carole had been born and swiftly made a ward of court. 'For her own protection'. Thomas Rhys seemed to have vanished into thin air. There was no mention made of a father in any of the case conferences. And no further accusations were made against him. Whenever Bianca had been admitted to hospital Carole had been cared for by the Social Services. And when Bianca was in charge the supervision had been close and daily. No one had apparently quite trusted Bianca to care for her own daughter. For Carole it hadn't been much of an upbringing. There was mention of her being teased and bullied at school and requests made to the Social Services that she be admitted to a residential children's home— permanently. But against all odds Bianca Rhys had largely brought her own daughter up. Megan cupped her chin in her hand and stared out of her window, towards the Slaggy Pool. No wonder there was this dichotomy of emotion between mother and daughter. Love and hate.

One thing did strike Megan as she scanned through the notes. Not once was there mention of a suicide attempt. There were plenty of references to her habit of self mutilation but no one had equated this with anything but a desire for attention. None of the razor slashes which striped her arms were more than skin deep. She had burned herself more than once with cigarettes. But not even a disturbed schizophrenic could believe she could destroy herself by this means. There were references too of her aversion to water.

Even a possible explanation, dug up by an unusually thorough counsellor. At three years old the young Bianca had fallen into an ornamental pond belonging to a stately home at the bottom of the valley, Triagwn House. Megan knew the place well. It had once belonged to the owner of Llancloudy mine, a huge, grand place with now neglected gardens. Today it was an old people's home. And Megan, Andy and Phil were responsible for the inhabitants as the attendant medical officers. Megan even knew the pond. Right at the front, with a cherub doing an ungainly arabesque across its width, water spouting from its mouth. Bianca's parents must have been looking round the gardens while the child had run off. Minutes later Bianca had been dragged from the water, unconscious, to be resuscitated by one of the gardeners there. Perhaps the memory of drowning had been implanted deep in the child's brain and led to her pathological phobia. Perhaps even the water spewing from the cherub's mouth had planted some seed inside an already vulnerable mind. Certainly long before schizophrenia had manifested itself the little girl was displaying an aversion to water, disliking the seaside, hiding when a trip to Porthcawl had been organised by the Sunday School of the Bethesda chapel. By the time Bianca was in her early teens she had begun to manifest one of the signs which later

70

characterised her illness: not bathing. More than once her despairing mother had brought her to the doctor. 'To see if anything can be done'. He had documented his hygiene talks to the child but to no avail.

*   *   *

Megan leafed through the notes, absorbed by a life long history of mental illness culminating in an untimely death. She knew as well as Phil Walsh that statistically it was not entirely unexpected. People with mental illness rarely saw out their expected lifespan. She put the sheets of notes together with the letters back in the beige envelope, pushed her chair away from her desk and sat very still, her eyes again fixed by the Gericault. To her relief the woman looked less like Bianca now. Phrases from the psychiatrist's letters crawled through her brain. Not a danger to herself. Her grip on reality is tenuous. Bianca will never be capable of independent living. She will always need close supervision. Above all one phrase stuck out in her mind as having some deep, hidden significance, It is not unusual for people who have delusions to retain a good deal of perception and keep in touch with reality. She wondered how much of Bianca's thoughts had stuck to reality. And who, if anyone, would know which was which.

There was another small clue. All her life

Bianca had been the focus of trained psychiatric personnel—nurses, psychiatrists, psychologists. They had shone the brightest of interrogation lights on her psyche with the result that her attitude to suicide had on more than one occasion been explored by asking her questions specifically structured to expose such a risk. And each time they had come up with the same answer. Bianca Rhys had been assessed a negative risk. Not a danger to herself.

Megan scooped in a long, deep breath. So was her doctor now to believe she had either deliberately or accidentally approached a body of water which would have filled her with the same amount of horror as a pit of spiders to someone with arachnophobia, having abandoned the safety of her fortress house for no apparent reason and . . . Again words from the poem seemed to spear her brain. 'In she plunged boldly.'

Or was it as her daughter had suggested that the voices had finally driven her Mad from life's history.

Glad to death's mystery? Swift to be hurl'd—Anywhere, anywhere Out of the world.

That truly must be the answer, rather than the unimaginative police suggestion that Bianca had wandered, her voices driving her forward, and she had slipped.

She folded Doctor Wainwright's letters

together and slotted them back in the Lloyd George envelope. Make no deep scrutiny into her mutiny? The Hood poem seemed to be telling her something else.

Her eyes flicked across to the wall. The mad woman was still watching her, her expression suspicious, untrusting. The sun had dropped far below the mountain so only the very tips of the hills were still glowing.

*　　*　　*

It was time she left.

CHAPTER SIX

She locked the surgery door behind her, setting the burglar alarm against the marauding youngsters whose greatest wish was to raid the cupboard for syringes, drugs—or simply fun. It livened up a quiet evening, setting off burglar alarms, waiting for the flashing blue lights to sweep up the valley. The noise, the shouting. It staved off boredom.

*　　*　　*

Sitting inside her own car it was that very same boredom which compelled her to dial the police station on her mobile phone and ask for

73

Alun. At least the hot, guilty embarrassment was better than the void which filled her life the moment she stepped outside her doctor's role. At the same time she lectured herself sternly that Alun was married now, with a child. She'd read both the announcements without emotion in the local paper a couple of years ago. A wife would naturally be suspicious of the motives of an old girlfriend, recently divorced, suddenly turned pally, who followed up a chance meeting with a phone call.

The answering voice was uncurious. 'I'm sorry, Police Constable Alun Williams is not on duty today. Who is it speaking please? Perhaps I can take a message.'

Megan's eyes drifted across the road at the dark slick which marked the Slaggy Pool. 'Yes,' she said slowly. 'Will you please tell him Megan Banesto rang. I'd like to talk to him.' She was anxious to explain that this was a professional call. 'It's about a case.'

'He's got your number, has he, Doctor Banesto?'

Anonymity was impossible in these valleys. She gave the officer both her home, mobile and surgery number and he asked her to hold on for a minute.

Put the ball into Alun's court. If he rang back, fine. She could pursue her line of reasoning to him. If not. Well. Nothing ventured . . . A swift flash of Alun, streaming off the rugby pitch, muddy and grinning, straight into her outstretched arms, made her blink with pain. Why hadn't she settled for him instead of committing virtual social suicide by hitching up with the Italian Stallion? Life would have been so simple. Predictable. Comfortable. She would have been happy. Only now she knew it. More than ten years too late. But she had left for Cardiff Medical School, leaving him behind in the valleys without so much as a backward glance. The world was out there. Waiting for her. She had felt a desperate need to escape. Escape had seemed more important than anything. And by the time she had finally returned to Llancloudy to take up a General Practice post it had seemed inappropriate to pick up the strands of an old relationship.

*　　*　　*

The police officer came back to her with his calm, reassuring voice, breaking into her thoughts before she could continue this awful, pointless agonising. 'Right. Well. I can't tell you when PC Williams is due back, Doctor Banesto, But I promise I will give him your message. All right now?'

'Thank you.'

Relief swamped her. She had taken some action. Now she could go home.

*　　*　　*

75

Home was one of the terraced houses that had its back rammed against the mountain. Number 37, Heol Caradoc. A well built, two bedroomed, ex miner's cottage with the luxury of a bathroom. Downstairs the living room and the dining room had been knocked into one and a kitchen built on at the back. It was small, basic and secure. She could lie in bed and hear movements in the houses either side of her. And downstairs she could hear neighbours' televisions, hi fis, the ping of a microwave and occasionally noisy, family rows. The tiny front garden which overlooked the road meant that sunning yourself was a public affair and the back was little more than a yard and a tiny tool shed. Privacy was at a premium in Llancloudy.

*   *   *

She had bought number 37 when she and Guido had finally split and sold the detached modern estate house at the bottom of the valley which had briefly been their marital home. From her 50% share she had bought this house outright. It was a solid practical place which she had largely decorated herself but it was basically sound, warm, cosy and she felt safe hemmed in and guarded by her neighbours. The only real drawback was having to leave her car out in the street, tightly parked and clamped against the gangs of out-of-control streetboys led by Joel Parker, a twelve-year-old psychopath who was capable of joyriding in the Calibra and smashing it up together with his band of law breaking mates. One day, she had promised herself, she would move. Only not yet.

*   *   *

Megan let herself into the narrow hall, picking up a couple of bills from the floor. She went straight into the sitting room and flopped down onto the cream sofa, flicked the TV on, channel hopped for half an hour, found nothing of interest then padded upstairs to run a bath. Her big toe was poised to dip in when downstairs the telephone rang. 'Bugger,' she cursed. 'Bugger.'

*   *   *

One of the nice things about living alone was that running downstairs starkers she was unlikely to encounter anyone. But she still felt embarrassed when Alun's deep voice spoke from the other end.

'They told me you'd rang the station, Megan. What is it?' He sounded very slightly irritated. Almost a stranger. Not glad to hear from her at all.

She could hardly ask him to wait while she put some clothes on so she perched on the bottom step, grateful for the retained warmth in the house. She began tentatively. 'I—I wanted to ask you about Bianca Rhys.'

'What did you want to know?'

'What the official line is, Alun.'

He gave a non committal 'Mmm'.

'And the pathologist said she had some stone in her pocket.'

He gave a loud burst of laughter. 'Well she was always nickin' something. Gave us no end of trouble. She must have pinched it from someone's garden.'

'Well what was it? Was it heavy enough to have weighted her down in the water? And why did she go up there in the first place?'

'I think . . . Hang on a minute.' There was a pause. He was shutting a door. 'I think I should buy you a drink and we can talk about this face to face, in a civilised fashion.'

Relief enveloped her. He had no idea how much she would like that. 'Yes. OK. When?'

'What are you doing now?'

She glanced downwards. 'Right now?'

'Right now.'

'Just about to have a bath.'

He chuckled again and she knew he knew she was wearing nothing.

'Are you free then for the rest of the evening? After your bath?'

'Yes.'

'I'll pick you up in an hour then, Megan.'

'OK. I live—'

78

'I know where you live.'

*   *   *

She washed quickly, shampooing her hair, blowdrying it, straight and sleek, around her face and pulling on some cream cotton jeans and a black silk shirt with black, leather mules. One of the rewards of being five feet eight inches tall and weighing eight stone was that she could wear most clothes without worrying whether her 'bottom looked big' in them. She left her face bare apart from a touch of mascara. The Alun he had known had disliked makeup. She finished her toilet with a spray of Chanel then perched on the window seat and peered out into the street, waiting for him. He would not be able to find a parking spot. She would need to meet him on the road.

*   *   *

Long ago on dates she had always made the men park their car, knock on her door—formally—while she counted to ten—slowly—before opening it. She had dropped such affectation years ago.

*   *   *

He turned up a few minutes after half past eight, pulling up adjacent to her car, throwing

79

open the passenger door of the Peugeot estate as she locked her front door behind her. A swift glance over her shoulder told her this was a family vehicle—there was a Brita child seat in the back.

Megan could swear right along the road curtains were twitching. A few kids across the street stopped passing their rugby ball to each other while they stared.

Alun waited until she had closed the car door behind her before he spoke. 'It's good to see you again, Megan.'

She looked long and hard at his blunt featured face and felt as though she had come home. 'You too.'

'Thought we'd go to one of the quieter pubs. Some of them here you can't hear yourself think—let alone have a civilised conversation. All right if you've got nothing to say. But . . .'

'Fine. Whatever.'

He accelerated down the road, drove swiftly to the head of the valley and climbed towards Llangefni, a small collection of scattered houses and an ancient pub. Once there he parked the car neatly in *Y Ddraig Goch* and they entered the lounge bar.

As pubs go it was OK. Not posh but not fake either. Round oak tables, a faded red carpet, the cloying scent of stale cigarettes, a fruit machine sparkling in the corner. Two girls beside it, a mobile phone silent on the table between them.

'He said he would phone. That's if he can get away. Bloody wife of his.'

Megan turned her eyes on Alun. He was blushing.

'What do you want to drink, Meggie?'

The name had been his pet one for her, the one that could turn her knees weak. Trust him to use it now, turn the clock back.

'A white wine, please.' Long ago Bacardi and cokes were ignored in a swamp of sophistication.

Alun returned from the bar with a pint pot for himself and a glass of wine for her. As he put it carefully on the table he spilt a drop and she had the satisfaction of watching him turn red again. She smiled to herself. He always had had this tendency to blush. Useful to know when he was lying. It had come to her aid before—on more than one occasion. She wondered whether he would blush when his wife asked him where he had been tonight. And with whom?

He took a deep draught then set his beer back down on the table. 'And how are you managing now, on your own?'

She shrugged.

'Must be a bit lonely after—'

She sidestepped the personal interest. 'What's the official version of Bianca's death? Are the police making any investigation?'

'Why do you ask? What's your involvement

in it? She was just a patient of yours, wasn't she?'

'Her daughter . . .' she began.

'Oh—Carole.' Alun made a face. 'She's been makin' all sorts of allegations. Police neglect—not caring. You name it. Actually we have been takin' statements as well as making a proper inspection of the area around the pool.'

'And?'

'We think Bianca slipped in sometime on Sunday night. She can't possibly have fallen in during daylight. Someone would surely have seen her. So that would mean after nine o'clock on Sunday night. We've taken statements from a few people who saw what they thought was some old clothes in the pool. It was her all right. There was light rain on Sunday night. That would have made the ground a little bit slippy.'

She remembered the rain, a soft, summer rain that had seemed to moisten the atmosphere without falling as raindrops. And the cloud of damp had lain heavy in the valley as a cloying, grey mist blotting out the mountains. She had escaped by spending the evening with a friend in Cardiff and had returned late—well after nine. By then Bianca must have been a floating corpse.

She looked enquiringly at Alun for further explanation.

'The pathologist thought she might have

saved up a couple of her pills and taken them all together, got a bit confused and knocked off, wandered up there, slipped on the grass, knocked her head and fell in. And the police surgeon agreed with this version. Apparently once she'd fallen in the water she never really drew breath. But she would have found it hard to scramble out of the pool anyway because her clothes had got tangled up in an old pram some one had dumped there. That's the official verdict.'

It was a logical explanation. But something didn't fit. Megan fumbled around trying to understand what it was. 'And the stone in her pocket? Would it have been enough to weigh her down?'

'No—not really. Goodness knows. It was something broken off an old statue or something. A piece of carved stone. Not very big.'

'What was it?'

'I don't know. Like a claw or something.'

'And where had she got it from?'

'I don't know, Megan.'

She picked up on his exasperation. 'And you don't think it's important.'

He shook his head, leaned forward, touched her hand. 'Meggie,' he said bluntly, 'all the police are concerned about is that no one else was involved. It wasn't murder. It might have been suicide. It probably was an accident.'

'But what was she doing up there in the first

place? Bianca was frightened to leave her house after dark.'

Alun looked amused. 'You're not trying to be a detective, are you? You should stick to being a doctor, Meggie. From what I've heard you're good at that. All I can say is we've finished our enquiries. We've handed our notes to the coroner and he's happy.'

She regarded him for a moment before asking, 'Have you seen anyone who actually saw her heading up the pool? Did anyone see her any time on Saturday or all day Sunday?'

Alun reddened. 'What are you suggesting?'

'And how do you explain the head injury?'

'She hit it as she fell into the pool.'

'What on? Have you sent frogmen down?'

'The pool's a few feet deep, Megan. The bottom is full of rubbish. There's plenty of stuff there she could have hurt herself on. I don't get where you're comin' from.'

'I'll tell you where I'm coming from, Alun,' she said quietly. 'Bianca was "three streets short of a city". If she had been a normal woman your investigation would have been more intense, more detailed. Because she was a schizophrenic you're hardly bothering.'

'No—it isn't because of that. It's because if Bianca had been any normal woman we could probably have worked out what she was up to. But with her anything is possible. Her voices might have told her to throw herself in—or go up there late at night. It was always the voices she blamed for shoplifting. All we care is that she wasn't deliberately pushed in or drowned. And think about it, Meggie. There wouldn't be any point to it besides it being a useless way to try and murder someone. She might have climbed out. You couldn't predict the fact that she would die of shock the minute she hit the water. If new evidence came to light we'd look at her case again. But as it is there's no justification for further investigation.'

'You're not searching for new evidence, are you?'

'We've done the necessary. We've carried out house to house. We've examined the ground beside the Slaggy Pool.'

'After half the population of Llancloudy had marked the area with their own footprints.'

'Hang on a minute. We came as soon as we were called.' Native honesty compelled him to add, 'Well—within the ten minute deadline anyway. We couldn't help it if people had already trampled around the pool destroying trace evidence.' He lifted his beerglass, his eyes never leaving her face all the time he drank. 'I wouldn't have thought your life was so lacking in drama you'd have to go searching for it in this sad accident to a pathetic old mad thing.'

She wanted him to understand. 'It's because she was a sad, pathetic old mad thing.'

He always had struggled to understand her commitment, her attitude, her responsibilities.

'And her daughter isn't happy.'

Alun snorted. 'Her daughter's never happy. Carole Symmonds is the sort who'd always say her family was being discriminated against.'

There was an element of truth in the statement.

'Don't bother turning over stones,' he advised.

'Because there might be toads underneath them?'

'No—because there's nothing and I wouldn't want you to waste your time and energy. It's not worth it.'

She sensed his anger was rising and so she was silent, disagreeing but not wanting a confrontation. She was enjoying his company—even the sparring. They always had been a quarrelsome couple. After they had parted Megan had realised that half of their quarrels had been encouraged for the passionate reconciliation.

Alun drained his beerglass and put it back on the table with sudden firmness.

She waited for the storm to break.

'How could you be such a . . .' he burst out. 'You were the prize catch of the sixth form. You could have had anyone. We all had the hots for you. How could you have married that . . . ? Why the hell did you, Meggie? It was obvious from the start what he was.'

She felt as though she'd been kicked in the solar plexus. 'Not to me it wasn't obvious.'

86

Alun looked incredulous. 'I don't believe you. You must have known.'

She gave a dismissive shake of her head. 'Don't—please—don't.' She stuck a bright smile on her face and touched his hand briefly. 'I went on holiday. The sun shone. I was away from work and the dullness and the stifling closeness of here. We lay on the beach and talked and talked. We made love. We swam, we ate, we slept. It seemed an idyllic existence. I couldn't know things would be so different when we came back here. He changed.'

'Rather a lot as I understand.'

She closed her eyes for a moment and nodded.

He hadn't finished. 'I couldn't believe it when I heard—falling for an Italian waiter like some cheap holiday romance.'

'He wasn't a waiter,' she said, stung. 'He owned the restaurant. He is a cultured and intelligent man with a huge appreciation of beauty.'

'And he likes men,' Alun said sourly.

'Alun,' she appealed. 'I know what the gossips say. Don't join them, please.'

'Well they aren't talking so much about you any more,' he said. 'They've got something else to concentrate on now.'

'Temporarily. Memories are long in this part of the world. They'll *never* forget. I'll always be labelled as the doctor who went on holiday, married an Italian waiter. And he preferred men. Even if I married again the gossips would follow me. As long as I stay here, in Llancloudy.'

'Why do you,' he asked. 'Why did you come back?'

'Because people here need me.'

'I needed you,' he said, looking away, 'once.'

'But not any more. You're married now.'

He nodded.

'And I hear you've a . . .'

He was already fumbling in his pocket, pulling out a photograph of a mischievous looking toddler. 'That's Gareth.' His pride was evident. 'Two next birthday. And another one on the way.'

'*You're* happy then.'

'Oh yes.'

The worst of it was that she believed him. Alun invariably blushed when he was lying. And he wasn't blushing now. If anything he looked slightly pale. Mentioning his wife had made him worry talk would trickle back to her about his drinking companion tonight.

Best to return to safe subjects.

'And you're happy that Bianca's death was simply an accident?'

'Yes.'

'One last thing,' she said. 'The piece of stone. What have you done with it?'

'It's down at the police station.'

'Describe it.'

'About four inches long, carved grey stone.

88

As I said, looks like a bird's claw—or something. Maybe not quite a bird's claw, Megan. More an animal's claw.'

He was distancing himself from her. The pet name had been dropped.

She stood up. 'Can I get you a drink?'

'Just a half. I'm driving. Wouldn't do for me to get copped over the limit.'

They both drank the second drink quickly, swapping information about ex-classmates. Alun drained his glass and glanced at his watch. Megan picked up her bag. She could take a hint. She smiled. 'We'd better make a move. Busy day tomorrow and all that.'

He answered her smile with a vague one of his own. 'It's nice to see you again, Meggie. You look—well.'

It was one of his typically clumsy compliments.

They left the pub, climbed back in the car. Alun drove carefully and silently until they reached the bottom of Heol Caradoc. There was a constraint between them and she anticipated his wish. 'Don't come all the way up the road. It's so narrow and there's nowhere to park or pull in. Just drop me here. I'll walk home.'

She would have preferred not to have read the look of relief that swept across his face.

'OK.' He leaned across to open the car door for her. 'Good night then, Meggie.'

Somehow she got out without a polite peck

on the cheek. She walked up the road self-consciously without even a backward glance and slammed the front door behind her.

* * *

It was a little past ten o'clock. Too early even for her to go to bed with cocoa and a paperback so she pulled her own pathology book from the shelf and began to read, conscious all the time that Alun had not invited her to make contact again even if she had more ideas, theories or questions about Bianca.

The evening had promised so much—and delivered nothing. Bianca was a real and memorable person to her. But to PC Alun Williams she was a nuisance, a statistic, a file; a pathetic, mad old lady who had slipped and drowned in a grubby little pond.

Sometimes it is easier if we depersonalise tragedy.

CHAPTER SEVEN

They loved funerals in the valleys. Paying last respects was an important ceremony. All who could would attend the funeral—even the funeral of an expired mad, sad creature like Bianca Rhys. She might have been lonely in

90

life, avoided by most, but in death she was far from abandoned. And her dramatic exit had ensured a full turn-out at her funeral. As the hearse crept towards the church people standing on the route dropped their eyes and the men doffed their caps. Catholics crossed themselves, Methodists muttered a prayer. Those with looser religious tendencies prayed for a peaceful soul while even the agnostics stopped whatever they were doing, eating chips, shopping, chattering on mobile phones to stand silently and watch the cars slide down the valley, a queue of motorists behind, some in black ties, others impatient to arrive at work. As the procession passed, the streets stilled for Bianca Rhys. In death she commanded more respect than she had probably ever been given in life. Megan trailed after the procession in her own car, shifting from second gear to first as they neared the church.

The hearse halted in front of the double doors and the bearers shouldered the white plastic coffin.

*   *   *

Carole Symmonds was amply supported by friends, relatives and neighbours. A stout woman wearing an elegant, wide brimmed hat helped her up the path. Meggie followed slowly, deep in thought. Her own grandparents had been buried here, as had been many of her ex-patients. When she looked up again Esther Magellan was standing right in front of her, blocking her route. 'I've been meaning to talk to you, doctor,' she began.

Esther had dressed for the funeral. In a bright red hat with a floppy rim that at a guess had been bought from one of the charity shops, it looked like a remnant of the early seventies and battered enough. Purple leggings which sagged at the knee and a long, black T-shirt completed her funereal outfit. Esther was plump and amorphous with a lardy complexion and huge, beseeching eyes. And as always she wore a smear of bright red lipstick and face powder randomly applied, Megan suspected, without the aid of a mirror. Her hair was heavily henna'd, sawdust-dry, brittle and badly cut. Her eyes were pale blue and quite vacant but devoid of malice. She touched Megan's arm timidly. 'Bianca isn't here today,' she said, 'at least she is here in her body. And in her soul,' she added cheerfully. 'She just isn't *here* any more.' She touched her eye with a grubby handkerchief. 'I don't know how I'm going to manage without her. She was my friend.'

Megan murmured something non-committal.

'Perhaps I should have looked after her better.'

Megan was swamped by the pathos of the

situation. Esther was not capable of looking after herself. Let alone Bianca, with her attendant problems. 'It wasn't your fault that she died, Esther,' she said. 'It was just an accident.'

'That's what they're sayin' but I wonder. Maybe it wasn't an accident at all. Maybe somebody pushed her. She couldn't swim, you see. She told me that—once.'

'She didn't need to swim. The pool was only shallow.'

'Oh.' Esther opened her eyes wide, as though this was news to her.

'You were her friend,' she continued happily. 'She liked you. She thought you would make her better, stop her from hearing those nasty voices.'

Megan nodded, again deliberately non-committal.

'Bianca was clever,' Esther said suddenly. 'She *understood* things.' She grabbed Megan's arm. 'She did *know* things. *Understand* things. Things *other* people didn't have the sense to realise. She could put two and two together and make . . .' she hesitated for a couple of seconds, her eyes shining with a vision, '. . . anything she wanted,' she finished happily. 'Anything.'

Megan looked back at Esther Magellan, who knew so little and understood less than half that. To her simple mind Bianca might have seemed wise. Knowing. Someone who

93

knew things. But far back her mind prickled with some animal alertness as though primitive instinct had been evoked. 'I'll come and visit you tomorrow, Esther,' she said. 'Late—after surgery.'

Esther nodded and vanished through the swinging doors. Megan took her seat at the back. She was not a relative nor a close friend. She half-listened to the prayers of commitment and filed out, with the others, to the churchyard. At the graveside she glanced around her at the ring of faces and saw sadness and deep, deep thought as though each person was remembering the strange life which had been wasted.

Wasted—gangland slang for murder.

But looking across the open grave she would find it hard to credit that anyone here believed Bianca's untimely death had been anything but a sad and unnecessary accident. There was a spirit of acceptance. Except for maybe one man. He was standing right at the back of the huddle of mourners. He was small and wiry and hopping from foot to foot as though he was angry. Angry? The emotion seemed misplaced. Why should anyone be angry at Bianca's death—except maybe Carole. And like the others she looked calm. Sad but tranquil. Megan took another surreptitious peep at the man and wondered what was making him angry. Bianca's death had been a chance event. So was he angry that

94

the pond had remained unfenced? Or that she had been unsupervised—did he blame her death on a lack of care in the community? Megan sneaked another look, wondering whether she had misread his fidgettiness. But if anything she had underestimated his emotion. He was a furious little man. Like Rumpelstiltskin—the angry, restless little dwarf of the child's fairy story, his eyes glaring around the room, cross with anyone they landed on. She turned back still wondering why he was so angry.

'Meggie.'

She knew it was Alun touching her shoulder without even turning round. She would have sensed his presence without him speaking a single word. She could smell his aftershave, recognise the firm grip. He had often gripped when he had meant to touch. She didn't turn around but tilted her head slightly backwards.

He leaned forward so his face was almost touching hers. 'Meggie,' he said again.

She turned her head around slightly to look at him. 'Do you make a habit of attending funerals?'

'Do you?'

'More often than you'd think.'

'Does that mean you're an unsuccessful doctor?'

She smiled at the clumsy banter. 'Successful or unsuccessful has nothing to do with it, Alun. Nature beats me hands down every time.'

She sensed he was smiling too. In the hot air around she knew he was feeling warm towards her.

'Not nature this time, Meggie.'

'No,' she agreed.

People were filing past, some nodding at her.

Alun glanced around him. 'Dismal affairs, aren't they, funerals?'

'I haven't been to many happy ones.'

'Oh—I don't know. Old people who've had a long and fulfilling life.'

'I know plenty of old people, Alun,' she countered. 'But not so many who've had a long and fulfilling life.'

'I intend to.'

She turned around fully then and met his eyes, read there the fierce determination that had seen him through plenty of tough rugby matches, muddy, cold and with fearful opposition. 'I know.' It was all still there—that hunger that she had once adored but now had almost forgotten about. He must have read some response mirrored in her face. He caught his breath.

But she knew people were watching and so did Alun. He responded with a fierce blush and a hand on her arm.

'Come for a drink with me again?'

She nodded.

*　　　*　　　*

On the following day Megan felt jaunty. The sky was blue, the weather warm but not too hot. The surgery had—for once—been emptied quickly of patients with minor problems and she had no visits—apart from this one she had promised.

*   *   *

Esther still lived in the small, semi-detached council bungalow she had shared with Bianca. Megan flicked open the red painted wicket gate and approached the front door via a straight concrete path. The garden was neat, sporting wallflowers and scarlet bedding geraniums—tended by the council gardener— and the house itself was recently painted. She gave a brisk knock and stepped back. It always took Esther a while to unbolt the door.

Eventually it was pulled open and her patient peered around it fearfully, her face brightening when she realised it was Megan. 'Hello, doctor,' she said, grabbing her hand. 'Hello. So you have come. Thanks. Thanks ever so much.' She was still wearing her purple 'funeral' leggings but today they were teamed with a blue polyester blouse which billowed over her wide hips and some very old fashioned brown slippers which slapped against her heels as she led the way to the sitting room.

The air inside was faintly musty; none of the windows were open and the curtains were still half closed allowing only the dingiest of lights to penetrate.

'I'm on my own now,' Esther said trustingly, dropping down onto the sofa. 'I can't get used to it neither. She's gone and she won't be back now. They buried her yesterday.'

'I know. I was there.'

Esther looked, child-like, at Megan. 'The council say they'll move me to a flat. I don't mind if they do.'

And although Megan knew she shouldn't do this she began, gently, to probe her patient. 'When did you last see Bianca?'

Pale blue eyes looked guilelessly into hers. 'One of the days,' she said with great, vacuous significance.

'Which day was it? Saturday?'

Esther nodded, smiling.

'Morning or afternoon?'

'I wouldn't know the time.'

Megan suspected Esther wouldn't even know the day. 'They told me they found her in the Slaggy Pool,' she continued calmly. 'They said she'd drowned. They buried her, you know. Yesterday.'

'I know. I was there.'

'You were?'

'We spoke.'

'Oh.' It was news.

'You told me something about Bianca?'

'I did?'

'That you thought . . .'

'Oh—I don't know what I thought. She used to say things, you know.'

'What things? What did she say?'

'About people. Bad things about people.'

'What sort of bad things?'

Esther merely flashed her a bland smile.

Frustrated now Megan tried again. 'Which people?'

'It's surprising really. You'd never guess it, who does what.'

'Who does do what?' Megan asked. 'What do you mean? What did she mean?'

But Esther's mind had tracked away. 'I miss her, you know.'

'I'm sure you do.'

'She was my friend. My—one—true—friend.'

'I know.'

'My best friend. My very best friend. The council say they'll rehouse me.' Esther smiled. 'In a flat. I don't mind if they do.'

So Megan gave up, checked whether there was anything Esther needed and left.

On the pavement she hesitated, tempted to knock on Doris Baker's door. But the police had already taken a statement from her. She had last seen Bianca on Saturday morning to give her her tablets. She would have nothing more to add. Any questions she directed to Bianca's neighbour would be classed as

99

interference. She sat in her car for a few minutes, half hoping Doris would appear. But there was no movement and after a while Megan started up the engine and drove off.

It was time to stop peering into the murky waters beneath *The Bridge of Sighs.*

CHAPTER EIGHT

But events conspired against her. A couple of weeks later, on Friday morning, the sixth of September, a request was filed for her to visit Triagwn House, now a home for fifty elderly residents and the responsibility of herself, Andy and Phil. The Social Services had been the rambling house's salvation. Unless a practical use had been found for the building it would have been pulled down years ago and the land used for a much needed housing estate. But in the early nineteen eighties, when the grand house had been falling into irreversible decay the council had anticipated a growing need for local nursing home care for the elderly. And so they had bought Triagwn House and adapted it.

* * *

As Megan threaded down the valley away from Llancloudy, towards the bottom of the valley, she was conscious of an unaccustomed sense of relief. Since Bianca had drowned, the village of Llancloudy had seemed particularly oppressive, almost claustrophobic. The weather had turned hot and the streets had felt even more cramped than usual. It had been noisy too with the streets filled with people, car windows open, blasting music into the air. The houses had looked different; front doors had been propped open, windows thrown wide, people sitting in what little front gardens they had. The patch of land opposite the surgery had been packed and one day Megan had even watched a small boy float a plastic yacht on the Slaggy Pool. To leave the crowded village behind felt like a welcome escape. The road, the river and the disused railway shared the bottom of the valley and she drove downwards until she reached the point where the valley widened out and the ground flattened. By the time she reached the town of Nantyglo and ran the gauntlet of the long rows of pebble-dashed, semi-detached houses she was singing along with the car radio and an All Saints record. The sun beamed in through the windscreen. The road gave way to a petrol station and a wide roundabout. Left and right would lead straight onto the M4, left to Cardiff, right to the West—Swansea and beyond to the narrow lanes of Pembrokeshire and the St David's Peninsula.

She drove straight on, towards the market

town of Bridgend, tapping the steering wheel in time to the music, then took a small lane to the right which led to a narrowing road and some tall, iron gates permanently propped open. The car rattled across the cattle grid and finally she faced Triagwn; a pleasing, square red brick building with a white pillared portico, vividly bright in the sunshine.

As she drew nearer to the house it was hard not to reflect how starkly different the mine owner's home had been from the tightly packed, higgledy-piggledy terraces of cottages which had housed his workers. Their homes had been as different as their working days, the one, mole-like, underground, the other living from it and above it in splendid luxury which must have astonished the miners the few times a year when, usually on Bank Holidays, the doors were flung open to the general public. Megan smiled, in no hurry to end her approach, for once obeying the 10mph speed limit set more for the safety of the sheep that roamed the grounds—having picked their way across the cattle grid—than the inmates who mostly stayed indoors.

It was ironic that some of the current inmates of Triagwn had once been employees of the mine owner. And now they lived here alongside their onetime task-master. Geraint Smithson, aged 94, resided in one small room of this great house when he had once occupied and owned the entire building and most of the land both around it and underneath it. Today he was probably the most troublesome resident of Triagwn, a cantankerous old man who still believed he was master of the mine. And of the house too, so he bossed the nursing staff around mercilessly. The only person he had any regard or respect for was his son, Arwel.

* * *

Arwel was the florid faced member of the local hunt, a 54-year-old bully who had his own delusions. He still believed he had the right to deflower any female who came within touching distance of his long reaching and ever groping hands. Arwel lived in the Woodman's Cottage, a few hundred yards behind the main house; set amongst the trees which had once provided the wooden pit props the miners had been so fond of. Megan remembered her grandfather telling the reason for this affection. 'Because, *cariad*, if they are goin' to break they tell you. They do crack first, make a noise, give you warnin', give you time to get out—most of the time—whereas steel. Well—it do just go.' His eyes had taken on a dark, unhappy look and Megan, the child, had visualised roofs crashing down and had held her hands over her ears to stifle imagined screams. But it was true that until the mines had closed the miners had trusted their lives to native wood and rejected

103

the steel manufactured just a few miles towards the west.

*   *   *

She was at the top of the drive. She skirted the fountain and resumed her recollections as she often did when she visited the big house. She was hazy when exactly the Smithson family had moved out of Triagwn and decamped to the Cottage, or when Geraint had been admitted back to his onetime home as a patient. She could vaguely remember walking up the drive when she had been a child, maybe ten years old, and the place had been derelict. She could recall peeling paint and dirty windows, gardens overgrown with nettles and weeds, threatening Keep Out signs, boards nailed across ground floor windows, threats that trespassers WOULD be prosecuted and tugging her father's hand, wanting to escape the forbidden place.

Even now, when she entered through the rear entrance she could still sense dripping gutters and damp ferns. In those days the cherub of the fountain had been coated in green slime and the pool filled with stagnant rainwater. A contrast to the pure diamond drops that spurted from the cherub's mouth today.

And when Bianca had made that fatal visit twenty years previously things must have been different again. She could picture it, the heyday of the house, the Smithson family throwing open their garden gates with pride and patronage a few times a year, inviting the locals to gasp at their wealth. It must have been on one of these public days, almost fifty years ago now, that three-year-old Bianca Rhys had visited Triagwn with her parents, fallen in this fountain and almost died. And so a pattern had been set for her strange and tragic life. Until finally she had died in a similar shallow pool.

*   *   *

During Megan's teenage years she had vaguely been aware that Triagwn was being energetically renovated for some purpose. And when the scaffolding was finally removed Triagwn had looked different, all remnants of neglect wiped away. Then the signs had been erected, announcing that it was due to reopen as a nursing home for the elderly. The climax had come late in the nineteen eighties when a local celebrity—a paunchy, ex-rugby player— had arrived in a stretch limousine with shaded windows to declare Triagwn House open. The first inmates must have arrived within days.

She remembered all this before swinging the wheel around and covering the last few yards of the drive, pulling around to the left and halting next to a mud splattered Land

Rover.

Sandra Penarth must have been watching for her. As soon as Megan reached the front door it was pulled open. Acting matron Sandra was a bright, competent woman in her early forties with thick, red hair which escaped from what probably should have been a neat chignon. But her hair was too heavy to stay up and flopped onto the nape of her neck. She was casually dressed in navy blue trousers with a turquoise shirt.

*   *   *

As usual the welcome was warm. 'Come and have a nice cup of tea, doctor, and I'll tell you about the few residents we'd like you to see.' Without waiting for an answer she bounced along the corridor, still chattering, the rhythm of her rapid speech tapped out by staccato steps on the vinyl tiles. The air was scented with lavender Airwick which failed to disguise an underlying odour of cabbage. And lurking beneath that was the unmistakable scent of old age.

*   *   *

The pictures that hung from the yellow walls lifted the atmosphere, depicting cornfields and rural scenes against cloudless, blue skies, the shadows starkly defined by bright, golden

106

sunshine. They sported the optimistic primary colours of a child's palette. Red, yellow, blue. Megan recognised a Van Gogh, a Rousseau, a Gauguin. No Gericaults here.

*   *   *

They turned at Van Gogh's Cornfield into Sandra's inner sanctum. Familiar, tidy, organised, neatly copied staff rotas pinned to a cork board. On a small table in front of the window stood a tasteful arrangement of fresh flowers—chrysanthemums and gladioli—and on either side a couple of framed photographs. The desk was light Ikea, the top clear except for a blue plastic pen holder and a maroon diary, closed, a long ribbon marking a page. The chairs were comfortable and new looking, upholstered in heather coloured wool. Megan settled into one, Sandra Penarth sat behind the desk, legs crossed, still talking.

'To be honest the biggest worry is old Mr Driver. I think he's got broncho pneumonia. His chest has always been awful and now he's got a bug on it to add to his worries. The trouble is that he doesn't want to go to the hospital and his relatives really don't want him to be forced to leave here. I mean, he's been here six years. I don't mind keeping him. As far as I'm concerned he can stay. He won't last long. The work may be heavy for the nurses but they don't complain. They just get on with it. The only thing that troubles me is it upsets the other residents when we get a death.' She looked up. 'You know, Megan, one death, someone they know so well. Brings things a bit nearer.'

'Need they know?'

Sandra's bosom jerked. 'Hah. Try keepin' it a secret. In fact try keepin' *anythin'* secret in this place. It's hopeless.'

They were interrupted by a knock on the door and one of the Care Assistants in lilac trousers and white top brought in a tray of tea.

Sandra handed Megan a cup, sipped and smiled, waited until the door had closed again before continuing. 'The other patient I've really got my worries about is old Mr Smithson. He's always been a difficult patient, bossy and demandin' but recently his mind's wanderin' somethin'awful. He's getting quite wild. He's telling tales so bizarre he's frightening all the other residents. And that's not good for them.'

Megan took her tea. It must have been the phrase 'tales so bizarre' that pricked her interest.

'What tales?'

'Silly old stories. Absolute nonsense.' Sandra put her teacup firmly down on the desk.

Megan persisted. 'What stories?'

She did not receive a direct answer. Sandra Penarth rattled on. 'You'll have to sedate him, doctor. He'll have to have more Largactil.'

'What dose is he on?'

'I'm not absolutely sure. We've been giving him a bit extra.'

'How much extra? You can't justify giving him extra Largactil on account of his telling tales.'

'An extra tablet or two a day. If we can't keep him under control,' Sandra said with the tiniest hint of a threat, 'he'll have to go to a mental hospital or somewhere better equipped to deal with him. And that would be a shame really to take him away from here. Being as it was his place all those years ago when he exploited the men of the valleys down his mine. I tell you what—I don't know how his conscience is clear listenin' to half the inmates coughing and spluttering up their coal dust.'

'They get compensation.'

'They'll all be dead by the time that comes through.'

'Well—what could he have done? He isn't personally responsible. It was the way coal mines were run in those days.'

'He could have done more.'

Megan was anxious to put a stop to the conversation. She stood up. 'I'd better see them all,' she said.

Sandra followed her out of the room and together they started the laborious ward round, stopped in the corridor by beslippered residents, all of whom had vague symptoms and vaguer questions. It was as though they needed to see a doctor purely to retain their health. But then they had little else to focus on. And all the inmates in Triagwn were over seventy-five years old. They were likely to have some pathology.

Megan talked to all of them but the phrase Sandra had used, 'tales so bizarre', had reminded her of one consultation with Bianca which had stuck in her mind. It had been about eighteen months ago, during a period when she had been at her uncontrolled worst, peering round the surgery door as she had entered, checking the telephone briskly for a bug and finally blurting out to Megan that the child was dead. She had fixed Megan with pure anguish in her eyes, her forehead wrinkled with worry. 'She's definitely dead,' she said. 'I know it now—for certain. I'd wondered before but when he told me, this time, I *knew* it was the truth. It was the way he said it, you see. I knew he'd done it. Such a sweet little girl she was too. Always chattering. Never shut up. Little Rhiann.' Her face had sagged, bleak and hopeless and tears had tracked down her cheeks. 'Isn't he awful,' she had finished. 'Why does he do it?'

Megan had given her patient her injection but half an hour after Bianca had left the room she had still been struck with an awful horror. For those few minutes she had glimpsed just how real and terrible Bianca's delusions were.

110

And now it sounded as though Smithson senior was suffering in a similar way.

* * *

Sandra Penarth was watching her, concern wrinkling her brow. 'You all right, doctor? You look miles away.'

Megan licked a smile onto her lips. 'I'm fine, Sandra. Just a bit tired. End of a bit of a busy week. If the weekend's sunny I shall head for the beach. Take my towel and a good paperback and brush up on my tan.'

Sandra grinned. 'Like the rest of the population? Sit in the queues all the way to Porthcawl more like.'

Megan laughed. 'Whatever.'

And yet she couldn't resist probing. 'What stories?'

'Sorry?' There was a pause. 'Oh—you mean Mr Smithson?'

'Yes—what stories?'

Sandra brushed aside a lock of stray hair. 'About the mines when they were working and having to sack so many men when they were slack. Then he goes on about not knowing about their lungs being so affected and what's that other thing—where their fingers go numb?'

'Miners' white finger.'

'Yes—that's right—from holding the drills. I just tell him. It's too bloody late now for all these regrets. The damage has been done.'

But these were not tales bizarre enough to upset the resident population of Triagwn nor were they the ramblings of an eroding mind. They were the truth. Smithson was an old man who had finally discovered his conscience. Sandra was right. It was too late for regrets. But the tales were not bizarre. There must be more. She kept her eyes trained on Sandra Penarth. 'And?'

'Some really silly old stories', she finally admitted reluctantly, 'about children who have disappeared, one of them buyin' chips. Another little thing who never stopped chattering. Then he talks about old ghosts,' she added reluctantly, 'people dying. Crawling through the mine workings. Vanishing when they shouldn't have done. A teacher who never turned up to class. They're bloody mad.'

'Does he mean mine accidents, do you think?'

'If he means mining accidents,' Sandra said severely, 'then he shouldn't talk about people's faces all covered in blood, about them still lying under the ground, tapping at the ventilation shafts, trying to crawl out, still covered in that horrible coal dust. Saying he can make people appear and reappear. Like he was some magician.'

Now Megan was smiling too.

But Sandra's blood was up. 'There's patients here who've lost family in pit

112

accidents. Old people dwell on these sorts of things. Tragedies. Upsets them. Mrs Price Morgan lost her husband in an explosion down the pit. He was only young and old Smithson going on about it brings it all back, see?'

Megan nodded. She did see.

'And he must have heard about poor old Bianca because he was sayin' he could remember her falling into the fountain when she was small and how they all thought she was dead. Then he really offended everybody by bursting out laughing and saying she drowned in the end anyway so why did they bother to pull her out. They may as well have left her there. I ask you . . . Gave a lot of offence. I mean Bianca was quite popular here.'

Megan felt her jaw drop. 'I'd forgotten,' she said slowly. 'I'd completely forgotten. She worked here, didn't she?' So it was explained. *Bianca had shared her stories with Geraint Smithson. And now Smithson suffered the very same delusions, mixed with guilty fact—that as the mine owner he was responsible for some of the suffering that had happened beneath the ground of Llancloudy. And as his brain aged he had become less able to distinguish between Bianca's mad tales and his own true stories. They had become muddled, jumbled together, inextricably tangled.*

Sandra was still talking about Bianca. 'She worked very hard. She wasn't lazy like some of the other cleaners. Didn't rest on her brush for

113

half an hour or have long tea and fag breaks. Oh—I admit. She was slow. Awful slow sometimes. I could have shaken her to move a bit faster. But she did her job. She was reliable and the patients here liked her. She was funny and strange but we knew her. It wasn't her fault that sometimes she'd seem like she was in a world of her own. She turned up. She was honest and she didn't mind what task you set her. Scrubbin' toilets, cleanin' floors. Never too proud to do the humblest of jobs. We'll miss her. And the way she died. Well. It was a horrible accident.'

'Yes. Yes.' Megan stopped outside one of the doors. 'Well—let's have a look at Mr Driver, shall we, Sandra?'

'He's got a visitor,' she said as she pushed the door open. 'An old friend of his from down the mine.'

The friend stood up as they entered. Megan knew him immediately. The small, wiry man, who had seemed so angry at Bianca's funeral. Here, then, was a connection and possibly an explanation. Maybe his anger had been justified. Bianca had been popular here. She had been held in some affection by staff and patients alike. Her death must have seemed an unneccessary waste.

'I suppose you want me to get out.' As expected his voice was truculent.

'Would you mind, Mr Jones. The doctor just wants to have a quick look at your friend.'

The man left but Megan could have sworn he muttered something under his breath. It sounded like, 'For what good it'll do.'

She shrugged and concentrated on her patient.

The matron was right about old Mr Driver. Barely conscious with a distinct death rattle in his throat and skin a pale waxy colour that meant only one thing. Megan listened to his chest and confirmed her initial suspicion that he had only days left to live. At ninety-one he would fail to reach his century. She discussed his care with Sandra, the visitor filed back to his vigil and they continued along the first floor corridor, visiting a few more of the inmates until they reached room four.

She bumped into Geraint Smithson just outside his room. He was a tall man with an aristocratic air only slightly marred by his cardigan wrongly buttoned, slippers on the wrong feet giving him the air of walking, crab-like, in a strange direction and trouser flies left undone.

'Good morning, Geraint.' Megan greeted him warmly, ignoring Sandra Penarth deftly dealing with the fly buttons.

He seemed oblivious to the attentions and returned her grin. 'Well, how are you, Doctor Banesto?'

He had called her by her married name even though she had changed it professionally only three years ago. It didn't fit in with senile dementia. Senility erases recent memory leaving its victims trapped in the past. Sometimes their ancient past. Octogenarians have been known to cry out for their mothers, their schoolfriends, brothers and sisters, forgetting they have spouses, children, children's children—and even sometimes great-grandchildren.

Her curiosity was pricked. 'I've heard you haven't been too well, Mr Smithson.'

He looked past her, straight at the matron. 'Can I have a word with you, doctor?' He spoke deliberately. 'In private.'

'Of course. Look, Sandra. I'll see myself out after I've chatted to Mr Smithson. He's the last of the patients, isn't he? Don't bother waiting around. I'll give you a ring if there's anything particular.' She didn't know why she was dismissing the matron. Only that he wanted it and that she should comply.

Sandra gave her a swift, warning glance which Megan ignored even though they both knew that interviews with disturbed patients were safer accompanied. By ignoring this first rule Megan knew she was silently questioning the fact that Smithson senior was disturbed. Certainly she felt no unease as she followed him into his single room and closed the door— breaking rule number two.

She sat on the chair, he on the bed, his eyes fixed down at his hands fiddling nervously with the cardigan. Something really was bothering

116

him. She waited until finally he looked up.

'Things have begun to prey on my mind, doctor,' he began. 'Things that happened many years ago. I had responsibilities, you see. As a mine owner I was in charge of the men.'

'But your family sold out to the Coal Board years ago.'

'I know that. But the harm was done by my family.'

'You shouldn't feel responsible. It was a different world then. So much less was known about the medical side effects caused by working on the coal face.'

'Things that were wrong in the nineteen fifties are wrong today. The same things.'

'I don't understand.'

The old man's eyes gleamed with a strange fanaticism. 'Then that's where you're not so smart as some that are labelled mad.'

She knew whom he meant and wondered what strange conversations he and Bianca must have held. Geraint Smithson returned her stare with a touch of defiance and something else. An unexpected and triumphant lucidity which felt more threatening than the senility she had been anticipating. Megan felt very uncomfortable— as though there were a third person here, in the room with them. Then she felt angry with herself. She was a doctor. With a patient in a bustling nursing home. She was surrounded by real people. Not alone. And certainly not

117

accompanied by ghosts. She was merely confronted by a man whose mind was surely beginning to fray at the edges. And she felt threatened?

Smithson continued smiling blandly at her until his eyes veered away—towards the window. And following his glance and straightening up a little she saw—quite plainly—the fountain; chubby cherub doing ungainly arabesque and spewing water from his mouth. She looked back at the old man and recognised that he saw much much more than simply the fountain. His vision extended to include not only current reality but past events, fact and fiction.

He stood up. Tall, much taller than she, and bent over her so she could smell his nearness—tobacco, old clothes, carbolic soap. 'I've been resident in this house for more than ninety years,' he said. 'I've seen plenty happen. Good and bad. I remember things that went on many many years ago, before you were born. Now I'm tired and I want to go to the grave with my slate wiped clean of all the memories. But no one will listen to me. They call me mad. They try and make me sleep twenty-four hours a day. They tell me to shut up. But they won't listen.' He sank back on the bed and covered his face with his hands. 'I only want to die with a clean soul' he said. 'A clean heart. *The Calon Lâm* of the song. It's not a lot to ask, is it, doctor?' He was wringing his hands with sudden, acute anguish. 'The trouble is I don't know how I'm going to achieve it if nobody will listen to me.'

Her judgement was clinical. The emotional liability was surely a sign of a failing intellect.

'Perhaps the clergy . . . ?'

Smithson responded with fury. 'I'm not a bloody Catholic. Welsh Methodist. That's what I am. Have been all my life. I'm not about to recant like a tortured infidel.'

It called for quick salve and a friendly hand on his shoulder. 'I wasn't suggesting you were, Mr Smithson. But surely—even the Welsh Methodists can give you some absolution.' Quickly she read his rejection of the word and substituted. 'Peace of mind.'

'Peace of mind, doctor?' The old man's face was screwed up in agony. 'Peace of mind? Who the hell do you think can give me peace of mind? Have you any idea what's playing around in my head? Sin and corruption. Children gone missing. Mothers going to look for them. And never finding them. Fathers grieving for their sons and daughters. Not knowing they're underneath? Underneath, I tell you. Right under their feet. Brothers. Sisters. Old people. Young people. All come to haunt me they are. Ghosts. They're still there, doctor. Underneath us. And *I* dug the grave.' His wild eyes dropped towards the floor.

And Megan knew now why the matron had tried to warn her. Beneath a cloak of politeness and normality, uncontrollable anger was welling up inside him. He had lost control. His id was no longer restrained by his ego. It was making him insane. She edged nearer to the door.

The old man advanced towards her. 'Now I've frightened you, haven't I? Want to get out now, don't you? Want to escape. Get away from the mad man.'

He was mocking her nervousness.

'I tell you, doctor. Maybe I am mad. It's possible. Even a sane person would finally crumble when locked inside their head are events so terrible I can't close my eyes. I dare not sleep. *She* knew. *She* could understand. She told me all about it, confided in me, see. I listened to *her.* Why will no one listen to me?'

Dignity abandoned, Megan walked out of the room as quickly as she could, her heart pounding.

Insanity has this effect on us. As though it was an infectious disease, we want to limit contact. Remove normal values and we panic.

And Wainwright's words sat at the back of her mind like a bag of stones.

'It is not unusual for people who have delusions to retain a good deal of perception and keep in touch with reality.'

*　　　*　　　*

She could not remember an occasion when she

had felt so intimidated by a patient. Even Bianca had not had this effect on her. She ran down the staircase and out of Triagwn then stepped outside into the clean, pure sunshine. She needed to calm herself.

*　　　*　　　*

Once through the garden door she was in a dark funnel of trees: yew, pine and other evergreens which leaned together to form a passage with a subterranean feel. Beneath her feet was a carpet of silent needles. In the few spots where the trunks were not placed too close together she could glimpse daylight; dazzling bright triangles of blue that gave an illusion of unreality as though she were peering from a darkened auditorium onto a lit stage.

*　　　*　　　*

Someone was coming towards her, whistling. A man. Tall. Bulky. Silhouetted in the deep shade. Striding purposefully in time to his tune. As he drew nearer she knew him. Smithson the younger. Arwel. Somewhere in his fifties, oft divorced. A member of the Llangeinor Hunt. Megan always had seen more of the bullying mine owner in the son than in the father.

'Doctor Banesto.' He had a loud, carrying

voice, louder and echoing, contained in the enclosed space. 'Sandra told me I might just find you out here. You saw my father?'

She took in his tweed jacket and plus fours. Straight out of a cartoon book. What Ho, Jeeves?

'Hello, Mr Smithson.'

As soon as he reached her he gave her a boisterous nudge. 'Arwel, Megan. You know me well enough to call me that. How did you find my father?'

'Very strange.'

Piggy little eyes bored into hers. 'His mind is going, Megan. What are you going to do about it?'

'There isn't a lot I can do.'

'Sandra suggests you write him up for some more sedation.'

'I *could* do that. Arwel. Your father is . . .'

'Senile—not to put too fine a point on it. Don't believe in all this politeness calling it Alzheimers. He's in his nineties and he's losing his marbles. A hooker short of a rugby team— as they say. Sandra can't keep him here at Triagwn House because she hasn't got the staff if he's going to be so disruptive and frighten the other residents with all his stupid stories. He's causing mayhem there. You heard about Mrs Price Morgan? Nearly had a nervous breakdown.' His chuckle contained no sympathy.

'Yes—but.' They had reached the end of the

tree tunnel and Megan could see Arwel Smithson's face very clearly. Too clearly. She didn't like what she saw. It was a dissolute face, podged up with alcohol, its muscles lax, the sort of face Caligula might have had. Cruel and unpitying. Arwel was as frightening as his father in a different way. He would have been a merciless master, the sort to tumble the maids then turn them out if they became pregnant.

'I want my father to be properly taken care of,' Arwel said as though he didn't expect to be argued with. 'I want him fed with something that will keep him quiet and out of trouble. If you can't do that he'll have to be put in a mental hospital and I wouldn't like that. You understand?'

Her hackles rose. She was a doctor. Not a scullery maid. Paid by the Health Service. Not by him. And yet, more than fifty years after his family must have last paid a GP's bill he still believed he could order her around like a servant.

'I'll do whatever I believe best for your father's health and well being, Mr Smithson. My judgement will be made on clinical grounds.'

'As you wish.' He tried to stare her out. And when that failed, Smithson turned on his heel and strode back along the yew tunnel.

Megan drew out into the sunshine with a feeling of intense fury.

123

*   *   *

Around the side of Triagwn House had once been a walled kitchen garden that must have provided fresh produce, flowers and vegetables for most of the year. But the vegetable plots had long since been turfed over, seats placed at the corners of the geometric paths, rose beds planted. There was little left of the original except a couple of gnarled trees which bore apples speckled with blight. A few of the residents were enjoying the warm weather and, knowing she was in danger of being called over for an impromptu consultation, Megan hurried through the garden and skirted the house until she was standing in front of the fountain. She sat down, on the stone rim, temporarily swamped by visions. Bianca being dragged from here, as a child, almost dead. The old man who was probably still staring out of the window, down at her, his decaying mind filled with ghosts and ghoulies. His son, determined he should be sedated until he cause 'no trouble'. Her mind drifted on, lulled by the sound of water spouting from the stone child's mouth. Megan focused on it and wondered whether Bianca had believed the stone child was drowning. She put her hand in the water and rippled the surface.

Look at her garments

Clinging like cerements
Whilst the wave constantly
Drips from her clothing.
The poem was still haunting her.

Maybe all drowned people resemble the woman of Hood's poem in one way or another.

And then for no good reason other than that she was still and allowing her mind to wander at will, as Megan sat against the fountain, her mind flicked to her own problem.

*   *   *

She should never have married Guido. It had been the stupidest decision of her life, one of the few made entirely with her heart totally undirected by her head. She stared into the waters and was at last brutally honest with herself. He had been a mistake. That was all. Her life was not irretrievably ruined. She had simply—made—a—mistake. She looked down into the water, at the reflection of the red brick facade and the smooth bottom of the pool. People had dropped coins in, perhaps believing it would bring them luck. Or maybe she was wrong and it was simply generosity. A lead plaque beneath the cherub proclaimed any profits from the fountain would be donated to the National Schizophrenic Association. Megan fished around in her own pocket, found a fifty-pence piece and dropped it in too. They needed money and she needed luck. Like the old man whose silhouette was framed in the upper floor window she needed to lay some ghosts.

Maybe fifty-pence was all it had needed. As Megan walked away from the fountain she began to put her life into perspective. 'Yes,' she said to herself. 'I made a mistake. But I am still in control. I am still a good doctor.'

And she felt a welcome peace.

CHAPTER NINE

The weekend, sure enough, turned out dull and wet. Megan visited her parents who had retired to Southerndown in a glass-fronted bungalow, and on the Sunday she walked the downs with her father. He had always been a fit, active man, a lifelong supporter of the local rugby club, still involved in their training. They enjoyed their country walks together, taking their binoculars to spy on the local birdlife. The pattern of their wings, their shape when perched, colour, habitat and habit were enough for them to identify most common species. Her mother always stayed at home, protesting she had the Sunday dinner to cook. But Megan knew the minute she and her father had turned the corner and Cymro, their Welsh Border Collie, had stopped barking his enthusiasm, her mother would retire to the sofa with the latest in a string of novels, borrowed from the library.

*   *   *

She returned to Llancloudy late on the Sunday night, invigorated by the sea air and her mother's cooking, and rose early on the Monday morning, still feeling the benefit.

But the first patient of her morning surgery was Carole Symmonds.

Bianca's daughter was hardly in through the door when she started to voice her reason for coming. 'I've been doing a lot of thinking, Doctor Banesto,' she began. 'And I'm really not happy.'

Megan ushered her in. Through the open door she took in the waiting patients' curious stare.

Briefly she touched her patient's shoulder. 'It's a natural grief reaction, Carole.'

Bianca's daughter sat down heavily and faced Megan across the desk. Her face was tense and unhappy. More lined even than she had been at the funeral. Yet Bianca had been dead now for more than a month. Yet grief wasn't the prime expression on Carole's face but bewilderment. 'No,' she said. 'I can accept Mam's death. At the back of my mind I've always had the feeling something would happen to her—that she might have an accident—get run over, fall—or something.

127

She always seemed so vulnerable. But it isn't that, Doctor Banesto. It's everything else.'

Megan waited.

'It's a few questions I've been going over and over in my mind. Since Mam died I haven't stopped asking the same old questions. Where the hell was she all day Saturday? Why did no one see her? Not a single person. I've asked in the video shop. I've asked in the Co-op and I've been to the chippie. She didn't go to any of those places all day Saturday. But Esther told me Mam left the house on Saturday morning and never came back again. All right.' She held a finger up. 'Esther's a bit *twp*. She might be mistaken. But not everybody else in Llancloudy. Not the entire population. Nobody saw her, doctor. *Nobody*. I've been askin' around. It's as though Mam became invisible. Doris Baker is *certain* that she gave Mam her tablets on the Saturday morning and never saw her again.

'The second question I've been asking myself is this. Why did she go up the pool so late? Why didn't *anyone* see her going up there? It's quite a walk from Mam's house to the Slaggy Pool but nobody saw her. Again it's like she became *invisible.*'

Megan opened her mouth to speak. And got no farther.

'And couldn't be seen again until they fished her out of that bloody pool on Monday morning.'

128

'Talk to the police,' Megan urged.

'Oh—the police.' Carole's tone was scathing enough for Megan to withhold any defence. 'Couldn't find out who's joyridin' the cars around here when the kids are drivin' up and down the damned housin' estates in full view of the people livin' there. Can't bring some of the little buggers to court for crimes everybody's seen them do. How the hell are they going to tell me what happened to my mam when they can't solve what's under their noses?'

'Talk to PC Williams.'

Carole Symmonds turned a shrewd eye on Megan. 'Sweet on him once, weren't you. When you were both at school.' She gave a knowing wink. 'Still—I suppose it was a long time ago. And he's married now. Though you are not. Not any more, anyway.'

Megan winced and Carole continued regardless. 'Water under the bridge, as they say. Tell you what. Alun Williams will probably talk to you. And my Mam was your patient. Why don't you have a word with him?'

'I can't. There's nothing to go on.'

'I've got an idea.' Carole glanced back over her shoulder, as though worried someone might be listening in. 'You know them kids?'

'Which kids?'

'The ones that went for my mam last year. The ones that hang around with Joel Parker.'

Megan was aware that she could say nothing.

129

Nothing. Because anything she might say could be repeated, possibly misquoted, definitely attributed—to her. She could hear the words that would be said. 'And the doctor said she thought bloody Joel Parker and his mates pushed my poor mother into the pool. They murdered her. That's what she said.'

'Look—Carole,' Megan said uncomfortably. 'You should talk to PC Williams yourself. I can't intervene. It wouldnt be professional. It's possible Esther's mistaken and your mum did come home that night then went out sometime on Sunday. Maybe she wasn't feeling well and just went to sleep. Then woke up, a bit disorientated some time on Sunday evening and wandered outside, ended up at the Slaggy Pool . . .'

'I don't think Esther's mistaken. And anyway I'm not relying so much on what *she* said as what all the people have told me who've got the shops where Mam used to hang out. The coroner told me the pathologist put the time of death as sometime Sunday night. She would have to have stayed out the way all day Saturday and all day Sunday. She didn't drown on Saturday. They found her soon enough on Monday morning didn't they. Because her clothes were visible on the surface. I've talked to Mervyn Jones and he told me. He was one of the ones that first saw her in the water. The clothes weren't there any time Sunday.' Her face suddenly sagged

130

further. 'Look, Doctor Banesto. I'm not saying she *was* pushed. I'm only saying I want a proper investigation. Better than what they've done.'

'Talk to the police,' Megan urged again.

Carole nodded, all her chins wobbling in unanimous agreement. 'I will. I can tell you. I certainly will.'

*   *   *

Megan finished surgery, took a list of visits from the receptionists and left, meaning to continue with her morning's work. But once inside her car she sat, immobile, finding herself thrown back to last month's events.

Bianca's death still felt like unfinished business.

With the result that she didn't even get as far as turning the engine over but as though in a dream, controlled by some force other than her own will she climbed out of her car, locked the door behind her and crossed the road to the Slaggy Pool. The water reflected the weather, the reflected grey further dulled by the dark sludge of water stained with coal dust. Megan tried to peer to the bottom but it was impossible.

A few folk were ignoring the damp to sit around on the wooden park benches but once there they lost their animation and sat, immobile, staring down into the dark waters.

131

All were dressed in sombre colours. Black, brown, navy macs, their hoods drawn over their heads, like monks. No one took any notice of her. They reminded her of an old Simon & Garfunkel song about old friends sitting on park benches like bookends. One of the 'bookends' looked vaguely familiar but it took a few moments before she remembered who he was—the angry visitor to the dying Caspian Driver. She nodded a hello and he moved his head in greeting before bowing it again. She did not greet any of the other figures and they did not acknowledge her while she stood for a moment at the edge of the pool and closed her eyes, this time wilfully conjuring up the words.

> *As when with the daring Last look of despairing*
> *Fix'd on futurity.*

Emotions are unchanged with the centuries.

Her eyes snapped open. She was deceived. The poem was the tragic suicide of a young woman who could not cope with the shame of being pregnant. She must stop being misled by it. *Look, Megan. Look.* The edges of the pool *were* muddy. They were also slightly slippery. But not very. Stones had been placed round the perimeter to prevent the banks from caving in. Large, round, flat stones, like the ones harvested from Southerndown beach by

Ground Force aficionados. Maybe Bianca had hit her head on one of these. She peered closer, stooping slightly. It would be easy to assume Bianca had stolen up here at dead of night in order to indulge her kleptomania—that irresistible temptation to steal that had led her through the courts on many occasions. Maybe she had wanted some special stone and had reasoned she must steal here after dark

That would be a logical explanation.

But it was not the right one. Bianca had never hidden her thieving.

The round, flat stones formed a perfect circle, grinning back like teeth.

Her eyes were caught by a splash of colour in the drab scene. On the surface of the pool floated a wreath, blown towards the sides, like a child's sailing dinghy. Dark red roses, the card soggily draped over the stems, like Dali's watches, the flowers already starting to discolour—to darken and curl. Megan hardly needed to make any effort to decipher the message displayed. She knew what it would say.

Er Serchus Cof, Anwyl Mam, and the name, *Carole.*

Megan turned away from the pool, returned to her car and resolutely rang the police station. It was not for her that she did it. There was no selfish motive. Only a desire for pure truth.

LIAR.

The same, friendly desk sergeant answered as before. And again he recognised her voice. There was no need to give her name.

'Police Constable Williams? He's in today Doctor Banesto. I'll just put you through.'

Her tension mounted as she waited for Alun's voice knowing whatever he had intimated at Bianca's funeral he would not be pleased to hear from her at work. People chatter. Seconds ticked away. She glanced at her watch. She would be late starting her visits. The sick would wonder where she . . .

'Meggie.' Irritation always made his voice gravelly. She had heard this before. When matches had been lost. When he had given away a vital pass. When she had told him of her decision to leave. A hundred times before she had picked up on this harshness. Too many times to pretend even to herself that she did not recognise its significance now.

Her anticipation had been right. He was not pleased to hear from her.

'What is it?'

'Answer me a question?'

'Depends what it is.' The distance in his voice was enough to make her cringe.

'The stone carving you found in Bianca's pocket. Where do you think it came from?'

'We've given it some thought but we don't

think it's of any significance.'

She waited.

'We did wonder whether it had been broken off something in one of the churches. You see—it was something like you'd find there, like a religious carving. And it had been broken off not long ago. The break was quite clean.'

'And?'

'Well—we drew a blank. None of the vicars seemed to recognise it.'

He was sounding uncomfortable. 'Sorry, Megan. That's all I can tell you.'

Nothing, in other words.

She said a brief goodbye, pressed the End Call button on her mobile, turned the key in her car and revved up, driving quickly to one of the ugliest council estates in the world. Grey, flat-roofed, squashed in like poor quality chicken coops. It fitted her picture of Russian Gulags but this was South Wales. This was also where her first visit of the day was. And it was where Mandy Parker, Joel's mother, lived.

Megan dealt swiftly with the bronchitic old man who lived in one of the chicken coops, wrote out a prescription for some Ventolin for his nebuliser and lingered outside Joel Parker's house, knowing it was ill advised yet unable to stop herself from wondering. What if . . . ? The garden was untended, like many round here. The grass grew high, the fence was broken, the front door had had a replacement

135

panel inserted. Still unpainted MDF. A dog barked from around the back. She heard its chain rattle. A curtain twitched in response. From one of the houses she heard the throb of hard house music. An upstairs curtain billowed behind a cracked pane of glass. People here could be brutal in their retribution and Joel Parker had upset plenty of inhabitants on this estate. A youth sauntered down the path. Leered at her. 'Lookin' for someone sick, doctor?'

It wasn't Joel but his younger half-brother, Stefan. Shaven head, earrings. An enormous, flame orange T-shirt, baggy shorts and trainers with thick soles. No more than ten years old. He eyeballed her fearlessly. 'Well are you?'

She met his defiant, world-hating eyes and wondered whether he knew anything about Bianca Rhys's death. 'No. I've just been visiting a patient.'

Stefan lounged against the gate and kicked at the rotten post. It crumbled under his shoes. 'What—old Parry?'

She smiled. 'Just a patient.'

'Sorree,' he said rudely. 'Forgot. You can't tell secrets, can you? Not that I could bloody well care anyway. See who you like. There's nobody sick in our house.'

'Good. Less work for me.'

He was still watching her as she climbed back into her car, seemed to wait for her to switch the engine on. She could still see him watching her in the rear view mirror as she drove back down the road. He seemed very anxious for her to go. She wondered why. A permanently guilty conscience? Or was there some particular reason why he wanted rid of her? She recalled Carole Symmonds' unhappy heart-searching and desperately wished she could talk to Alun about her own misgivings.

Instead she drove to her next visit, to one of the semis on the new estate and a baby with croup.

It was as she was again climbing back into her car that her mobile phone rang.

Number Anonymous.

Although it had been her wish she was startled to recognise Alun's voice. 'Megan.'

He still sounded stern. 'Have you been egging Carole Symmonds on?'

'I don't know what you mean.'

'She's been down here making allegations that could end her up in court.'

'Well it's nothing to do with—'

'She said she'd discussed it with you.'

'I said hardly anything.'

'Well she's got the impression that you're along with her about her mother's death. That there's more to it than accident. And now she's insisting on a full investigation.'

Megan was stung. 'She's entitled to that, isn't she?'

'There isn't any point.'

She felt a sudden surge of indignation. 'This

isn't to do with me, Alun.'

'No?'

'No.' But there remained one question that had been burning her curiosity. She might as well be hanged for a sheep as a . . . 'Where was Joel Parker on Saturday night?' she asked recklessly.

'With his dad in the bloody Rhondda for the weekend.'

He wasn't just irritated. He was furious. *And* he'd been anticipating her question.

'Megan. You saw Bianca Rhys on Friday. Joel Parker was at school all day and his dad picked him up outside the school gates. Understand? He stayed with his dad all weekend and he was dropped off again Monday morning back outside the school gates.'

'Convenient.' The word slipped out before she could stop it.

'That he's got an alibi, you mean? Well it's a bloody good job he has otherwise tittle tattlers like you and that bloody daughter of Bianca's would be . . .' He was too angry to continue.

Megan waited.

'Honestly. Talk about giving a horse a bad name.'

'It's a dog, Alun.' Megan desperately tried to summon up her last vestiges of dignity.

'I don't care what bloody animal it is. Bianca drowned. Unfortunate. But there isn't always someone you can blame for the unfortunate.'

138

One more Unfortunate, One more Unfortunate. The phrase spun around in her head. *One more unfortunate.*

Megan was silent, listening to the words and hearing Alun's rapid breaths down the phone. More puffed by anger than by a race up the pitch to the twenty-two line.

'Was there anything else?'

'Alun, I'm sorry. I promised . . .'

'I know who you promised, Meggie. And I understand that Carole's upset but she mustn't go around spreading rumours.' Already he was melting. His anger had always been quick to raise, swift to subside. By the time the ref had reached him he was invariably already apologising. She knew his style. Only now was she realising just how well. 'This is a small place, Meggie. Rumours start all too easily. You and me going for a drink, Carole Symmonds making allegations about Joel Parker. This isn't a big city like Cardiff where you can get lost. Mud sticks.'

'Alun—'

'Leave it.'

She thought she understood him completely, read into the two words an instruction to abandon both the examples he had quoted.

She was silent and again his apology was swift.

'I'm sorry. Meggie. I'm being a bit short with you.'

Yes you are.

'No. No. It's OK. You're right to warn me off.'

He was silent for a moment and when he spoke again she could hear the concern in his voice. 'Meggie—are you all right?'

'Of course I'm all right. Why wouldn't I be?'

'It's just that. Well—you're getting yourself in a stew all about an accident. I've been years in the police force. I *know* there's nothing suspicious about Bianca's death. I can't understand the way you're carrying on. You don't like Joel Parker. OK. You're not alone there I can tell you. But to start throwing mud at him. I mean—what are you suggesting? You're not being rational. Meggie. It's not sensible. It's not *you*.'

He was right. It was not her. Not sensible Megan, Megan the swot, Doctor Banesto. But Doctor Banesto was not always sensible. She had gone on holiday, had a flirtation with an Italian, brought him back to the valleys. And married him. Megan Banesto lacked judgement. She was impulsive.

'I think you're working too hard. And the strain of the divorce—it's starting to show. I think you should go away far from here, Megan, and have a good holiday.'

*   *   *

She thanked him politely and formally.

140

CHAPTER TEN

Days drifted by during which Megan did manage to forget about Bianca. Her life was filled with work and visits to far flung friends. As autumn approached the surgery grew busier and she was further distracted.

And then early in October she received a summons to attend the coroner's court on the following Friday.

In cases where there was doubt burial normally took place after the coroner had pronounced his verdict. But coroners are busy people and relatives tend to want expedient burial. It aids the grieving process. And so the police and the coroner had come to agreement that Bianca could be buried before judgement was finally pronounced.

*　　　*　　　*

The inquest had been set for 11 am in the morning in the coroner's court in Bridgend. As Megan set out she had a feeling of underlying calm, a sense of hope that justice would be seen to be done, that some explanation of Bianca's death would be forthcoming. The other inhabitants of Llancloudy had forgotten about Bianca. Even Carole Symmonds had not returned for a repeat prescription of her sleeping pills. But Megan was uncomfortably aware that Bianca's death still lay at the back of her mind. Had she been a superstitious woman she might have believed Bianca's restless soul roamed the earth. But it was not in her religious repertoire. So as she turned right into the court car park she looked forward to a resolution.

*   *   *

The first person she saw as she pulled into a parking bay was Carole herself, the centre of a cluster of people, one of whom was wielding a reporter's notebook; another wafted a large, furred microphone in front of her. Megan gave her a quick smile which Carole returned before diverting her attention back to the woman in jeans who was scribbling everything down at a furious rate. Behind her, just climbing out of a police car, was Alun—in uniform. He gave her a brief nod and walked straight into the coroner's court. It was the cue for the others to file in behind him.

The interior reminded Megan more of a schoolroom than a courtroom. And like a schoolroom there was no doubt who was directing the proceedings. The coroner, Ieuan Griffiths, sat at the front, frowning over some papers. He was hardly known personally to Megan though she had spoken to him and his office frequently over the phone. He was short

142

and stocky with pale skin, black curly hair and blue eyes, the type thought of as physically typical of the Welsh. He cleared his throat, looked up and the room fell silent.

*   *   *

The coroner addressed Carole Symmonds first, in a voice so soft and quiet the others could hardly hear. But Megan could tell by his tone that they were words of sympathy. He was patently well used to dealing with anguished, grieving relatives. And angry ones too. Whatever he did say Carole Symmonds looked instantly calmer and partially appeased. Megan glanced around the courtroom and wondered who everyone else was. Relatives, Press, friends? Alun was sitting two seats to her left. He glanced across and gave her a warm, chummy smile. At that very instant he felt like a good friend. A really good friend, someone she could trust and rely on—implicitly. The coroner cleared his throat and addressed everyone in the room. He spoke with heavy authority, setting out his remit like a strict teacher or as clearly as a lawyer. 'My job here today,' he said loudly, 'is to establish the facts surrounding the death of Bianca Rhys. It is not my job to point the finger although it might be appropriate for me to make certain recommendations.' He cleared his throat again. 'Perhaps we could start with you, Police Constable Williams.'

Megan watched Alun move towards the front with the heavy, rolling walk of a sportsman. He began at once, referring to his notebook frequently and giving evidence clearly and unambiguously.

Times, dates. All the facts with no interpretation and no emotion. Ieuan Griffiths listened with approval.

'I was summoned to Llancloudy Pool on Monday the fifth of August at 10 am with the information that a body was visible in the pool. Myself and Police Constable Jarvis Watkins arrived at the scene within ten minutes.' He glanced up, his broad face troubled for an instant. 'Quite a large crowd had gathered and we saw, in the water, what looked like a bundle of clothes. Myself and PC Jarvis Watkins waded in, brought out the body of a woman and lay it on the bank. I recognised it straight away as Bianca Rhys.'

'How?' interrupted the Coroner.

'She was well known to us.' Alun flushed, 'She had very—distinctive hair, sir.'

Carole Symmonds gave a noisy sob into her handkerchief and the woman sitting by her put her arm around her. The coroner gave her a swift glance and asked for a glass of water to be brought. Carole took a few sips and put it down beneath her chair.

The coroner continued with his questions. 'Did you make any attempt at resuscitation?'

'No, sir.' A swift, apologetic glance at Carole. 'The body was quite cold. I was of the opinion it had been in the water too long for us to be able to bring her round.'

'Were there any marks around the pool to indicate she might have fallen in?'

Alun had beautiful eyes. Very dark green-brown, fringed with thick black lashes. Megan leaned back in her seat and watched him answer the coroner's questions.

'I didn't know what to think, sir. The ground around the pool was heavily footmarked because so many people had gathered.' Megan looked at Carole. She was watching Alun with a definite challenge in her face.

'I see.' Ieuan Griffiths looked displeased. 'And then what did you do?'

'In cases like this,' Alun said slowly, 'it's advisable to have life pronounced extinct at the scene.' He risked the tiniest of smiles at Megan. 'Doctor Banesto's surgery is just across the road so I summoned her.'

'I see.' The coroner adjusted his glasses, glanced down at his notes and looked Alun straight in the eye. 'And, Constable Williams, did you have any reason at your preliminary assessment of the case that death was in any way due to other than natural causes?'

Alun did not hesitate. 'No, sir, I did not.'

Megan knew both the deliberation and choice of words had been selected to put Carole Symmonds' mind at rest. She risked a swift glance. Carole was staring fixedly at Ieuan Griffiths as though she had absolute trust in him.

The coroner gave a brief summing up and Megan knew she would have to give her statement next.

She was called.

As she stood up she caught sight of Esther Magellan sitting alone—right at the back—apart from everyone else. The seats around her were unoccupied. As usual she was bizarrely dressed in a flowery cotton skirt and a vividly coloured flowered blouse. Her face was frozen of all emotion except one. She was suffused with intense disappointment as though Megan was letting her down. Megan felt irritated. What did Esther expect her to say?

*   *   *

The coroner addressed her from her left. 'Doctor Banesto. Perhaps you'd continue.'

'When I arrived at the banks of Llancloudy Pool,' she began slowly, 'I could see Bianca Rhys's body lying on the bank. I touched her. As Police Constable Williams has already said she was quite cold.' On the tips of her fingers Megan could still feel the chill of Bianca's skin like a dead, uncooked fish.

'Rigor mortis was present. I was of the opinion she had been lifeless for some hours.'

Megan ran a swift check on the faces watching her. 'I checked for a heartbeat with my stethoscope and formally pronounced life extinct.'

'You didn't take her temperature or form any opinion as to how long she'd been dead?'

'I didn't take her temperature.' The words were sticking in her throat. She was having a struggle to retain control. Taking the temperature would have meant a very public intrusion. Not for the world would she have exposed Bianca's sad skinny little body to the watching public. She met the coroner's eyes and knew he read her—perfectly.

'I formed the opinion she had been dead for at least twelve hours. There was some wrinkling in the skin suggesting she had been in the water for some length of time.'

The coroner gave her the briefest of smiles. 'Thank you, Doctor Banesto.'

As a contribution it felt very little. Megan sat down, her mind still struggling to blot out the flashbacks. The dress, sodden and dripping, Bianca's mouth, slightly open, filled with the filthy, coal-black water of Llancloudy Pool.

The police surgeon gave his evidence concisely, that Bianca 'appeared to have drowned' and that he had authorised removal of the body, suggesting they bag up her hands to preserve any trace evidence and finishing with the sentence, 'Then we awaited the results of the postmortem.'

The coroner next turned his attention to a tall, slim man in his early fifties who introduced himself as Franklin Jones-Watson, pathologist. He was clear and very precise about his postmortem findings. Too sure. Megan listened intently.

'The deceased was a poorly nourished female of fifty-seven years old. She looked older, Mr Griffiths. She weighed forty-five kilograms when stripped. On speaking to Doctor Banesto, the deceased's general practitioner, I understand Bianca Rhys was a paranoid schizophrenic undergoing regular therapy. I formed the opinion that she slipped and fell into the pool, hitting her head, possibly against the side or even on some object in the pool. A large amount of debris was present at the bottom of the pond. I believe that the fall combined with even such minor trauma caused her to die of shock. That would be consistent with my postmortem findings.'

'Were there any marks on the body?'

'Only the one bruise on the deceased's occiput done at around the time of death. The deceased's nails were broken and mud was retrieved from beneath them furthering my deduction of the mode of the deceased's death.'

He was looking complacent. It made Megan uncomfortable—tempted her to mistrust him.

148

She looked across at Alun. His gaze was fixed firmly forward. But she could tell from his profile that he accepted the pathologist's statement without question. And why not? It had been thorough.

'How long did you think Mrs Rhys had been dead for?'

'I examined the body at two pm on Monday the fifth of August, four hours after the body was first discovered. At that time I was of the opinion she had been dead for something more than twelve hours. Possibly up to twenty-four hours. It's very difficult to be precise after prolonged immersion in water. Added to that the weather was warm with temperatures well up into the seventies.'

'Was there anything else discovered at postmortem which might indicate the circumstances surrounding Bianca's death?'

'I took some blood for serology,' Franklin Jones-Watson said. 'They showed a high level of hypnotics—namely Chlorpromazine—or Lagactil.' For the first time he seemed aware of Carole Symmonds. He looked at her for a brief moment before continuing. 'She might well have been prescribed that for her general condition.'

'Was she, Doctor Banesto?'

Megan nodded. 'Yes, sir.'

'And this was . . . ?'

'Normally administered by a neighbour who gave her her daily tablets.'

149

'So an overdose . . . ?'

'I didn't say an overdose, sir, but enough to make her quite drowsy.'

Now Megan found herself admiring Jones-Watson's precision.

'And your opinion was . . . ?'

'These were large amounts but some schizophrenics are sedated quite heavily.'

The coroner addressed his next question to Megan. 'What dose was Mrs Rhys prescribed?'

'100 mgms, three times a day.'

The coroner nodded. Both a doctor and a legal man he thought he understood perfectly. Bianca had hoarded her medication, probably pretended to swallow it, spat it out and saved it 'for a rainy day'.

'I'd also like it mentioned there was an injection site on her right buttock.'

'How old was the injection site, doctor?'

Jones-Watson peered at her through rimless glasses with his intelligent grey eyes. 'A day or two.'

The coroner glanced down at his notes and nodded. 'I believe Doctor Banesto mentioned in her statement that she had administered an injection to the right buttock on the Friday before the deceased's death. And her lungs?'

'It was a dry drowning,' Jones-Watson replied. 'No water was found in her lungs, only in her mouth and some in her oesophagus. She did not breathe beneath the water.'

The coroner spoke to Carole Symmonds.

150

'Would you like all this explaining to you?'

She nodded and the coroner, still speaking in the same gentle tone, clarified all the postmortem findings. It gave her a free moment to ponder.

*   *   *

As she had watched the pathologist give his evidence she remembered the primary rules of forensic pathology. You don't construct facts around the forensic evidence but analyse both separately before slotting them together. Jones-Watson was ignoring slices of forensic evidence because they failed to fit in with his initial theory. Namely the bruise on the occiput. How did she do it? If she had tumbled in the pool surely she would have fallen head first. Knowing Bianca's fear of bodies of water Megan could not imagine her standing with her back to the pool yet close enough to the edge to fall in.

*   *   *

Bruising should have been found on the front of her head—if anywhere. Not on the back. Theories should have come last in his statement—not first. Listening to his self assurance she had begun to mistrust his conceit. She would have preferred a more balanced pathologist, one who didn't make

151

premature assumptions. Was she the only one to have these misgivings? Again she glanced across the aisle at Alun. He looked contented. She swivelled round to see Carole Symmonds. But Carole was holding a hankie up to her eyes. Not enough of her face was visible to know whether she accepted this version of events or not. As Megan scanned the courtroom she realised that she was the only person dissatisfied with the proceedings. Even Caspian Driver's visitor was nodding approvingly at the pathologist. It seemed he too was convinced.

Megan turned back to the front to hear the coroner's summing up. And knew he had decided the verdict before the proceedings had begun. The open court had been a sop to Bianca's daughter, a means of reassuring her that everything that should, had been done. The coroner was already shuffling his papers together, fastening them with a giant paper clip. He was satisfied. He had probably already filled his verdict in. He addressed one last question at Alun. 'Are there any ongoing enquiries, Constable Williams?'

'We're still trying to find witnesses,' Alun said, 'but we don't feel there's any question of foul play.'

'And no suicide note was found?'

'No, sir.'

Again Alun gave Megan the briefest of glances. And so the coroner made his statement—that there was no evidence to indicate that Bianca Rhys had intended to take her own life but it seemed she had fallen unintentionally into Llancloudy Pool.

Death by misadventure.

He was accepting Jones-Watson's version of events.

In fact all professional people, Alun, the coroner, the police surgeon, the pathologist—as well as the family and friends accepted the verdict without a hint of misgiving.

*   *   *

So why couldn't she?

CHAPTER ELEVEN

Megan stood up with everyone else and filed out slowly.

She had expected to feel reassured after the coroner's court. But she didn't. Instead she felt troubled—as though something was wrong. It felt as though everyone had glossed over Bianca's death, without taking the trouble to explore the alternatives. What about the head injury? She couldn't see how anyone could hit the back of their head either against the side of the pool or on the bottom. Or exactly when she had tumbled—unseen by anyone. Neither had they addressed the puzzle of where Bianca had been from Saturday morning to Monday morning—invisible to everyone in Llancloudy. Nobody had asked the simplest of questions. Was there trace evidence on the stones at the side of the shallow pool? Had anyone even bothered to look? How had she walked up there without anyone seeing her when it was a distance of a little over a mile?

The silent explanation to every unasked question was the same. Bianca was irrational therefore her movements would not be explained rationally. And no one bothered to ask.

In a sudden fit of frustration, Megan caught up with Alun outside the courtroom, tugging his arm.

'And are you happy with that?' she demanded.

Again he looked angry. 'Of course I'm happy Megan.' He glanced around to see who was watching or listening. Carole Symmonds was, her eyes brightly inquisitive.

Alun shook his arm free. 'As happy as I can be after an accident.'

'Misadventure,' she corrected.

He interpreted her sarcasm correctly. 'That's right, Megan. Misadventure. That's what the coroner said. That's the official verdict. Now just drop it, will you. Don't go looking for toads under stones.'

'Because they might be there?'

'They're not, Meggie. They're not.'

They stood for a while, staring at each other. Megan turned away first. She was reading coldness and rejection in his face. They were expressions she had never read before and they both shocked and hurt her. He might like her. Love her—a little. Lust after her. But behind all that something deep within him was beginning to dislike her too.

She mumbled something and crossed the car park to where Carole Symmonds was shaking the Coroner's hand. Megan waited until he had walked on and then asked Carole the same question.

'Are you happy with the verdict?'

'Very happy,' Carole said. 'I feel much happier—more settled about Mam's death now. I can picture what happened. And the coroner's told me quite certainly that she didn't suffer. It was instant. She never really knew what happened to her.'

And neither will we.

'Knowing Mam didn't suffer makes it easier for me, doctor.' Carole was smiling in the direction of the coroner's dark green Audi indicating to turn right out of the car park. 'You really feel you can trust him.'

Megan unlocked her car with a feeling of exasperation which was tinged with isolation. She was the only one to voice any misgivings.

She drove straight home without speaking to anyone else.

No one wanted trouble.

Bianca had been interred. The verdict had been passed. She wasn't quite happy with the verdict but what was she going to do about it?

And so Megan did nothing. Life moved on. She took up the invitation to dinner with Phil and Angharad, she copied one of the TV chef's dinner parties and had a riotous weekend in Torquay with a couple of med. school friends who were kind enough not to mention Guido's name for the entire weekend.

She even spent an evening at Cardiff's new Festival Hall listening to a concert of Harp & Mozart. And the man who had invited her was what her mother laughingly called, 'a bit of a charmer'. So life was good. Too good to ruminate over the tragic death of a sad, mad woman.

She even visited Triagwn once a week, as was contracted but she was not asked to see Geraint Smithson.

* * *

And then, on the first day of November—a Friday—Megan found a note in her pigeonhole asking her to ring Arwel.

He picked up on the first ring and as usual his voice was abrupt and peremptory.

'I asked you, Doctor Banesto, if you would sedate my father to relieve his wanderings and help the staff. They have informed me that you have done no such thing. Now they are finding him so difficult they are threatening to have him transferred to one of the psychiatric establishments.'

'He's already written up for appropriate medication.'

'Well he needs more.' A pause. 'Or something else. Something stronger. He's causing chaos there.'

He always got under her skin.

'I'll go and see him today,' Megan said sharply. 'I'll use my clinical judgement to decide how best to deal with him.'

Arwel's answer was a loud snort and Megan put the phone down.

*   *   *

The colours of November appeared dingy and unwashed when compared with August's bright tints. Megan brushed the surgery blinds apart and looked at today's ice grey sky. Soon every last vestige of colour would be drained from the valley. Rousseau and Gauguin would be lost; the hues would be that of Gericault, despairing, muted, depressing greys, blacks, charcoal.

She hated the winter.

Maybe she should follow advice and visit

157

the travel agent in Bridgend. She was owed a couple of weeks' holiday. India, Africa or the Caribbean could always provide heat and colour. A few hours on an aeroplane would soon make her forget a Welsh winter.

As she drove towards Triagwn she dreamed again of Italy as it had looked when Guido had first welcomed her to his restaurant, the faded red terracotta, brilliant scarlet flowers, the scent of herbs growing in pots. And he had looked so different, his shirt super-white against the olive skin, his eyes very very dark and his oiled black hair. No wonder she had tripped and fallen for him.

She smiled.

*   *   *

Normally she would announce her arrival but this was an unofficial visit. She had been summoned by Arwel Smithson to visit his father. She did not want to be escorted round by Sandra, to see everyone who had an ache or a pain and wanted to speak to the doctor. One patient would be enough. She wanted to drive to Bridgend and plan a short escape.

So she parked the car round the back of Triagwn and walked in through the kitchen entrance. No one saw her. The nurses must be busy elsewhere. And no one knew she was coming except Arwel. The corridor was deserted. At this time of the morning it was in the kitchen that activities were centred. She could hear the clatter of pans and the hum of kitchen gossip, the radio providing old pop tunes to work by. Megan passed straight by and walked upstairs towards room four. She was anxious to find out for herself how much disruption Smithson senior was really causing.

It was obvious before she reached the top of the stairs.

She could hear the old man shouting from the end of the corridor. 'Why will no one believe me? I tell you it's true. It's *all* true.'

'Oh, shut up.' The voice replying was unrecognisable as the matron's.

Smithson again, 'Look. *She* told me. Right?'

'No one believes you, Mr Smithson. You're just makin' trouble here, upsettin' people. But then when has that ever bothered you?'

'I don't care what you think of me. I know there's people here who must hate me. I understand that. But I'm not confused.'

'You don't know anything.'

Another different voice. Scornful. Disbelieving. Valerie. 'Val' they called her. Valerie Simpson. Second in command to the matron. Megan drew nearer room four and heard Geraint Smithson break down, a note of sheer desperation making his voice gravelly. 'I can't remember the exact year, I tell you. It was a long time ago. I don't know exactly. I've forgotten. The sixties. The seventies. Look it up, I tell you. Look it up. Perhaps you'll believe me then.'

'We'll *never* believe you, you—'

Megan could only guess at what Sandra Penarth had been about to say. She had reached the doorway and the matron had spotted her straight away. Immediately her face changed. Guilt swiftly replaced by a bold, defensive look. Megan took in the scene in an instant. The two nurses were bent over the old man giving him an injection. Smithson's eyes were filled with fear. He appealed to Megan. 'Doctor Banesto.'

Megan approached Sandra, tried to keep the nurse from reading the shock in her eyes. She had never before witnessed cruelty here at Triagwn. Only kindness, humanity, consideration. Was it all fake? As much a facade as was the stone porch fixed on the front of the house?

'What are you giving him?' she asked.

Sandra Penarth had finished pressing the plunger on the syringe. She withdrew the needle. 'Only a sedative, Doctor.'

'But who's written him up for an injection?'

'Andy said if he became too noisy we could give him the extra Chlopromazine.'

'By injection?' Megan didn't intend to make it sound so much like an interrogation.

'Yes. He wouldn't take his tablets. He spat them out so Andy agreed over the phone that we could give him his Largactil by injection.'

'Has Andy examined him?'

160

'No—he didn't *need* to. He *listened* to what we told him. Not like some.' The two nurses exchanged conspiratorial glances. Megan knew they had been talking about her. Val had her hands on her hips and was staring at her, unblinking. It was a direct challenge. Geraint Smithson gripped her hand. 'Please,' he pleaded desperately. 'Please. All I ask is that you believe me. Listen. Just listen.'

Megan nodded, not even half understanding what was happening.

Not yet.

'You see,' Sandra said briskly. 'He's very disturbed. He definitely needs the extra sedation. He's agitated.'

Smithson's eyes were begging her.

'How much are you giving him?'

'Five tablets three times a day.'

'What strength?'

'A hundred milligrams.'

'That's over the maximum recommended dose. And the injections too?'

'He's agitated.'

Smithson's hand shot out to grasp hers. 'I just want them to listen. The little girl was going to buy some chips . . .' He was beginning to sag. His grip was loosening by the second. His eyelids were drooping. His face took on a vacant look.

And knowing she was not doing the right thing but undermined now by both her partner and the nursing staff Megan took the prescription chart from the bottom of the bed and cancelled the injections but to appease the nurses added on yet another oral tranquilliser, Haloperidol, a drug specifically prescribed for the disturbed, elderly, confused patient.

The only adjective out of the trio that she knew described him accurately was elderly. The rest was open to debate.

CHAPTER TWELVE

But the fates have us in our grasp.

*   *   *

It was the following Thursday, November the 7th, Megan's half day. And once she had waded her way through the morning's surgery and done a couple of home visits she would be free. She drew the blinds right back and made her decision. She would ring a friend. Even though the weather was blustery, there were hopeful glimpses of cold blue in the sky. It was a bright, energetic sort of a day, ideal for a trip to the coast, a brisk walk along the sands of Porthcawl and a gossip in one of the hotels which served dinner. They would pass Coney Beach, the fairground, closed for the winter. Out of season there would be only the faintest, lingering scent of vinegar and chips and none of the rattling and screaming that made it such a nightmare in the summer.

She always had loved it more out of season when its seediness and flaking paint hinted at some of the fairground parodies of the past: the fat lady, the tooth-pulling man, the strange creature from Africa. The rickety rides also had a charm of their own—the waterchute, the roller coaster and best of all the carousel, its fiery horses awaiting the call to gallop round and round, their names painted along their necks: Valkyrie, Thunderbolt, Battle Scar. It returned her to her childhood and herself clinging on for dear life, Bonnard's Bareback Rider, risking life and limb as the world spun past her.

As a child Megan had loved the thrill of the fairground at the same time as she had been frightened of its illusions. The Hall of Mirrors, the Cake Walk, Over the Falls. As she drew her surgery blinds together she could almost hear the faint strains of jingling, compelling music. She unlocked the bottom drawer of her filing cabinet and picked up her handbag, impatient now to be gone. But she made the mistake of glancing across at the Gericault and could have sworn it was not envy that she read in the mad woman's face but mockery. To be taken in by such cheap illusion. Defiantly she closed the door behind her and wandered into the reception area to find that Andy and Phil had already left the surgery leaving a message that they would manage the two visits without her.

She was free.

*　　*　　*

And then the door opened.

Catherine Howells, the psychiatric social worker breezed in. 'Ructions,' she said, flopping into the nearest chair in the waiting room. 'Absolute bloody ructions. They're moving Esther Magellan into a flat. She can't stay in the house now she's on her own. It's for dual occupancy only and nobody would share with Esther now Bianca's gone. At least nobody in their right mind.'

'So is Esther objecting to the move?'

'Not to the move as such. She seems to have accepted that. It's the junk she wants to take with her. Merthyr Crescent is stuffed absolutely full of rubbish. The backroom's a health hazard. Full of boxes of old newspapers, bottles, washed out food tins, old clothes. You name it, she kept it. And now Esther won't let us chuck anything away. Keeps saying they were Bianca's. They were precious and she promised her she would keep it all. I ask you. It wants takin' down the tip. But I can't budge 'er. Stubborn as an old mule she is.'

Megan frowned. 'Can't you move Esther into her new flat and then dump the stuff?'

'We could but I think she'd create. A couple

164

of the boxes she's huggin' to her like it was worth something. And it's *all* junk. The flat's been newly decorated and I'm not having her messin' up the new place with rubbish. Some of the stuff goes back years. The food tins are vintage, mouldy, the bottles are ancient and some of the newspapers are thirty years old. I found one boxful going back to 1971.'

Maybe it was the mention of years gone by that awoke Megan's interest. Or simply the detritus of Bianca's life in the form of valueless old junk. Perhaps Megan sensed that the reason the social worker had arrived at the surgery was that she had hoped Megan would offer to help. Or maybe there was no reason that made Megan offer to act as mediator. It simply happened like that.

'I wonder,' she said slowly, 'if she'd let me dispose of some of the junk?'

Catherine looked relieved. 'We-e-ll—she does trust you. That's for sure.' She sat up straight as though Megan had already provided a solution to her problems. 'It'd be worth a try. For sure *we're* getting nowhere fast. Would you?' She was already on her feet.

So Megan followed her colleague's bright blue VW Golf to the Llangeinor Road, winding through the estate of council houses before turning left into a crescent with a patch of sodden, muddied grass in its centre. She pulled up behind Catherine's car outside the small, council bungalow which had until recently housed the two women. It was easy to locate the source of the social worker's concern. Esther was standing in the middle of the front path, struggling with a man in a beige overall who was attempting to lift the armchair of a three piece suite into the back of the three ton lorry. 'Don't you dare,' Esther was screaming at him, tugging his arms. 'These are *my* things. You *can't* take them away.'

The removal man was patient. 'I'm not trying to take them away, Miss Magellan. We're movin' them. Like I told you. They are going to your new place.'

Esther took a step back, hands on wide hips. 'How do I know?' she demanded. 'You might be stealin' them. And me just lettin' you.'

The man gave a deep sigh. Catherine was already beside her, her arm around Esther's shoulders. 'It's all right, Esther. They're taking all your furniture to that lovely new flat I showed you last week. Remember? The one with the yellow door. And I said that all the garden belonged to the flats and you could walk through them. Remember?'

Esther's face looked confused for no more than a moment. Then it cleared and she beamed. 'The house with the yellow door,' she repeated.

'Flat,' corrected Catherine. 'Up the stairs. Remember?'

'I remember the garden,' Esther said, smiling. 'There was a tree in it. A tree.' She registered Megan's arrival. 'Doctor?' she said uncertainly.

'I've heard you've been a bit troubled by some stuff you promised to look after for Bianca.'

Esther nodded vigorously. 'Bianca's,' she said. 'I promised. She didn't want it thrown away.'

'But she doesn't need it now, does she?'

'I *said* I would keep it for her.' Catherine was right. There was an air of donkey stubbornness about her.

'But you won't have enough room in the flat.'

'N-o-o.'

'There aren't many cupboards, Esther,' Catherine put in helpfully. 'You won't have anywhere to put all that junk.'

Esther looked troubled. 'But I promised,' she repeated.

Megan touched her arm. 'What about if I look after some of the things for Bianca?'

Esther looked confused. 'Which things?'

'Let's have a look, shall we?'

Esther put her finger on her chin, the age old gesture of a child—puzzling. Then she beamed again. 'All right, doctor,' she said. 'That'll be all right. Bianca always trusted *you*.' Behind her patient, Catherine's eyebrows lifted but she said nothing.

Megan's heart sank when she opened the door to what must once have been a dining

167

room, a room which she had never visited when both the inhabitants of 42, Merthyr Crescent had been alive. Searching her subconscious she could now recall the sound of an interior door being pulled shut when she had knocked at the front door. As though a room inside the bungalow had held a secret. She scanned the contents and knew now. No secret. Only an imagined one. Behind the door had been a roomful of rubbish. Boxes were piled up in the corner, some of them collapsing under their own weight. One or two bore stains as though liquid had seeped out and soaked the cardboard. The air was sour and stale. There was a faint smell of cat pee. Megan swallowed. The room smelt like a rubbish rip. She would *have* to dump it all.

*   *   *

Mentally she cancelled the trip to Porthcawl and felt a hollow sadness as the tinkling fairground music slowed and faded to nothing. There was a lot of junk. The boxes would need two trips. Her Calibra was hardly a load carrier. The tip was a few miles away and she would need a bath after touching this stuff. She picked up another waft of strong, animal scent. The car would probably need cleaning too. She must be mad. Public Health would have shifted it. It was hardly one of *her* duties. But Esther touched her arm timidly, gazed at her with trusting eyes. It was a more eloquent plea than any words that existed in the English dictionary.

'Esther,' she said, trying to stifle her disgust as she lifted the top of the first box and pulled out a rinsed-out baked beans tin. 'Some of this must be thrown away.'

Esther moved nearer. 'Not the papers,' she hissed. 'I promised Bianca I'd *never* throw those papers away. She wanted me to keep them. They're important. *Very* important.'

'All right, all right.' Megan knew she had to agree to this. Policed by a protesting Esther she spent the next hour loading up boxes of junk into the back of her car. She had been right. There was too much for one trip. And it was going to take up the entire afternoon. The dump was only four miles away but the journey took double time due to a set of roadworks blocked by irate drivers who passed through on red only to be forced to lock bumper to bumper to assert their rights on green. Megan sat and fumed as the lights flicked through their sequence, unwillingly inhaling the stale smell of the car full of litter even though she'd opened both windows. She was tempted to put her hand on her horn simply to blast out her own frustration. But she would soon be recognised as the doctor. And it didn't do to express anger. What made it worse was that above her the clouds had rolled away to reveal a Wedgwood blue sky. She checked her watch and cursed November. It might be just two o'clock but only a couple more precious hours remained of daylight. On top of that her car now stank like the municipal tip. Feeling angry with herself for having got involved, she finally reached the recycling centre, pulled up in front of a huge skip and unloaded the carload of boxes, slamming the doors shut before heading back to Esther's house.

*   *   *

Esther had vanished, presumably with Catherine to take up residence in her new home, but the van was still outside, the men almost ready to roll the doors down on the shabby contents. Megan went straight back into the dining room and loaded up the last of the boxes, four of them filled to the brim with old newspapers. She hardly glanced at them but placed them side by side on the back seat which she had protected with a green waterproof sheet usually used for picnics. And now she had a dilemma. She had promised Esther she would not throw the papers away. Hands still on the steering wheel, she turned around.

They were just boxes of old newspapers. Nothing more. She began heading towards the tip. But the traffic was building up, the roads now clogged with cars full of schoolchildren. Megan sat impatiently in her car, fingers

170

drumming the steering wheel, a Britney Spears tape blasting out to distract her. A swift glance at her car clock told her her journey would be fruitless anyway. It was three o'clock and the tip closed at three thirty.

Besides, her conscience still nagged her. *'You promised Esther you would not throw these newspapers away.'*

She did a five point turn in the road provoking an angry blast of car horns before reluctantly heading for home, reasoning that in a month or two Esther would have forgotten their existence. She could dispose of them then.

For now she could put them in her garden shed. There was plenty of room there.

*   *   *

And so through a simple set of events, by a thread as fine as the blink from a set of traffic lights, lives are changed. Maybe all is coincidence. There is no divine plan except one—the law of entropy, of chance, of chaos.

*   *   *

So she headed home, parked her car outside and carried the boxes into her hall one by one. One of the penalties of living in a mid terraced house was that access to her garden shed was through the house. She was ready for a drink so she stacked the boxes near the back door and opened the fridge, reaching in to the far corner of the bottom shelf for a can of Red Stripe.

The flap of the box had dropped and the top newspaper almost slithered out. So it was that she read part of a sentence.

'. . . going to buy chips . . .'

She had heard that particular phrase recently.

Smithson had used it.

'I just want them to listen.'

'Listen to what?'

'The little girl was going to buy some chips.'

Megan was intrigued. If Smithson *had* been referring to this case—why? What had been of such significance that he had struggled to bring it to their attention?

She pulled the can out of the fridge, closed the door, and sat down on the floor.

She slid the box towards her and reached out the top newspaper, flattening it with the palm of her hand until the headline was clear.

Schoolgirl goes missing.

In 1988 a ten-year-old girl named Marie Walker had been on her way to buy some chips and had never been seen again.

It was a not uncommon story. She studied a school photograph of a girl with long, dark hair and a small, mean mouth and wondered what had happened to her.

So had Geraint Smithson been referring to

this case? And if so why?

Megan pulled more newspapers from the box. Each one contained an article about the missing ten-year-old who had vanished on November 23rd, 1988—almost fourteen years ago. Some were entire newspapers, others carefully snipped articles. Bianca must have collected every single piece written about the disappearance of a little girl and Megan read right through them. The articles were peppered with quotations from friends and family. *'Going to buy some chips, she was.' 'Nice little thing she were.' 'She was my best friend at school.' 'We'll miss her somethin' awful.'* For weeks the editors of the *Western Mail* must have racked their brains to keep the name of Marie Walker on its front page, hoping that the little girl would be found. There was a variety of headlines.

The Parents Who Wonder
The School That Mourns
The Friends Who Miss their Playmate
What Happened to My Little Girl?

Each headline was accompanied by pictures of sad-faced people who stared into the camera with only one question . . . Where was she? Megan pulled out more and more newspapers, scattering them all over the kitchen floor, wondering whether there was, finally, an answer.

But even though the newspapers spanned months, nowhere was there mention of Marie

Walker being found, dead or alive. As time passed the articles moved from the front page towards the back, eventually resting in the 'Other news' sections. The interval between features lengthened and finally rested in the *Er Cof*, the In Memoriam. Megan spread the newspapers right across the kitchen floor and read through again, this time noting every single detail.

The basic story was this:

On the night of November 23rd 1988 at nine o'clock, Marie Walker had been given five pounds to fetch the chips for the family who were sitting watching an old video of *Jaws*. Bored with a film she had probably already seen too many times, she had offered to go to the chippie and her stepfather and two stepbrothers had thought nothing of it. It was, according to the *Western Mail*, a trip she made a few times a week. Her mother had been working late as a barmaid at The Oddfellows Arms—otherwise she might have insisted one of Marie's stepbrothers accompany her daughter. By ten o' clock the three men had grown hungry and, assuming Marie had 'bunked off' with the money and the chips, had cursed the girl's delay. It was only when Marie's mother had returned home at a few minutes before twelve that the family's threats of tanning Marie's hide had translated into belated and worried action. They had made phone calls—to every single one of her friends.

And drawn a negative. Marie had disappeared. At half past twelve they had called the police.

Megan swigged at the Red Stripe and continued reading.

According to the server in the fish and chip shop, Marie had bought four large portions of chips and put the salt and vinegar on herself. Witnesses testified she had left the shop with her fingers already dipping into one of the bags as she had started walking home. She had been spotted on her way still pulling at the chips and threading them into . . . Megan looked again at the picture and visualised the child's thin little mouth greedily pulling at the greasy food. Again, witnesses had seen Marie walk along the main road and turn right into St Leonard's Terrace. This would have been the direct path home, turning right again into Railway Terrace where she lived. Somewhere between the two roads she had vanished. And never been seen again.

The police opinion was that Marie had been heading straight home.

Megan hunched over the papers and absorbed the stories.

But, however deep she delved, Marie Walker never had been seen again. Years later her name cropped up only in the *Er Cof* column. Every year on November 23rd.

And Bianca had preserved even this lingering contact. Strange how she had become absorbed in this case.

Megan sat back against the wall. Why had Bianca hoarded these articles of a missing child, charging poor old Esther Magellan with their custody? What exactly had she told Smithson? Had it been *these* stories she had shared with the old man, adding to his agitation?

And why had Smithson, in turn, tried to pass on the tales to the nurses and herself with such desperation?

Had Bianca's stories disturbed him to such an extent? After all, she reasoned, Smithson would have been familiar with the story already. He would have read the newspapers. Megan glanced across the kitchen floor. There were plenty of headlines. What had made this story stick in his mind? And why did she not remember the case? Megan did some quick arithmetic. She would have been eighteen when Marie Walker had disappeared, and in the November when she was eighteen she had been a fresher at Cardiff University. That was why she didn't even recall the child's name. She had been living the riot of a first-year medical student. Hardly a time when she would have pored over the local newspapers. But it was strange that while she had been unaware of a child vanishing from her own home town for some reason it had been

176

significant enough for Smithson to quote it more than ten years later.

And Bianca had not only hoarded the relevant newspapers but had charged Esther with the custody of them. And at the back of her mind sat the words from Wainwright.

'It is not unusual for people who have delusions to retain a good deal of perception.'

What, Megan wondered, had Bianca 'perceived'?

*   *   *

She reached another Red Stripe out of the fridge.

There were three other boxes.

She replaced all the articles into Marie Walker's box and studied the others. Each one had a different name on the side, all written in the same writing, in black felt-tipped pen. Bleddyn Hughes was the name on the second box; Rhiann Lewis was written on the side of the third. 'Rhiann Lewis'. The name was vaguely familiar but she couldn't quite place it . . .

*   *   *

She lifted the lid and read the date on the top newspaper. 1980. Twenty-two years ago. Perhaps her parents had mentioned the name in front of their ten-year-old daughter as a warning.

She eyed the last box. On the side were penned two names, George Prees and Neil Jones. The year against the headline was quite recent. 1992. Ten years ago. But again the names brought no recognition. In 1992 she would have been twenty-two, a fourth-year medical student. According to the article the boys had vanished in June when she would have been abroad, working out her elective period in Lusaka, studying the effects of malaria on an unprotected African population. A million miles away from Llancloudy and its mysteries.

Whatever they were.

Megan lifted the 'Bleddyn Hughes' box onto the kitchen table and started pulling the newspapers out. Hughes had been a maths teacher at the local grammar school until 1971 when, like Marie Walker seventeen years later, he had simply vanished. Homosexuality was hinted at. He was, the paper said, 'fond of children', an ambiguous phrase. He had, apparently, run extra curricular activities at the school and in his free time—a chess club, swimming lessons, maths coaching. And then one Monday morning Bleddyn Hughes had failed to turn up for class.

Megan stared at the kitchen wall, her eyes unfocused. 'A teacher who had failed to turn up for class.' It didn't sound much of a story.

She bent over the newspaper and continued

reading.

Bleddyn Hughes had not shown nor telephoned all day and the headmaster, none too pleased at the non-appearance of one of his teachers, had visited Hughes' rented room to find he was not there and had not been seen since Friday night. The headmaster had been the one to alert the police who had then raided his rented lodgings and uncovered a number of 'suggestive' magazines.

In fact the tone of the articles displayed less concern at the disappearance of a suspect maths teacher than the sudden vanishing of the ten-year-old child sixteen years later. The assumption Megan read between the lines was that Hughes had 'gone to London' to pursue his activities in a more enlightened environment. The photographs showed an unprepossessing man, bespectacled, anxious, staring fiercely into the camera.

Interest had quickly waned even though there was no mention of his owning a car or having been seen at either the coach or the railway station.

But there was only one road out of Llancloudy unless you crossed the mountains— by foot.

The pile of papers was half the size of Marie Walker's. And there was no *Er Cof*. Bleddyn Hughes had not been 'a local man' and the speculation had only lasted a few weeks. Two months after Bleddyn Hughes had gone from

Llancloudy there was no mention of him at all.

Megan gathered the papers up and returned them to the box. She would find no explanation here. In fact, reading between the lines she sensed the sentiment that the authors of the articles believed Llancloudy was a better place without Bleddyn Hughes, Maths teacher.

She put the box back on the floor next to Marie Walker's and turned to the third box.

Which contained the saddest of stories.

Of a little girl, Rhiann Lewis,

'Little Rhiann' whom Bianca had mentioned, her wrinkled cheeks dripping because Little Rhiann was dead. 'Definitely dead.' And she knew 'he'd done it'.

For Goodness sake, Megan thought. What was this? And so she read about Little Rhiann.

The child had been just three years old, playing in her own back garden, behind a bolted door while her mother and her grandmother sat in the house, sharing a pot of tea. There was no way out of the garden except through the house or the bolted door out onto the street.

Little Rhiann should have been safe.

But the child had not been safe. Half an hour had elapsed between them hearing her singing and chattering as she bathed her dollies in a plastic paddling pool and the discovery of a door swinging open.

Rhiann Lewis, the little girl who sang lullabies and was 'always chattering', had vanished.

And as Megan scanned the column inches she realised that, like the other two, Rhiann was never seen again.

*   *   *

And now Megan was disturbed. Llancloudy was only a small village. Less than three thousand people lived here. Condense the three vanishings to boxes sitting on her kitchen floor and it seemed a strange town, a dangerous town, a black hole where people disappeared without trace. A town where a mad woman vanished on the Saturday morning only to reappear, drowned, in the shallowest of pools, on the Monday.

Bianca, with her warped understandings of time lapses and disregarding hinted explanations put out by the Press, had preserved the newspapers because . . .

*   *   *

Because they had intrigued her? Frightened her? Interested her? Because she thought she had an explanation? Or because she sensed a connection?

'She's definitely dead. I know it now for certain. I'd wondered before but when he told me this time I knew it was the truth.'

Who had told her? Her 'voices'?

Megan read right through the hoarded newspapers searching for some clue. Mine shafts were mentioned, together with the accompanying photographs of miners, their lamps ablaze, as they prepared to search the warren of tunnels beneath Llancloudy. Strain etched lines across the face of Rhiann's mother so she was indistinguishable from Rhiann's grandmother. Rhiann's grandmother. Megan recognised a much younger—and thinner—Gwen Owen. There was a photograph of the child's father, gaunt and haunted-faced as he joined every single man in the town to look for his little girl while the women comforted the family, as women had done ever since the mines were first opened. But this was no pit accident. The mines had been searched and nothing found. Then the talk had turned to veiled hints of child snatchings, paedophiles, abduction. But the problem always returned to the fact that the police believed that the child herself had shot back the lock on the door of her safe haven.

Mother and grandmother spoke of hearing the child chattering as she had washed her dolls. The dolls themselves had been found, slippery with soapsuds, still with dripping hair. Only the child was missing.

They couldn't say when the child had stopped talking. It had been no more than a background tune to their mother/daughter gossip.

182

Megan took a long time looking at the photograph. The toddler laughed straight back at her, displaying beautiful milk teeth and a face framed by a shock of curly black hair. The picture had frozen her clapping her hands at some unseen photographer. And even through the yellowing pages of the *Western Mail* the child's happiness was palpable—as was her parents' grief in later pictures.

Megan leaned back against the kitchen wall, hardly seeing the smart white kitchen with its blue ash units. Instead she saw faces, the thin-lipped child, the asthenic teacher, the happy three-year-old, clapping her hands, Bianca's tear streaked face, powder washing down her scrawny cheeks, Smithson's earnest pleas for someone to listen. The disappearances had spanned more than twenty years. Each had been under a different set of circumstances. Had Bianca simply been fascinated by the unusual and the inexplicable? Or was there some other explanation?

And there was a fourth box, still holding its secrets. But *like* Pandora's box she knew it held nothing pleasant. And once the lid was opened . . .

She didn't want to know.

Who knows how long she would have sat still. She was snapped out of her reverie by the insistent tone of her mobile phone. She fished it out of her bag and read the caller ID. A local number. One she did not recognise.

Always apprehensive it might be a patient she answered hesitantly. 'Hello?'

'Meggie.'

It was a shock to hear his voice unexpectedly. 'Alun?'

He laughed, embarrassed. 'We never did have that drink.'

'No-o.' She wanted to meet him again and at the same time she didn't. A deliberate assignation would be fraught with difficulties. *Someone would see them. And the further away from Llancloudy they met, in the eyes of its inhabitants, the more surreptitious their relationship. And someone would be sure to spot them. Wales is a small country.*

Typical Alun, he lobbed the ball into her court. 'Well?'

Her eyes roamed the kitchen. And she suddenly realised if anyone was party to the background behind the stories Alun would be. He was a police officer, had joined the local force straight after his A-levels. He might well have been involved in the two most recent disappearances. She stroked the newspaper on her lap. 'I never realised so many people went missing from this little town, Alun.'

He laughed back at her. 'You what?'

'Bianca hoarded old newspapers. I've inherited them.'

'Whatever for?'

'Esther was making a fuss about the council workers dumping them when she had

184

promised Bianca she would keep them.'

'You're not still on about all that, surely?'

'Bianca was my patient. And Esther is too.'

Alun spluttered out another laugh. 'I know modern day doctors are into this holistic nonsense—but isn't this carryin' things a bit far?'

'I've found them interesting,' she replied stiffly.

He sighed and his voice fell flat. 'Oh.'

He was losing interest.

'Every box of papers deals separately with a missing person.'

There was a pause before he spoke again. 'How many boxes?'

'Four.'

'I don't remember four people goin' missin from Llancloudy. There's been a couple of kids.'

'What happened to them?'

'We searched everywhere—with sniffer dogs. Extra police were drafted in from Cardiff. Everybody from Llancloudy turned out to look for the children. We found nothing. Not a trace.'

'Were the mine shafts searched?'

'Of course they were. But it's a bloody city down there. You can't search the whole place.'

A swift, awful vision of a child, wandering in the black nothing of a coal mine flashed through her mind. 'No.'

'So who were these unfortunates?'

One more unfortunate. His choice of words was terribly apt. 'Marie Walker,' she ventured.

'I remember that,' he said. 'One of the first major incidents I was involved with. We never found her. Some paedophile got hold of her, I think.'

'Rhiann Lewis?'

'I've heard about the case,' he said. 'Didn't she unlock the garden gate and get lost somehow? There was no evidence anyone snatched her. She let herself out of the garden. She would have been safe if she'd stayed behind the door.'

Megan turned her head sideways to read the names on the side of the fourth box. 'George Prees and Neil Jones.'

'Buggered off to London if you ask me. Pair of juvenile delinquents.'

She asked the last name knowing Alun would hold as little knowledge as she. 'Bleddyn Hughes?'

'Haven't heard about him.'

'Way before you joined. 1971 he went missing.'

Alun laughed again. 'As you say—way before I joined. So the disappearances span quite a few years then.'

'Thirty.'

'We-e-ell. Not that many really.'

Was he right? Was this the normal wastage of a village? Was it simply Bianca's mind which had distorted events into a mystery?

'Now about that drink.'

Megan arranged to meet him on the following night.

CHAPTER THIRTEEN

As she lay in bed that night, Megan tried to supply a rational explanation to Smithson's and Bianca's interest in the disappearances. But her dreams were filled with Alun, who kept running towards her then swerving at the last moment while she held her arms out, waiting. She awoke to a dull, blustery morning and a feeling of disappointment tinged with worry. It was not a good idea to be meeting Alun tonight.

She dealt deftly with the morning's patients and picked up the requests for visits—amongst them Triagwn.

She walked into the hall and was immediately met by Sandra Penarth. 'Morning, doctor,' she said warmly. 'And how are you today?' There was no hint of either embarrassment or aggression.

Megan was anxious to repair the damage. 'Fine, just fine. And how are my patients?' She spoke more heartily than normal.

'Well, Mr Smithson's been quiet since you started him on the Haloperidol.'

'No more weird stories?'

Sandra made a face. 'No more than usual but at least he is quiet. And we haven't had to have him transferred anywhere else, which suits Arwel better.'

'I'm sure.'

'After all—it would a shame to move him from here after so long.'

'Quite.'

*   *   *

Megan felt a snatch of guilt that she had been responsible for robbing the old man of what little fight he had had left. She had reduced him to yet another easily controlled geriatric when he had been such a demanding man all his life. Now he was everything the nurses liked—obedient, quiet and pliable, robbed of his tendency to spill out disquieting stories and disturb the calm of the old people's home.

'I'd like to see him.'

'Fine.'

They ran the gauntlet of the patients in the ground floor sitting room before climbing the stairs towards room four. And already Megan was noticing how much quieter the place was. She entered the small room and realised. Even the smell was different. She knew instantly what they had done—given him a wash, sprayed him with plenty of deodorant, and the room with air freshener. Smithson had been sanitised. The room now bore the corporate

188

scent of Imperial Leather and lavender Airwick. He was sitting in his chair, staring out of the window. He did not turn as she entered. A trickle of saliva dribbled from the corner of his mouth. She sat in the chair opposite. And finally he turned and looked at her.

'Well, Doctor Banesto?'

He had lost weight. The skin hung down from his face. But his eyes still had some fight in them. 'Hello, Mr Smithson,' she said.

Give me the fighter—anyday.

'It's OK, Sandra, you can go now. I'll talk to Mr Smithson. If I've got anything extra to say I'll pop in the office on my way out.' The nurse was irritating her, hovering in the doorway.

To her interest Smithson's face flickered as the nurse moved away.

Megan leaned in close to the old man so she wouldn't have to talk loudly. *Walls may not have ears. But people do. They say old men's ears grow bigger as they age. It helps them to hear better. An evolutionary process? Old men have more enemies than young ones. They have had a lifetime to watch the numbers multiply.*

'How are you today Mr Smithson?'

His world weary face locked in to hers. 'I'll survive,' he said. 'I expect.' A pause. 'For a while, anyway.'

'You must miss Bianca,' she ventured.

He nodded. 'A bit. Not much. No harm in the woman. A bit loopy. But not evil.'

'No. Not evil.' She hesitated. 'Was it from

189

Bianca that you heard about Marie Walker?'

Smithson was shaking his head.

'The girl who vanished on her way back from buying chips?'

He said nothing but stared at her.

'She did tell you stories?'

Smithson nodded, hooding his eyes with the wrinkled old lids.

'Stories about missing people?'

Smithson nodded again. More slowly this time.

'Rhiann Lewis?' Megan ventured very quietly.

'Poor kid,' he said.

'What happened to her?' Megan waited.

Smithson was silent.

'What did Bianca think had happened to Rhiann?'

'Look, doctor,' Smithson said slowly, 'Bianca was not right in the head. Everyone knew that. Anyone who believed her stories . . .'

'But you believed them.'

'Let me finish,' he said. 'Anyone who believed Bianca's stories must be halfway to nutty themselves. Understand me?'

'But the disappearances are fact. I've read the newspapers, Mr Smithson.'

'That might be fact,' he said, 'but not her explanations. They *can't* be true.'

His eyes were closing.

'What happened to the others, Geraint?'

Smithson's bony hand shook on the arm of

his chair.

'What did Bianca *think* had happened to them?'

'She didn't *know* what had happened to any of them. How could she?' Smithson's eyes had flicked open and were boring holes into hers. 'How could she,' he repeated. 'She was just a mad old thing.' His eyes dropped. 'Like me.'

Megan stood up. She had a terrible feeling that she had asked questions just a little too late. She would have got more out of Smithson a month ago.

She would learn nothing now. But as she reached the door Smithson spoke to her. 'Llancloudy' he said, 'is not a safe place. You have to be careful.'

She halted in the doorway. 'What do you mean?'

'It is not a *tolerant* place. Look around you, doctor. The valley is narrow. There never was the room for all these houses. People are squashed together and it makes life difficult. Nobody'll put up with anything. And it causes problems. That's all I'm saying.'

He dropped his chin onto his chest and gave a couple of soft snores. She gave up.

*　　　*　　　*

But she felt almost released as she walked outside the nursing home and into the walled garden. The colours were flattened now to their subdued winter tones. Black, brown, grey. Back to the subtle, depressing tones of Gericault; Rousseau and Gauguin suppressed. A couple of care assistants were braving the weather to puff on their cigarettes. Like most buildings allied to the medical or nursing profession, Triagwn operated a No Smoking policy. Megan tossed them a smile and carried on, towards the rim of pines that marked the edge of the trees. 'What's wrong with you, girl,' she scolded. 'You've been getting this thing right out of proportion. Bianca just slipped and drowned. She had a love of sensational headlines. And like most schizophrenics, she cottoned onto one idea and simply stuck there.'

*   *   *

'First sign of madness,' one of the care assistants called after her. 'Talkin' to yourself, doctor.' It was typical, chopsy South Walean banter. But it sent a shiver running through her.

Once you have conferred on yourself an aspect of strangeness, you begin to analyse your every action and then you are lost. She had seen it happen to a fellow medical student and had watched, horrified, as he had talked, late into the night, about the shaky issue of sanity, neatly and logically turning the discussion into a desperate plea for some

192

precise yardstick by which he could prove he was not mad.

There is not one. There is no yardstick which proves sanity. Catch 22 had dallied with this concept. Is to question one's sanity itself an insane process? Or a sane one?

*   *   *

She wandered towards the back boundary of Triagwn to the point where its own land ended and the dereliction of an old railway line had been transformed into a cycle track. Here a path threaded through the woods. And this was where—quite unexpectedly—she found another piece of the fragmented puzzle. The back wall which marked the boundary of Triagwn was built of stones; large, round stones like the ones found on Southerndown Beach. But over the years they had tumbled and been left where they had fallen. Brambles had adopted the undergrowth and crept along the floor with stinging nettles. They formed an inpenetrable barrier.

No one came here.

But her attention was caught and held by a tiny bird flittering near the floor. Probably a wren but she was curious and stepped forward. She banged her foot against some heavy, stone object and had something else to excite her curiosity.

She bent down.

It must have stood near the wall, a sentry to guard against intruders, a stone carving of a gryphon, the winged monster of mythology, head of eagle, body of clawed lion. Only one of the claws was missing. Megan instantly knew where it was. She had taken little notice of Alun's description of the contents of Bianca's pocket—the animal claw. But as she bent down she knew that Bianca must have come here, probably knocked against the fallen statue as she had done, and broken off one of the gryphon's claws. It was an explanation. The police had believed the claw had been broken off a statue in a church. But they had been wrong. Welsh churches were notoriously Low. They did not go in for rampant gryphons and such High idolatry. Only the owner of Triagwn had. Mythology, devilry, idolatry were all in his repertoire.

She studied the cruel beak of the eagle. So Bianca had walked this way shortly before she had died.

Was it significant?

She did not know. But she did want to see the claw for herself.

*　　　*　　　*

She glanced at her watch. Half past three. She must return to surgery.

Friday evening surgeries are, traditionally, the worst surgeries of the week. *Everyone*

194

wants 'checking out' before the weekend. Patients suddenly realise if they don't squeeze into the Friday night slot they will have to manage without for two more whole days. And so they pile in. For prescriptions, sick notes, advice, results of tests. The waiting room was heaving when Megan entered and for two and a half hours she could not afford to think about Bianca. She was even unaware of Gericault's Mad Woman surveying her critically from the walls.

*   *   *

But as soon as the last patient had left the room Megan's mind was again busily working overtime.

One person might have an explanation to the newspaper cuttings.

Bianca's daughter.

*   *   *

Megan had to park in the pub car park and walk back to Carole's house, a similar place to her own, small and terraced, cars jammed nose to bumper the length of the road. She could see the television on as she squeaked open the gate. Immediately, someone rose from the armchair and peered out suspiciously. By the size and shape Megan knew it was Bianca's daughter.

195

The door was flung open. 'Doctor?' Carole said uncertainly.

'Yes. I was passing. I wondered how you . . .'

'Come on in. Come and 'ave a cup of tea. I was just about to make a brew. Well. It seems funny to see you here.'

Megan waited while Carole filled a brown earthenware teapot with teabags and boiling water then briskly stirred and finally poured out two mugs of tea.

She handed one to Megan and leaned against the units. 'We-ell,' she said.

'Shall we sit down?'

In deference Carole turned the sound of the TV down and switched the main lights on. Then shrewdly she sat back and waited. Megan's eyes drifted around the room and fastened on to a large, framed photograph. Carole crossed the room and picked it up. 'It's by far the nicest picture I've got of Mam,' she said, handing it to Megan. 'She always was at her ease with children. Loved them she did.'

A terrible thought flashed through Megan's mind. What if? It was true. Bianca had loved children. She had naturally related to them, playing with their toys, giving them sweets, talking innocent nothing talk. What if? Four of the missing had been children. Might Bianca have abducted them? She stared at the strange face, framed with pink hair which smiled innocently out of the frame and immediately felt ashamed. Bianca could not have done that.

Even if she had been at her very worst and had been capable of murder she would not have been able to dispose of a body.

Not even if her voices had directed her? . . . And there she stopped. Because Carole Symmonds was staring at her. 'Are you all right, doctor?'

No—not even then.

'Carole. I don't know whether you've heard, but Esther has been moved to a singles flat.'

Carole nodded, waiting.

'She made a great fuss about moving.'

'I'm not surprised.'

'She made a particular issue about some boxes.'

'Oh yes. The rubbish my mam used to keep.'

Megan smiled. 'Most of it I took to the dump.'

'Best place for it.' Carole took a long, noisy slurp of tea.

'Some of the boxes had old newspapers in.'

'Yeah—I know. Mam used to set great store by them.'

'They were all about missing people. People who'd vanished from Llancloudy.'

Carole nodded. 'I know.'

'What did your mother think had happened to them?'

Carole gave a great chuckle. 'Somethin' different every day. One minute someone had murdered them all. Next thing it was aliens

197

come down in a space ship. Sometimes she'd say there was another city underneath Llancloudy with all the old miners in and they were there. Goodness knows.' Another long slurp of tea. 'Why, are you interested then?'

And suddenly Megan realised that Bianca's own daughter, much more familiar with her mother's delusions than her doctor, had discounted any logical connection between the disappearances. Megan drank her tea, explained that she had inherited the boxes only because the dump had been closed and she had made a promise to Esther, and made her escape.

She hardly even glanced at the fourth box, still unopened, on the kitchen floor. She had less than half an hour to shower and change before Alun arrived. And now she was nervous. She had a favour to ask him. She wanted to see the claw, to hold it in her own hand. Maybe she would divine something from the object. More likely it was just silliness. At the same time she already knew that Alun mistrusted her interest in Bianca's death. He interpreted her obsession as a sign of her own mental instability. And she didn't know how best to handle this. She didn't know what he expected of her—or what she expected or asked of him. She almost retraced his number on her mobile phone and cancelled the entire evening.

But she didn't.

CHAPTER FOURTEEN

She'd deliberately dressed down in black jeans and a white fleece, brushed her hair and applied very little make-up, mascara, a tiny amount of blusher, lipstick. She drew back her front curtains and waited for the headlights.

Half eight, he'd said.

At nine o'clock she saw the lights sweeping up the road, and she jumped up, locked the door behind her and walked towards them. He threw the door open. Even in the dimmest of car lights she could sense he felt awkward. He was not naturally a dishonest type.

'Just one drink, Alun,' she said. 'Then we'd better call it a day.'

And as he pulled out of the road she knew he was relieved. That this was setting the parameters for the evening, a quick drink, no awkwardness, no involvement. Simply friendship. An old friendship. Comfortable and warm as a pair of slippers.

*   *   *

He drove silently to the pub at the head of the valley. Little used, old fashioned, quiet except for three men sitting in the corner, playing dominoes. The swingers of Llancloudy did not visit here. No music, little company, a scruffy, old fashioned bar. But it was quiet. The domino players hardly looked up as they entered. They were far too engrossed in their game. And even the landlord kept his eyes on his paper while he poured a pint for Alun and some lager for her. He took the five pound note and handed over the change, still saying little, except one word of explanation. 'Crossword.'

Megan smiled. They took the drinks and settled in the corner, Megan opening the conversation.

'How's your wife?'

'Gettin' bigger,' Alun said sheepishly.

'How long does she have to go?'

'Six weeks, four days. One hour.' He grinned.

'I expect you'd like . . .'

He knew what she was about to say. 'Yes— another little boy,' he said. 'Then I can coach them both in the Minis.'

She laughed, terribly at her ease with a man who saw everything through the perspective of a rugby ball. Alun reminded her of her father. He laughed too, knowing what would strike her as funny.

'But girls can play rugby too,' she teased lightly.

He almost choked on his beer.

Heartened by the detante between them, she leaned forward. 'I had to visit Triagwn today.'

200

'Oh? The old people's home?'

'The old people's home where Bianca used to work. I think I know where the piece of stone came from.' She sensed she needed to remind him. 'The claw that you found in her pocket.'

His eyes scanned her over the cream froth.

'I was wandering through the grounds of Triagwn. Near the back boundary I found a statue of a gryphon. It must have fallen from the wall. It was missing a claw. And it looked as though it had been broken recently.'

He put his beer down. 'Well—there's an explanation then. I did wonder where it had come from.'

'She must have been wandering through the garden some time before she died. I'm surprised she wandered up there. She was a woman who stuck to regular routines.'

She took a deep breath and plunged in. 'Alun—is there any chance I can *I* see the claw? I'd love to know if it did match.'

He ran his fingers round the top of his beer glass. 'Still on about that then, are we?'

'Aren't you interested?'

'Now, Megan.'

'I don't think you've reached a satisfactory answer, have you?'

Alun pushed his finger round his shirt collar as though he was having trouble breathing.

She leaned forward. 'I know you think my interest is strange—unhealthy even.'

He said nothing.

'Did you know she collected newspapers about people who have vanished from this town?'

'Yes—you already said.'

'What if there is something in it? I mean—people did disappear.'

'What are you suggesting, Megan?' He sounded bored.

'I'm not really suggesting anything, Alun.' She tried a tentative smile. 'But what if she had stumbled on the fact that there was a connection between the people who had vanished. Wouldn't that give someone a motive for wanting her out of the way? She was beginning to talk about it, you know.'

'Well as it happens I do know. She was in the habit of ringing the station practically every week. Sometimes four or five times a day.'

'But you weren't listening to her.'

'You can bet your bottom dollar we weren't listening.'

'*You* weren't. What if someone else was? Someone who did take her allegations seriously?'

'Like who?'

'Geraint Smithson?'

Alun started laughing. 'Another lunatic. An old man confused, senile, living in a nursing home. Anybody sane, Megan?'

He was mocking her. There was a clatter of

202

collapsing dominoes in the corner.

'Meggie,' Alun's hand was on her arm. 'This has gone far enough. The inquest has come to its conclusion. Everyone's happy. The coroner, the police. Even Carole Symmonds. Everyone except you. For some unknown reason you're still harping on about Bianca's death as though it was the unsolved murder case of the millennium. You're making some of the wildest allegations. Now then. Just between you and me your theory about Joel Parker was more likely than any other notion. But he was away. And that, I believe, is the truth. Nobody killed Bianca because she was collecting newspapers or because she was always ringing us up making various allegations.' He was remaining assertive and calm. He needed to be. Megan was boiling over, her interest refusing to sleep.

'What exactly were her allegations? Against whom?'

'I can't say. It wouldn't be . . . There was no truth in any of it.'

'What if there was?'

'There wasn't,' Alun said firmly. 'Believe you me. There—was—not. I can't discuss all the cases that she got so obsessed with, but I do know about the two boys who disappeared at the same time.'

'The fourth box.'

'George Prees and Neil Jones.' Alun smiled. 'Must be eight or nine years ago that

203

those two vanished from Llancloudy. Neil was one of the ugliest little tykes I've ever seen. Red hair, great big front teeth, ears that stuck out like Dumbo the elephant's. Father worked up North somewhere—on the oil rigs. Mother—goodness knows. Bit of a bicycle she was. George Prees had a dad who never sobered up. And his mam had vanished a year or two before her son. We never found her to tell her he'd gone missing.'

'You never found the boys either?'

'Mavis Prees had gone off with one of the itinerant workers who tarmac the roads. Irish chap he was. We alerted the Guarda but we didn't have much detail on 'im. She'd been seen various places in Ireland.' His face turned a sudden fiery red. 'The newspapers were full of the story of the missing boys. She must have seen something or someone must have told her. But she never contacted us. Some mother.'

He sucked his lips in almost piously. 'The boys—neither of them—they didn't have much of a life.'

'So what happened to them?'

'We don't know,' Alun said. 'All I can tell you is this. It was a Monday morning in June. They were due to sit their end of term exams. Boilin' hot day it was. And they were spotted near the bottom of the valley, hitch hikin', school bags on their backs. We wasted months of police time lookin' for the runaways. But who knows. They could easily have taken a ride off to Coney Beach.'

Faint tinkles of fairground music reminded her of how such places tempted children.

'There's lots of itinerant workers hangin' around that place. They could have gone off with them, joined the travelling people. Nothin' was found, Meggie. Not ever. The two little buggers weren't seen again. And there's many that would have said "good". Like I said to you. Every case in Bianca's little boxes was different. You can't lump them all together because they vanished from one village. They are not the same. It isn't one unsolved case but four. Every one's got a different explanation.'

Megan nodded, for the first time seeing the disappearances through a more balanced viewpoint.

This was the voice of reason. She drained her glass and stood up. 'Thank you,' she said. 'I see now why the police did not connect the cases. There was more than simply a time span. There was no pattern.' She leaned forward and kissed his cheek. 'You should get back to your wife now, Alun,' she said gently.

*   *   *

They were both quiet in the returning car. As they sped down the valley, Megan felt disorientated by the passing lights. Rain was falling in heavy sheets so she confused pavement with road, walls with sky, shops with houses. She closed her eyes to blot it all out.

Alun pulled up at the end of the road and again she leaned over and kissed his cheek. It was soft. He must have shaved just before he had come out. And splashed some aftershave on. In the darkness she smiled at her private knowledge, knowing he would take her comment the wrong way.

'You are a simple fellow,' she said and felt him stiffen. 'I don't mean that you are stupid but you are uncomplicated.' She stared ahead, through the windscreen constantly being washed with rain. 'This is something I love about you. When I was younger I didn't value this quality enough. I do now.' She drew in a deep breath. 'I wanted you to know that.'

Without waiting for an answer she slipped out of the car and hurried along her street.

She had reached her front door before she saw his lights pull away.

* * *

She had realised months before what a luxury it could be to live alone. She poured herself a glass of wine, switched the heating up and pulled her book of poetry from the shelf. She wanted to read Hood's poem right through. The rhythmic phrases soothed her, the picture as clear as ever it had been of a desperate woman, unhappy, hopeless, driven to suicide and the sympathy of the poet who had translated her plight into such beautiful words. Lulled, she stared into the fire. Gas and fake coal but the heat was real enough. She half closed her eyes and recalled one of the many curious consultations she had had with Bianca.

'I wonder about those UFOs, doctor. I don't think they're flying objects at all.'

One could be fooled by Bianca's face when she made these statements. It never held the crazy emotion of Gericault's woman but looked serious and considering, intelligent even. Had it not been for the diagnosis of schizophrenia and the pink hair which made her look different Megan might have thought the statement an invitation to discuss science. There had been a subtle but elusive intelligence about Bianca, something fly-by-night that vanished as quickly as it had appeared, to be replaced by something unmistakably weird.

So when Megan had asked her, out of curiosity, one day, what she meant by not being sure about the UFOs Bianca's reply had been. 'They come down. They land. But they are with us all the time. They stay.'

Doctor-like, she had been trying to gauge Bianca's understanding. 'You mean they're in the car park?'

'Not so as you'd see them.'

'How do you know they are there?'

'They take people. And the people are

207

never seen again.'

'I don't understand.'

'I think lots of people here, in Llancloudy, don't understand,' Bianca had said. 'And that's because they are shuttin' their eyes and their ears. They don't believe me because they think I'm crazy. Instead they believe what the police tell them to believe.'

'And why would the police want them to believe something which wasn't true?'

Bianca had stared at her with a look of soft pity. 'Because it saves work. That's why. And money. Once they've got an explanation they can wind down the investigation. See?'

It was true. Megan could not argue this indisputable point. So instead she had veered off at a tangent. 'Who disappears?'

Bianca's look of scorn had shocked her.

'Read your papers.'

And Bianca had swept out of the surgery leaving Megan staring at the Gericault.

The encounter had intrigued her because Megan had come off worst.

When learning about psychosis, as a medical student, the entire concept of detachment from reality had frightened her. To be blissfully unaware would be one thing. But to have any insight into the condition must be to sit on the steps of Hell. And in the last seconds of the consultation she could have sworn Bianca Rhys knew exactly what was happening to her. She had been lucid, logical, perceptive. And had rejected her doctor because she had not listened.

Two weeks later, as though continuing the conversation Bianca had again broached the subject.

'UFOs might not be real at all.'

'Some people would agree . . .'

'They could be a clever device.'

'Ye-es.'

'Made up to explain the inexplicable. Understand?'

'I—think—so.'

Bianca had picked up on her hesitation.

'You don't believe me either, do you?'

To confront a psychotic with doubt can be a mistake. So she gave a non-committal answer.

'I wouldn't say that.'

Bianca had picked her handbag up from the floor. 'I don't believe him,' she'd said. 'It's him, see. And he doesn't like me asking questions. At least, not the wrong questions. He doesn't mind if they're the right ones.'

'Never you mind.'

'And another thing.'

Megan had already begun filling the consultation in on the Lloyd George notes, struggling to select the appropriate Reed Code.

'They can't be saucers. They wouldn't be big enough, see. Flying plates. That's more like it.' And she had gone.

So tonight Megan smiled into the fake fire.

She could have pursued the line of questioning but Bianca had been *twp*. A Welsh word not quite parallelled by its English equivalent of simple. The word *twp* held affection while simple did not.

Something struck her. One would have expected a schizophrenic to *believe* in UFOs rather than question their existence. Their nightmares consisted of being overlooked and overheard, frequently by extra terrestrials.

She loosened the zip on her fleece, suddenly uncomfortably hot. Because, riding on the wings of these revelations, was the unwelcome thought that however high her ideals of returning to the Valley to help its inhabitants, she had failed one of her most needy patients. In failing to follow through Bianca's precious flashes of clarity she had not recognised that—like glimpses through a keyhole—these confidences were part of a bigger story. And now the light was permanently switched off. Bianca was dead. The picture had gone. The room was dark.

What if, she thought, Bianca had pieced together a story which no one else had fully understood, because a rational mind searches for rational explanations? But what if she had been the one to hit on the truth? That five people in this small town had been murdered. And only she and the killer knew it. Was it such a giant step then to assume that she had herself been abducted and later murdered.

Smothered maybe, and her body dumped in the Slaggy Pool?

Was it a flight of fancy, a stretch of the imagination? Or could it possibly be—the truth?

There was one huge difference between Bianca's story and the fate of the other five.

Her body had been found.

She pulled the last box towards her.

CHAPTER FIFTEEN

This box looked newer than the others, the cardboard less bleached and brittle. And Bianca had sellotaped the top down. Megan pulled at it fruitlessly before resorting to a pair of scissors.

*   *   *

Inside were the papers, neatly folded, with the dragon rampant of the *Western Mail* showing on top. Megan lifted the top one and read through the lead article. She already knew the details—Alun had given her a graphic description of the background to the disappearance of the two boys. And he had described them. But she wanted to see their photographs.

Faces of two eleven-year-olds, in school tie,

V-necked sweaters, scrubbed faces and combed hair peered back at her from the piles of newsprint. She could guess which one was Neil Jones: 'the ugliest little tyke' Alun had ever seen. Crooked teeth, hair that stuck up like Dennis the Menace's, a pair of defiant, cynical eyes. The other one, George Prees, looked quieter, a little afraid of something.

She spent a while searching their faces. They didn't look 'little buggers' even though their addresses were some of the worst roads on the estate and it was tempting to tar all inhabitants with the same brush. But in the police quotes on pages two and three she could read between the lines. They were *known* to them. There had been *suspicion of truancy*. They had been *cautioned* on previous occasions. And like the sniff of neglect present in the Marie Walker case their parents had not reported them missing until very late at night. These were not children closely watched, as Rhiann Lewis had been, but kids who had roamed the streets with their friends in gangs, finding and creating trouble. Just like Joel and Stefan Parker. Megan felt a sense of inevitability about this most recent disappearance.

As though to agree with her observation she turned the pages and found, on page four of the *Western Mail,* a brief interview with Samuel Parker, Joel's older cousin, about his missing 'mates'.

Megan read through curiously.

'I did wonder when they didn't turn up for the exam. See, the teacher had told us anyone missing the maths end of terms would automatically fail—whatever the excuse. But I thought that Neil and Georgey probably had such brilliant excuses they'd get away with it, see. That's what I thought. So I didn't say nothin'.'

Megan smiled. Samuel Parker had invented the Parker stamp for his two younger cousins. Currently in prison for supplying marijuana to almost the entire valley he would soon be free to set up his business again. Megan knew him quite well. She had signed his doctor's note to avoid Community Service more than once. There was no real harm in Sam. Buying and selling marijuana had seemed, to him, a perfectly reasonable way to supplement his income from a variety of poorly paid careers in Llancloudy.

*   *   *

She pulled a sheaf of papers from the box and settled down to absorb the detail. The facts were now familiar. The two boys had last been seen walking towards Llancloudy Comp., school bags on their backs, uniform on—as though they had been intending to attend. One report said that two boys, answering the description of Neil and George had been seen at the side of the road, hitching a lift out of the valleys. But it only appeared in one article. The witness had not known the boys personally so identification was uncertain.

That meant there was a chance that George and Neil had never left the valley.

Which would mean another vanishing.

Which would mean, in turn, that in the last thirty years five people had disappeared from the small village of Llancloudy. *None* had ever been seen again and there was no explanation.

Bianca had saved the newspapers, Esther Magellan had been charged with their custody and she, Megan Banesto, had ended up with them.

Make no deep scrutiny.

The Hood poem again, wrong context but apt words.

Make no deep scrutiny. That was exactly what she was doing. *Too* deep a scrutiny. Megan gathered the papers back together, put them carefully back into the box and folded the lid down.

It was late.

*   *   *

She lay in bed still chewing over the possibilities. Fact: People had disappeared. *Something* must have happened to them. Megan pulled the blanket right up to her chin.

She patted the pillow and closed her eyes,

214

ten minutes later flicking them open. She could not sleep with these shadowy visions of a killer who liquidated people every few years. She padded downstairs and made a cup of tea. Then she took a paperback to bed with her and distracted herself with Denise Mina's *Garnethill* until she fell asleep.

*   *   *

The weekend passed quietly, cleaning the house and necessary shopping on the Saturday; a visit to her parents for Sunday with the tradition of her and her father wrapping themselves up against the elements and taking the dog for a brisk walk across the beach and her mother curling up in front of the fire with a book. But when they returned, the scent of roasting Welsh lamb made her salivate. And the mint sauce was freshly made from mint grown in the greenhouse. Megan hugged her mother and ignored the lurid cover of a thriller which peeped out from behind a cushion on the back of the sofa.

After tea, she and her father settled down to watch the rugby on television, her father making sound and critical comment on the performance of the teams. They both stood up and cheered as Rupert Moon belted up the pitch and hurled himself—and the ball—right over the try line giving the Scarlets yet another victory. 'Good lad there,' her father said.

She could have asked them about the disappearances over the years from Llancloudy but she didn't want to blight the weekend. Problems simply didn't belong in this peaceful retirement bungalow.

She left late.

*   *   *

For a few years, the eleventh hour of the eleventh day of the eleventh month had been marked by a two minute silence. Megan kept an eye on her watch. She always observed it. Not because she had any experience of war but because she did have experience of suffering. And to her the terrible slaughter of the two World Wars was something she felt never should be forgotten.

Morning surgery presented the usual plethora of minor complaints, the medicine easy to dispense but the lifestyle problems, as usual, insoluble. At ten to eleven her last patient arrived.

It didn't take a brilliant process of deduction to see that something had upset Gwen Owen.

And for once she seemed at a loss for words. She sat and fiddled with the strap of her handbag, a cheap, plastic thing she always housed on her lap, her eyes flickering around the room like a nervous wren, her forehead deeply furrowed.

'I don't quite know how to say this, doctor. I'm afraid you'll think I'm . . .' There was despair in the heavily powdered face.

'My doctor gave me some tablets for it.' She hesitated. 'They seemed to help.'

Megan had an inkling of what was the problem.

It was five minutes to eleven.

'You probably don't remember. Years ago my little granddaughter let herself out of the garden. We never saw her again.'

'Rhiann?'

'You remember that?'

'No—not really. I was too young.' Megan felt agitated. 'The name—that's all.'

'It was awful. We thought she was safe. We never imagined . . . But it *must* have been her who unbolted the gate.'

'Why would she . . . ?'

'It must have been someone she knew—someone she trusted. You see—we were always telling her not to open the door to strangers. And I can't think she would have done so. And that's the worst of it, doctor.'

It was eleven o'clock. Gwen Owen had not noticed.

Megan was puzzled. 'So why are you particularly thinking about Rhiann now, Mrs Owen?'

Gwen Owen dabbed her nose with a dainty cambric handkerchief which she then crumpled up. 'Well—Bianca used to . . . I

217

mean lots of people used to say they knew what had happened to Rhiann. But they couldn't have. Nobody knew. Not the police nor anybody else.' She was wringing her hands as though applying a softening skin lotion. But the sound was rasping and dry.

'And Bianca?' Megan prompted.

'She used to upset me. Made me quite cross once or twice. Gave me awful dreams.'

'What did she say?'

'That Rhiann was with other people. That they were all together.'

'What do you think she meant?'

'I used to wonder if she was tryin' to comfort me, that she was sayin' she was with other people in Heaven. But the trouble was she might just as well have said aliens had taken her along with other people from Llancloudy.'

'What other people?'

The question was unnecessary.

'Oh—she set great store over some teacher who went back to London to avoid facing some angry parents. And years later, after we lost Rhiann another little girl—quite a bit older—was abducted on her way to buy some chips. One of those paedophiles took her I wouldn't be surprised. I hope . . .' She was screwing her handkerchief up into a tight ball. 'I can't bear to think that anything like that happened to Rhiann. But if she'd just wandered off and got lost we would have

218

found her, wouldn't we? Everyone was looking for her. But they never did find her, doctor. They never found anything. Not a sign of her. And then Bianca starting making out she had some knowledge what had happened to her. At one point I did wonder whether to call the police in again—to talk to her. After all—if she knew something it's only right she should tell them. But I came to the conclusion she never knew anything really. Like us she didn't have a clue. On another planet she was. Sometimes,' Gwen stared towards the window, 'sometimes I'd wonder and I'd ask her. I'd threaten her even. *If you know. Then tell me. For God's sake tell me where my little girl is.* Got quite vicious I did with her one day. I could have hurt her. But I stopped myself, doctor. She couldn't help how she was. But now.' Her eyes were drifting towards the vertical blinds which carved the outside into narrow slivers of pictures.

'Bianca's been dead for nearly three months, Mrs Owen. Why are you thinking about what she said now?'

'I didn't think of it at first. But what if Bianca *did* know what happened to my little granddaughter? She'll never be able to tell me now, will she? And then the other night I thought of something else. Bianca wasn't right in the head. What if she knew what had happened to my little girl because—whatever it was—she'd done it?'

Ten past eleven. The room was silent now.

'I can't stop thinkin' about it.' To illustrate what she meant she held out both her hands. They were shaking, pink-painted fingernails vibrating.

Megan reached for her prescription pad.

CHAPTER SIXTEEN

She met up with Andy and Phil for coffee. 'So—did you observe the two minute silence?'

'No, Andy. Sometimes it seems that talking to the living is more important than remembering the dead.'

Phil Walsh glanced up from the pile of prescriptions he was signing. 'You're a bit profound for a Monday morning, aren't you?'

She gave him a playful punch. 'Kind of goes with the job, doesn't it? Now then. When can I have a couple of weeks to soak up some sunshine on a long-haul holiday.'

They chatted for almost half an hour before leaving the surgery to do their separate visits.

A sudden cloudburst forced her inside the car. Rain spattered her windscreen and she felt a dreadful sense of boredom, of a lack of colour in her life and in the valley. People walked quickly, wearing dark, dull clothes, hoods hiding their faces, hands deep in pockets. She felt a desperate yearning for colour, for warmth, sunshine, flowers. Italy.

*   *   *

On impulse she decided to call on Esther Magellan, now presumably settled in her new home; she had received no pleas for help from Catherine Howells. She took the road south out of the valley, diverted across the old stone bridge and drove up the side of a low hill towards the flats. These more modern homes were prettier than the Parkers' estate, built of red brick with pleasing design and good views back down the valley. The Social Services had looked after Esther well. The small block of maisonettes looked clean and civilised. The grass was clipped, there was no graffiti and it was quiet apart from the distant bark of a dog and faraway traffic. Peace was a rare commodity in the valleys where one family in two had a man's best friend employed to bark at strangers and protect the family home.

Megan let herself in to the entrance through an unlocked wired glass partition and climbed the steps to the yellow front door. From inside she heard shuffling, slippered footsteps. She started planning her interrogation. It would be tricky. Direct questioning was unlikely to bring any results. Esther would simply clam up or cry. They were her defence mechanisms. On the other hand if she was too circumspect she would learn nothing. Esther was quite capable of rambling on for hours in her flat, monotonous voice without giving away much of substance.

Behind the door the shuffling footsteps had stopped. Megan could hear adenoidal breathing and she knew Esther was waiting, listening. She knocked again, impatiently, wondering not for the first time exactly how much Esther did know or retain in her suet-pudding mind. The truth was obscure. Still. However confused Esther Magellan was, she was the best chance Megan had of learning the truth about Bianca. For while Carole Symmonds had been close to her mother it would have been in her flatmate, her 'one true friend', that Bianca would have confided.

She called out. 'Esther?'

The door was pulled open half an inch and a voice spoke, 'I don't want any milk today, thank you. Not today.'

'Esther?'

The door was flung open and Esther was tugging at her arm. 'Oh it's you, doctor. I am sorry.' She gave a self-conscious giggle. 'I thought it was the milkman. Even though he already came today. I didn't want more milk, see.' Her face fell. 'But I'm not ill, doctor. I don't know what you're doin' here.'

'I just came to see how you're getting on in your new flat,' Megan said brightly, following Esther inside and closing the door behind her. She didn't want anyone hearing her questions about Bianca.

Esther flopped, ungainly, onto the sofa, legs wide apart, pink knickers showing. Megan eyed them and wondered where on earth you bought knickers like them from.

She trained her eyes back on Esther's face. 'How are you Esther?'

'I'm very lonely,' Esther answered happily. 'I miss her, you know. Bianca was my friend. My good friend. I wish she was here now. Today.'

'I'm sure you do.' Megan glanced around her. 'It's very nice here though. It's a lovely flat.'

Esther pulled herself to her feet. 'Would you like to have a look around?'

It was as good a method of breaking the ice as anything else so Megan enthusiastically inspected the area. It was clean and tidy, though small. And freshly decorated in contemporary colours, bright blue walls and a white breakfast bar which divided the kitchen from the living / dining space.

Proudly Esther marched her into a small bedroom with cream walls and an orange duvet and a bathroom with a white suite and walls painted the same shade of blue as the living room. When flats were built for single people that was exactly what they meant. Comfortable but tiny as an egg box with four little pockets. Megan felt a suffocating sense of claustrophobia. She would have found it hard to live in such a tiny place. Esther led her back into the sitting room and she stood and admired a couple of Constable prints screwed to the walls. What the Social Services had provided was not removable.

*   *   *

Central to the living area was a gas fire, turned full on, making the room uncomfortably hot and stuffy. Maybe it was the claustrophobic atmosphere that added to the impression that this was a place too little even for one. Perhaps even Esther thought so. She'd opened the steel framed window as far as it would go, exchanging some of the dank, November air for the fusty interior. Megan crossed the room in three steps and leaned out of the window to take in a couple of lungfuls of damp air, winter grass, mountain streams and the plaintive bleating of sheep. Her eyes trailed along the valley as she wondered how best to broach the subject of the newspapers.

Esther did it for her. 'So what did you come for?' she asked innocently.

Megan took the plunge.

'If Bianca was still alive you wouldn't be living here in this nice place, would you, Esther?'

Sometimes folk we label as simple are not. Esther focused a pair of dark green eyes on her. And for that split second Megan was convinced she read intelligence. The next

224

moment it was gone. Esther's eyes now appeared black and empty. 'I might,' she said flatly. 'I might still be living here. They might have put me here and Bianca too.'

'No,' Megan corrected her. 'These apartments are for only one person, you know. If the two of you were still together you'd still be in your house in Merthyr Crescent.'

'I could live here and she could live next door to me.'

As usual Esther's blunt logic was impossible to argue with. So Megan agreed.

Esther was still fixing her with a stare. 'Why did you come? I'm not ill. I don't need a doctor.' Esther's abrupt question might have thrown Megan had she not had her answer ready waiting in the wings.

'I've come as a friend.'

'Like Bianca was?' The eyes were marginally less trusting. She was not taken in by Megan's mild deceit.

And now Megan knew she must get to the point quickly or lose this chance. 'Sort of. I'd been thinking about Bianca quite a lot lately. I was wondering about those newspapers. Why she kept them.'

'Because the people disappeared.'

'What did Bianca think had happened to them?'

'Lots of ideas she had,' Esther said. 'Lots and lots.'

'And what were they?'

'Flying saucers.'

'Do you believe in flying saucers?'

Childlike Esther's hand flew up to her mouth to suppress a giggle. 'Of course I don't. You'd have to be very stupid to think they'd gone into a flying saucer. It wouldn't be big enough for a start. They'd have to be Flyin' Plates. And big ones at that.'

Megan had a sneaking feeling that Esther's comprehension of a flying saucer was more literal than scientific but she didn't want to sidetrack so she let the idea hang in the air and tried again. 'Did she have any other ideas?'

Esther frowned. 'That they'd been taken by the—'

Megan leaned forward eagerly. She was on the edge of discovery. 'By the . . . ?'

'By the trolls.'

Megan exhaled with disappointment at Esther's dumb lack of understanding.

'What did she mean?'

'She said that there were people living underground. Trolls she called them. She said they kept bodies down there.'

'Why—why would they do that?' She was still desperately searching for some logical, rational clue.

'To eat them,' Esther said cheerfully. 'Bianca said the children had been taken by the trolls because they wanted to eat them. Only no one knew—except us. And it was a secret.'

226

Megan could well imagine Alun's guffaw to this explanation. And the headlines in the *Western Mail*.

In her unfettered mind Bianca had connected trolls with caves and subterranean passages, with bodies stored and hidden, never again to see the light of day. An explanation indeed of what might have happened. If trolls had existed.

Megan felt disheartened.

She left Esther sitting in front of the television, munching chocolate biscuits, hardly looking up when Megan closed the door behind her. The impression she carried with her was of a large cow, contentedly chewing the cud.

CHAPTER SEVENTEEN

She sat outside Esther's house, staring down at the valley which still seemed stained with coal dust, dull black, dirty grey. She fiddled with her mobile phone, tempted. She could do with talking to a friend. Someone balanced, someone sympathetic. But it was not fair to burden Alun with her doubts. He had his own life to lead, a wife, a child, soon to be joined by another baby. For her to keep contacting him would do him harm.

The police had dismissed the cases years

ago after full investigation. Alun wasn't interested. And why should he be? It was history.

*   *   *

She began the slow, wet crawl up the valley towards home, hemmed in by cars. And yet something was still stopping her from entirely abandoning her ruminations. To distract herself she switched the car radio on, listened to the jaunty ramblings of the two presenters on Red Dragon radio and moved at fifteen miles an hour. Until she reached a grey-stone detached house halfway between the upper part of the village and the lower group of houses. A place where the slag heap had been flattened to provide a rugby pitch, a few swings, a roundabout and this one house with a pristine, pocket handkerchief front garden, windows polished like jet and perfect white paintwork. On impulse she pulled to a halt.

She found the front door unlocked, caught no response to her call and walked in. Barbara Watkins was a woman whom many called on unannounced. She was always waiting for—expecting—someone.

A retired headmistress who had once taught Megan, she had lived in these valleys all her life apart from a brief spell at university learning her trade and a year or two working in North Wales under the shadow of Cader

Idris. Rumour had it that her one solitary love affair had ended in a fall from the heights of the mountain about which so much folklore had originated. Tales of madness and poetry, of violent death and disappearance, insubstantial legend, hints of mists and druids, bards and poets. Maybe that great mountain was influencing her still—even from afar. She had an uncanny knack for sensing the truth, a reputation, in spite of her prosaic profession, of being fey.

The hall was narrow and dark, fussy with bits of polished brass and a pair of ancient portraits foxed with damp. Megan announced herself as she entered. It was the custom here, to shout out and prevent Barbara from being surprised.

She appeared in the kitchen door, a tall, angular figure with short, well cut straight grey hair and piercing blue eyes, wiping her hands on a cotton apron, her face breaking into smiles when she saw who it was. 'Megan. What a surprise.' She laughed, holding out her hands. 'I'm not ill, am I?'

Megan laughed with her. 'No. No you're not ill. And I do wish people would stop making that assumption whenever they see me unexpectedly. I wanted to ask your advice. Well—your opinion, really.'

'Well—you can have my advice and my opinion,' Barbara said tartly, 'but you'll have to come into the kitchen or my Welsh cakes'll burn. Nothing's free in this life, Megan.'

Megan followed her through, already salivating at the scent of the fresh Welsh cakes and relishing the anticipation of her one time headmistress' penetrative wit. She sat at the end of the scrubbed pine kitchen table, stuffing one of the Welsh cakes into her mouth and watching while Barbara deftly flipped fresh ones over on the griddle. When she'd finished and a pile was cooling on a wire tray she made them both a cup of tea and sat opposite Megan.

'For the chapel,' she explained. 'We have a fête on Saturday to raise enough money to extend our churchyard. So many people are dying.' She shot Megan a steely glance, poured them both a second cup of tea and cleared her throat.

It gave Megan a starting point. 'In a way,' she said, 'that's why I'm here.'

'Oh? Not about to make a dreadful confession, are you?'

Megan laughed. 'No.'

'Good—you haven't been killing off your patients?'

'Absolutely not.'

'Thank goodness for that. So?'

'Would you say that Llancloudy has a high crime rate?'

Barbara gave a deep sigh. 'Yes—juvenile crime, petty vandalism, car crime. Yes, I would.'

'People disappearing?'

'No, I wouldn't.'

'But quite a few people have vanished from here.'

'Go on.'

*   *   *

'Bleddyn Hughes?' Megan watched closely for Barbara's reaction. 'Do you remember him? As far as I know he was the first. He vanished thirty years ago. In 1971. A teacher.'

Barbara appeared to relax. She poured another cup of tea for them both. 'Oh, I do remember Bleddyn. Funny bloke. I always knew there was something different about him even when he first came to Llancloudy. A maths teacher who offers to coach the boys in rugby. Put in a lot of time after school hours if I remember rightly. I had a sneaking feeling that he wasn't a hundred per cent bona fide. But then it wasn't my place to point a finger. And you've got to remember, Megan, the climate was different then, thirty years ago. People weren't so aware of things like child abuse. But his wasn't a disappearance. There was nothing odd about it.'

'He vanished, didn't he? So what did you think had happened to him?'

'He was hounded out of the valley. No doubt about it. He just went somewhere else.'

'But his money, his passport, his clothes?

I've read the newspaper articles. He took nothing. Only the clothes he was wearing when he went.'

'I still don't think anything happened to him. I really do think he just left. Things were gettin' really difficult. When he started work in the school we had our suspicions but the rumours just grew and grew and a couple of the parents were starting to make complaints. Someone was bound to listen in the end. And he would have known it.'

'So you think he really did go away somewhere, maybe to London or a place where the climate was a little more tolerant and he would be anonymous?'

The retired teacher nodded.

'Leaving everything behind him?'

'He was panicked into it. There was a meeting of the Parent Teachers Association on the Friday. He left over the weekend. How much more evidence do you want?'

Thirty years ago Barbara Watkins had made up her mind. And no finger pointing by a middle-aged schizophrenic was going to change that very certain opinion. Megan breathed in the scent of hot Welsh cakes and began again. 'OK. So what about Rhiann Lewis?'

Immediately Barbara's expression changed to show sympathy, grief, pity. 'Oh, that was different. Terrible for the family. Lovely little thing she was. Great mop of dark curls. She would have been pretty when she'd grown up.'

'I know the story,' Megan said. 'I've read all about it in the papers. Seen the pictures too. She was a beautiful child. So what do you think happened to her?'

Barbara ignored the hint of irony in her voice. 'Someone else thought she was beautiful too,' she said softly. 'Someone took her away. I doubt even that she's dead. Some couple who wanted a child of their own took her. She was only three. Broke the family's heart. But I don't believe she's dead.'

'And Marie Walker?'

The retired teacher narrowed her eyes. 'She was the little ten-year-old, wasn't she? Went missing sometime in the late eighties? Buying chips. Saucy little thing. I always thought she was murdered. Assaulted and her body hidden somewhere. A couple of years after a man was arrested exposing himself right outside the same chip shop, Valley Chippie. They tried to make him confess but he said he didn't know anything about her. Completely denied it. No one believed him, of course.' Her eyes were directly focused on her. 'We *knew,* Megan. Knew as though we'd been there ourselves and witnessed it.'

'And the man?'

'Left the valleys. I heard he had a motorbike crash and was badly hurt some years after. Poetic justice.' There was more than a hint of chapel hardness in her face. 'Don't know anything more. Except he never did confess.'

'So what about the two boys who vanished together? Not so long ago.'

'What was it? Five or six years?'

'Eight.'

'George Prees and Neil Jones. I remember their names. Little monsters they were according to their teachers. I was glad, in a way, that they were never my problem because believe you me, Megan, they would have been a problem—all their lives. Perhaps it's being a teacher all my life, having no family but watching what people make of themselves. Makes us cynical. We can recognise a rotten apple in the barrel early on.'

It was true. Barbara had a hearty scepticism when assessing children's characters and potential. And again she had a rational explanation for the disappearance of the two boys.

'They hitched a lift out of the valley and disappeared—like many other truants, probably in London or Brighton or one of the other places the homeless gravitate to. Or maybe they just fell down a mine shaft.'

'So why weren't their bodies discovered?'

'Haven't you got any idea what's down there, Megan? It's like a city. The catacombs of Rome aren't more intricate than the tunnels beneath these valleys. We were sitting on coal. Tons and tons of it. Like an ocean beneath our feet. And there's still plenty there. It's just that nobody wants to dig it up any more. Old-fashioned, coal is. Like these poor little valleys. Sold our souls to the Japanese and their light industry. Anything from badges to microchips. But that isn't what's at the heart of these places, Megan. Those boys could have fallen down a shaft and no one would ever be the wiser no matter however hard they looked. They could have wandered in, got lost down there. The tunnels go for miles. One day they'll be found. Together like they always were, either in a city or under our feet. Always in trouble that pair. Tell them not to do something and it was like waving a red flag in front of a bull. They were the most rebellious kids I've ever known in my entire teaching career. And I've known some Che Guevaras and Pol Pots in my time, I can tell you. I was glad they never got to the comp.'

Megan sat still, uncomfortable with Barbara's words as well as with her underlying attitude. She was so judgmental, so unpitying, so unsympathetic. But she had been a witness to all the disappearances—an impartial observer who had known at least one of the victims well. She was undoubtedly sane and rational—unlike Bianca Rhys.

Her version of events must be the right one.

Poor Bianca had looked at the cases and threaded them together with explanations so bizarre no one had taken any notice. Even ringing the police with her suggestions of 'flying saucers' and trolls had been understandably treated as a very good joke.

It was more rational for her to agree with Barbara.

The only other person who had listened to Bianca's strange wanderings had been Smithson.

She looked up as Barbara poured her a second cup of tea. 'So what do you think happened to Bianca?'

'She fell in the pool.' It was the simple answer.

*   *   *

A message was flashing on her phone to visit Triagwn. And so she turned right out of Barbara's house, away from her own place and back towards the point where the roundabout crosses the M4. Turn right for Swansea, left for Cardiff, Newport and England. Megan drove straight over then took the narrow lane, first right after the roundabout.

She pulled up right outside the front door of Triagwn House and sat in her car for a moment, watching the cherub spout his stream into the pool below. A few drops bounced into the water, rippling its glassy surface. She climbed out of her car, slamming the door behind her and thought of the little girl who had fallen in, too terrified to save herself. It had all been so unnecessary. The pool could have been no more than a couple of feet deep. If the child had stood up her head would have been well above water. *And years later the same event had happened in the Slaggy Pool.*

If Bianca had stood up . . . she had a brief vision of Alun's trousers, wet to the knees and corrected herself. If Bianca had been able to stand up.

What if she couldn't. What if she had been already dead?

The sun escaped for a brief moment from behind the thick cumuli and framed Triagwn in a rainbow arch giving it a sudden, surreal beauty. Megan was reminded of a quote she had read by Herman Melville. *'Who in the rainbow can draw the line where the violet tint ends and the orange tint begins? Distinctly we see the difference of the color, but where exactly does the first one visibly enter into the other? So with sanity and insanity. In pronounced cases there is no question about them. But in some cases in various degrees supposedly less pronounced, to draw the line of demarkation few will undertake.'*

But there was no doubting Bianca's insanity. Only now was she appreciating the deep and chilling truth expressed by Herman Melville more than a hundred years ago. In sudden frustration she splashed some water. Droplets sprayed up, caught and captured the sunshine but the cherub's face itself was thrown into deep, sullen shadow. Not a chuckling angel but a wicked and malicious little faun.

She glanced up, hoping to see Smithson's face watching from the window. She was, in a way, fond of the old man and the sedatives were surely wearing off by now. There would be a return of the puckish, sharp wit.

People in the valley have funereal traditions. They don't stare at the funeral cortege but concentrate on their feet, on the pavement, elsewhere. They bow their heads and wait for the hearse to go by. Out of respect they do not peer into the funeral cars but avert their eyes from grief, from grieving, from suffering. The men wear black ties, the women their hats and their 'tidy' black. Children are not welcome, certain hymns are sung. Abide With Me. The Day Thou gavest, Lord, is ended. The men boom out their bass; the tenors add rich harmony as full and satisfying as the gravy poured on a Sunday roast.

And in the house of bereavement the curtains are drawn.

Megan squeezed her eyes tight shut and flicked them open to evaporate the mirage.

She had not been mistaken. The curtains to Smithson's room were drawn.

She pushed open the front door and walked very quickly to the door marked matron.

And all the time she knew that Smithson was dead.

The room was empty, the chair pushed back. The desk was littered with papers. As Megan stood, motionless in the centre of the room the telephone rang.

No one answered it. For the first time ever she was alone in Sandra Penarth's room. She glanced around and saw the framed photographs on the coffee table in front of the window.

Her grandparents? A painfully thin man with his arm around a plump woman in a print apron. At a guess the man had not long to live. The picture had been taken in the nineteen-forties or -fifties.

She put the picture down and approached the staircase, aware that the nursing home seemed deserted. No one knew she was there. The silence on the staircase was more than threatening. It was deafening.

She could hear a soft exchange of words as she neared Smithson's room.

'Just straighten out his legs. See if his eyes'll stay shut.'

They were laying him out.

The old man who had babbled would babble no more.

Valerie Simpson turned around and saw her. And Megan would have sworn to a court of justice that guilt flashed across her face.

Sandra Penarth broke the silence. 'We'd just rung the surgery.' She glanced down at the bed. 'He died this morning. Bit of a surprise.'

'It's a shock.' Megan spoke firmly. 'There was nothing to suggest . . .'

'You never can tell with the old.' Sandra spoke with full authority. 'I expect his heart just gave up.'

She was putting words into Megan's mouth, suggesting a diagnosis.

'His heart was fine.'

'Acute,' Sandra countered.

'He was ninety-four years old,' Valerie said mildly. 'Can't you just put old age?'

'Old age doesn't kill.'

'Heart failure does.'

'You want to fill out the death certificate then, Sandra?'

'You know I can't.'

'And I won't.'

'Look, doctor,' Sandra said reasonably. 'He was an old man. He obviously died from natural causes. What does it matter exactly what he died of? The family won't want him all carved up. I'm sure they'd much prefer a death certificate than a postmortem.'

It would have been so much easier to acquiesce.

Megan shook her head and read a judgement in their eyes.

She's been a right old bag ever since that business with the Italian bloke.

And in a way they were right. Had she been making whoopee with Guido, Bianca's death would have passed unnoticed.

Her examination of Smithson was brief but thorough. There were no physical signs. Merely an absence of life. No heart beat, no pulse, no pupil reactions. He felt cool to the

240

touch but not cold. He'd been dead for less than an hour. Had she not stopped by Barbara's house she might have been present at Smithson's final moments.

'All right, doctor?'

Megan nodded.

She would ring the coroner from her own mobile phone in her car from where she could not be overheard.

She left Triagwn.

CHAPTER EIGHTEEN

She waited until she was alone in her car before dialling the coroner's number and giving him the details. And as she had expected his attitude was relaxed. 'Do you feel in a position to issue the death certificate?'

She felt on the defensive. 'I think the relatives would prefer a death certificate. He was ninety four and the nursing home staff want a certificate as well. But he was so vigorous and cantankerous I can't explain his dying so suddenly.'

'You feel we should go ahead with a postmortem?'

'Yes.'

'I see.'

'It was an *unexpected* death.'

'And you saw him only a week or so ago?'

'He wasn't moribund then.'

The coroner gave a brief, dry laugh. 'All right then, Doctor Banesto.' He was humouring her.

And she felt a sudden and irrational hostility towards him.

Go on, chortle away, you complacent old man. You may soon be in for a surprise.

* * *

She drove back up the valley feeling this time she had, at least, taken some positive action. On impulse as she passed Barbara's house she decided to call in again. She stopped the car and climbed out.

A game of rugby had started up on the flattened tip. She watched someone pick up the ball and start to run—not far—no more than a few yards. Two players, one either side, caught him and pulled him down—lionesses dragging down a wildebeest. Even the snarling face of the grounded animal was the same. But it wasn't until the ruck dispersed, the ref blew his whistle and the player finally emerged that she recognised Alun. He gave a vague, rueful smile in her direction and trotted back up the pitch. She wasn't sure whether he had seen her or not.

* * *

Then Barbara was standing at her side, bulky in a hooded anorak, her eyes directed towards the field. 'Lovely game, isn't it? Poetry in motion. I do enjoy it when they do their training up here. Often come and watch, cheer them on. It's the police, you know.' She hesitated then gave Megan a brief, tentative smile. 'Do you know what I fancy? Having dinner out.'

'What a great idea.'

'Wait a minute and I'll put something a bit more glamorous on.'

Twenty minutes later they were climbing into Megan's car. 'Now—do you need to get changed as well? I know a great place to eat.'

A little over an hour later Megan was dressed in a grey, net mini dress smothered over by a fake fur jaguar coat. They had manoeuvred their way through the Cardiff Docks Regeneration Scheme and were pushing open the door of *La Casa Guido*. Barbara's idea this—to lay the ghost.

Guido swarmed forward to meet them, greeting Megan with the warmest of kisses on both cheeks. 'My darling, Megan. *Cara Mia*. It is good to see you.' He held her at arm's length. 'I forgot how lovely you are. I didn't think you ever would come here. I am glad to see you. Really.' He didn't stop talking all the time he was removing their jackets and sitting them at a table as though he had a thousand things to tell her in his curious blend of spaghetti talk. 'I missed you, Megan. I missed you. I really did.'

She'd forgotten how good he looked—and smelt. Tall, slim, black haired, snake-hipped, the scent of garlic, fresh herbs and something exotic in the spice line seeping from his pores. Beautiful, white teeth. Olive skin. She didn't love him any more but she suddenly realised how much she liked him—and missed him. She hadn't been so misled. He was a warm, attractive, affectionate man. And he loved her. He just didn't want to be married to her—or to sleep with her—or any other woman for that matter. So . . . ? It was no longer a problem.

Barbara peered at her over the rim of her glasses. 'As I said, Megan. There comes a time when you have to lay the ghosts.'

And she was intensely glad she had come. Because she knew she could still feel this fondness for her ex-husband, one particular part of her sealed up heart was opened up again. She knew now exactly who she was. It was as simple as that. Her judgement had not been so completely wrong. Only slightly. She had misread his sexuality. Maybe, in fact, he had too. Marriage had forced him too close constantly to a woman and for him it had only served to expose his preference for his own sex.

She glanced around the restaurant. The place was crowded. A small queue waited at the door although it was still early. There was an atmosphere of Mediterranean energy around. Behind a counter the chef was ostentatiously spinning pizzas. Maybe he was Guido's paramour. He gave her a broad wink and a dazzling grin and she grinned back, without rancour. Light guitar music was playing in the background. Glasses chinked. And there was the sound and the smell of cooking. She leaned right back in her chair and stretched her legs out, for a brief moment all the concerns of the last few months wiped out. She had forgotten how very good it felt to be in a contintental type restaurant, breathing in the combined scent of garlic and red wine and enjoying herself so thoroughly. On impulse she reached across the table and touched Barbara's hand. 'Thanks,' she said. 'You're right. It *was* time to lay a few ghosts.'

Guido snatched the menus away teasingly. 'You let me choose,' he said. 'I know what you will like.'

'And me?' Barbara asked archly.

'I can guess. I understand the palates of women.'

Megan raised her eyebrows and she and Barbara burst out laughing, feeling like a couple of young girls, giggling over a clumsy advance. Guido took no offence. Barbara met his eyes boldly.

'In your hands then, Mr Banesto.'

The food came thick and fast. Far too much to eat, Guido brandishing the huge pepper grinder like a sub machine gun and sprinkling fresh Parmesan cheese liberally over every course. He had done well in this place; this studious attention to detail was paying off, the check tablecloths, carafes of good house wine, even the frenetic, dextrous service. It was a family run trattoria on the edge of the capital city of Wales. Megan made a silent pact with herself. One day—soon—she would return to Italy. She would indulge in their hedonistic aesthetics again.

* * *

They left the restaurant at ten, threading their way through the late evening traffic of the city before crossing the M4 and turning up towards the valleys. Llancloudy seemed dark and quiet after the hurly burly of the metropolis. Although Barbara's house was further down the valley Megan invited her back for a coffee with a promise of a lift home. The house felt a little cool as they entered and somehow sterile after the colourful atmosphere of the restaurant. Barbara took in the white walls, pale carpet, cream sofa and the large abstract painting which hung over the fireplace. 'Is this what they call minimalist? I've always wondered what it looked like.'

Megan laughed. 'My own brand of it. A full blown minimalist would disown the books. But I like the feeling of emptiness. Like a glacier.

It helps me think. Coffee?'

'Mmm. That would be nice.' Barbara continued to prowl around the room, peering at the books. When Megan headed off towards the kitchen, Barbara followed her so the first thing they both saw when the lights were switched on were the four boxes, still standing against the wall. She had meant to remove them to the garden shed but one day it had been raining, another she'd had a bath and didn't fancy lugging the boxes up the garden path. And so they still stood. She would move them in the morning. Megan busied herself filling the cafetiere and carried it through to the sitting room where she kicked off her shoes and they sat in front of the fake-flame fire and gossiped about the lives of the girls who had shared Megan's year in school—the ones who had succeeded, the others who had fallen by the wayside. Some classmates Megan kept in contact with, others still sent cards and/or letters to Barbara and a few had simply vanished from view.

At eleven thirty Barbara picked up her handbag with a sigh. 'I don't want to go but it really is time I was off, Megan. You've got work in the morning. It's been lovely talking to you, reminiscing.'

Megan uncurled from the chair. 'Yes,' she said. 'I'll drive you home. Thanks for the great evening. We'll do it again.'

*   *   *

They were silent in the short car journey back to Barbara's house, the lights of Llancloudy spinning passed them. The roads were quiet, the pavements deserted. The cold and wet must be keeping people indoors.

Barbara thanked her politely for the lift and ran through the rain towards her front door. A swift fumble with the key and a second later the lights came on. Megan turned around near the rugby pitch and headed for home.

She let herself in with her key and took the coffee cups back into the kitchen. Yes, she thought, turning around. 'Tomorrow I must tidy up and throw the boxes away.'

But on the following day she didn't carry out her resolution because she woke up to the news that Stefan Parker had vanished.

CHAPTER NINETEEN

It was her custom to set the radio alarm for seven even though she didn't need to be at the surgery until nine. It gave her time to listen to the local news bulletin, pad downstairs to make a drink while the adverts were on and bring the mug of coffee back to bed.

That morning her eyes were still shut when the radio alarm clicked on. She heard the pips followed by the announcement, 'This is the news on Tuesday November 12th. You are tuned in to BBC Radio Wales.' Then there was the usual pause.

'The police are still searching for missing ten-year-old, Stefan Parker.'

She sat up, her eyes wide open. 'Stefan has not been seen since early Monday and police are concerned for his safety. His mother left for work yesterday at eight o'clock but Stefan failed to turn up at school yesterday morning and has not been seen since. Mrs Parker has appealed for her son to return home. Police have started searching the area around Llancloudy and are conducting house to house interviews. If anyone does have any information about the missing boy would they please ring Llancloudy police station at . . .' The telephone number followed.

Megan stared around her bedroom and felt cold. It was another disappearance. She flung the covers off and went downstairs. While she waited for the kettle to boil she stood, staring at the boxes in the corner and rubbing the side of her head with her fingertips.

She took her coffee back to bed and listened to an extended news bulletin with a heart-rending plea from Mandy Parker for Stefan to return home. There would be, she tearfully stated, no recriminations.

Megan drew back the curtains on the dullest day in November and stared out over rows and rows of slate roofs dripping with rain. Beyond them must be the mountains. But she couldn't see them.

*   *   *

On her way into work she bought the *Western Mail.* Stefan had made headlines here too.

Megan scanned through the stories as she sat in the car, reading the story beneath the lead, *Missing Llancloudy Schoolboy.*

Using the description, schoolboy, made Stefan sound an innocent—nothing like the little tough-head he really was. As she read through the story she was struck at the similarity between Stefan's disappearance and George Prees and Neil Jones. Like the two boys, eight years previously, Stefan frequently missed school. He was one of the aimless kids who hung around the chip shop, the video shop, the recreation ground or hitched a lift to one of the nearby towns to hang around there. Maybe he would trip to the seaside on a fine day. But Monday had not been a fine day. It had been cold and drizzly. A truant would have been more likely to haunt a coffee shop or the house of a friend. But Stefan's friends, Mark Pritchard and Ryan Jenkins had been at school and claimed not to have seen Stefan since the Sunday night.

According to his mum Stefan had been up and dressed in school trousers and a clean

250

white shirt, his brown and red striped school tie knotted around his neck when she had left for work at eight o'clock on the Monday morning. But he had not gone to school. Afterwards the police had looked at the Attendance Register. And by his name was a large, black cross—one of many.

Mandy Parker hadn't worried when he was late home for tea. He would often get that from the chip shop anyway, wander the streets a bit, call on a few mates. When he hadn't shown up by eleven o'clock on the Monday night she still didn't worry but rang round a few of his buddies—and drew a blank. None of them had seen him all day. They hadn't thought anything of it and neither did she. She still wasn't worried. She knew her son. He was a wanderer, streetwise, tough, one who could look after himself.

So she hadn't raised the alarm but had waited and waited for him to turn up, her anger compounding by the hour. Afterwards she said she did think about ringing the police but had rejected the idea. It would have been a foreign act to have spoken to the police, she had explained. Stefan wouldn't thank her for alerting *them* when he got home. Which he would. And Mandy Parker had already decided she'd give him a 'bloody good hiding' for not even bothering to telephone her. At that point she thought he might have hitched a lift to the Rhondda to see his dad. She had

251

tried to ring there but had had no answer. Only a jaunty answerphone which had invited her to leave a message. So she had waited four more crucial hours before finally alerting the police at three in the morning. And by nine am they had followed her enquiries with more of their own. No one had seen Stefan since his mother's last sighting, except for one neighbour who had spotted the boy letting himself out of the front door at eight thirty-five—and had assumed he was heading for school. It was now Tuesday morning and no one had seen him since. Not his mum, nor his dad, his *Mamgu* or any one of the cronies he usually hung around with.

Stefan Parker had vanished.

Each subsequent news bulletin described how the search intensified. Inhabitants of Llancloudy turned out to search the hillsides. Some began to explore the old mine workings. And the police formed road blocks to question motorists.

*   *   *

Through the slats of her surgery blind, Megan could sense the heightened action. Police cars raced past and vanished into the beyond. Figures loomed around the Slaggy Pool, and shapes formed and disappeared through the mist on the hillsides beyond. The lunchtime news contained no sightings, only a repeat of the morning's appeals. And when darkness fell early at three-thirty, Stefan was missing for the second night. When the evening paper dropped on the mat at six o'clock Megan picked it up and scanned the headlines with a feeling of inevitability.

He would not be found but would join the list of the vanished.

The photograph that filled half the page of the *South Wales Echo* only emphasised the fact that Stefan Parker had plenty in common with the two boys who had disappeared in 1992. So loosely supervised as to be practically vagrants. And there was something else which Marie Walker, George Prees and Neil Jones all shared—an air of jaunty, defiant, cheeky bravado. Megan stared down at the picture of the boy's face, smiling at her from the front page, one chipped incisor, gold sleeper in his left ear, number one haircut making him look tough enough to be an escaped convict—had he not looked little more than six years old. Stefan was small for his age.

Megan took the paper into the kitchen and spread it out on the kitchen table, perching on the chair. She didn't move until she had devoured every single word written about the boy's disappearance. The main article she folded into four. Then she took a pair of scissors from the kitchen drawer and carefully snipped around every column which mentioned the missing boy. He had been gone for less then forty-eight hours, yet there was a small pile by the time she had finished. The story had received plenty of coverage. A missing boy was the biggest story to have broken in South Wales that day and plenty of people had plenty to say—on truancy, on the safety of children, even—strangely—on the lack of recreational facilities in the valleys. The columns were full of conjecture.

But like the other vanishings in which Bianca had been so interested, there was no clue as to what could have happened to Stefan from the time he had left his home. Megan sat and stared at the clippings wondering what to do with them. Then she walked through the back door, along the concrete path to the garden shed, unearthed a cardboard box and carried it into the kitchen. She dropped the cuttings in, the full sheets floating to the bottom. Next she found a black felt tipped marker pen which had been anchored to her shopping list with a length of green thread. She snapped the thread. And on the side of the box she wrote Stefan's name in large, neat italics. Only then was her feeling of agitation replaced by one of peace. She had done what *should* be done. *Someone* must care. But as she peered into the bottom of the box she sensed that what would fill it would be speculation. *He would not be found. That was the pattern of events.* That was what had filled all the other boxes—surmisement. In years to come the papers would print *Er Cof, mab annwyl,* beautiful tributes and no answers.

This was not how she wanted it to be. She lined the box up against the wall, next to the others. But when she stepped back she had to acknowledge what she was doing.

Acting like Bianca.

And now she felt frightened. Her behaviour was not quite rational. She was being over-curious. Stefan Parker's disappearance was not personally connected with her. Putting the clippings in the box was not *her* direction but a blind following in another's path. And that other had been a documented paranoid schizophrenic. What had been Bianca's mad obsession she had adopted for her own. She felt a suffocating need to escape and flung open the front door. But there was no escape. The lights were paddling around the hill. They were still searching.

They will not find.

Bianca's voice. Not hers. She was still in touch with reality. Why should they not find a naughty truant?

But she stayed on her doorstep and watched them search as though it were a computer game. Dark figures, flashing lights. A missing child—a goblin—a troll in pursuit. Nothing but a gameboy. Far enough away to lose its reality. Even the sound effects were dead right. Distant traffic. Short blasts of pop music as doors opened and closed. Shouts that echoed from far away, doors slamming. And to make sure the players knew this was a Welsh game there was, in the background, the plaintive bleating of sheep. Over her head she saw in the light polluted, orange glowing sky a lone shooting star. Nothing else. She listened to the people's voices to gauge their tone. But there was no excitement there. They hadn't found him. The game was still running, the fugitive still pursued.

She moved back into the house and closed the door behind her.

But it was not possible to think or concentrate on anything else.

At nine o'clock she switched on the Welsh news. Here too Stefan had made the headlines. But the child experts dragged in to pad out the bare fact—that he had gone missing—offered only one explanation—that he might have run away to escape some unspecified family conflict.

This item was followed by a touching appeal from his dad—with a veiled accusation against the boy's mother that she had not cared sufficiently for his son. It seemed they had had 'words' the night before and Stefan had retired to bed on Sunday night in a sulk.

$$*\qquad*\qquad*$$

Mandy Parker was mascara-smudged for her thirty seconds of fame and she looked as though she had not slept for a week, or combed her hair which was heavily bleached and gelled, pinned with ugly looking clips. Her words were part appeal for her son to return and part defence—that she had not been that angry, that the row had not been that fierce.

*   *   *

The entire focus of the first ten minutes of the evening news was an appeal for the prodigal son to return, pick up a phone, and be forgiven. Only as Megan watched a home video of Stefan passing a rugby ball to his older brother she knew he would not return. She was tempted to switch the TV off. There was no point in these heart-rending appeals. They were a waste of time.

The programme returned to the studio for a brief resume of the rest of the Welsh news before returning to the main story, this time showing a panoramic view of the masque Megan had just seen enacted outside her front door; the searches of the surrounds of Llancloudy, the old mine shafts, the mountains, the derelict buildings, the winding wheel which had once lowered the miners to the coal face and was now carrying the searchers below ground to the catacombs in the hope of finding a lost and frightened boy. Even the river and the Slaggy Pool were scanned by helicopter. The aerial view was an unfamiliar one but she could recognise the flat top of the surgery building, the road between, the small, black area which was the pond, a cluster of houses and the river beyond. But Bianca's death was not mentioned. Neither were any of the other 'vanishings'.

No one had connected them. No one except Bianca. And she had been mad and was now dead. And Smithson. He had been—not mad—simply old and strange, but he was dead too. And now her. Megan hugged her arms around her and carried on staring at the TV.

The next clip was of a motorist being stopped at a road block and shaking his head regretfully. A jerky camera followed the police making a few house to house searches. And more shaking heads. They were in the street next to hers. But she didn't recognise the police officers. Maybe they'd been drafted in from Cardiff. Extras. She watched the entire news, all twenty minutes of it with a feeling of unreality, detachment. This had happened before.

Only they didn't know it.

She switched the television off and wondered who would listen to her.

No one.

She sat in the chair, staring at the blank screen knowing there was nothing she could do—apart from clip cuttings from the newspapers like a mad woman.

She was wrong. On the Friday, three days after Stefan's disappearance had officially been acknowledged, she was washing her hair at the bathroom sink in the early afternoon when there was a knock at the front door. She wrapped the drips up in a towel and pulled it open. Alun was standing outside in his uniform. She felt as awkward as he looked. 'Meggie,' he said quietly. 'I was just passing. Saw your car in the road. Knew you were home. Maybe it's time you and I had a little talk.'

She nodded and backed into the house.

This time she had learned her lesson—to allow him to take the lead. To be circumspect and wise. She sat down on the sofa and watched him drop heavily into the armchair.

He gave an amused glance at her headgear. 'Hadn't you better finish your hair off?'

'Umm . . . Yes.' She patted the towel. 'I'll be a minute. Can you wait? There's beer in the fridge. Help yourself. Pour me one. I've just got to rinse the conditioner out.'

The water splashed everywhere, soap stung her eyes. She half dried it with the hairdryer, gave up on the rest. When she returned to the sitting room he had opened two cans of beer and was leaning back on the sofa, looking around him. 'Nice,' he said approvingly. 'It's really nice in here. Clean-looking. Light. Bit

259

soulless though.'

'Glad you like it.' She eyed him over the rim of the beer can. 'So?'

'Was it you up at the tip on Monday night?'

'I was calling on an old friend.'

He smiled. 'I thought it was you—before I got pulled under.'

She nodded. 'It looked rough.'

'Mmm.'

She was determined he must be the one to broach the subject. She wasn't going to help him.

'We went to Guido's restaurant.'

'Oh?' He was uninterested.

'So?' she said.

'I came round to bring you something,' he said. 'I thought you'd want to see it.'

She knew what it would be even before he opened his hand to show a shaped piece of stone, about five centimetres long. Megan picked it up, studied the green moss that stuck to all sides of the gryphon's claw except where it had recently been broken off. This was granite grey, clean and sharp.

She looked up at Alun. 'And this was in Bianca's pocket?'

He nodded.

She handed it back. 'Another piece of the puzzle,' she said.

Alun nodded. 'I didn't take any notice of you,' he said, 'when you talked about people going missing from here. I thought. Well, you

260

know what I thought. I thought you'd been misled. I mean, it was typical of Bianca that she should pick up on something and make a science fiction story out of it.'

'The flying plates?' She laughed.

'Quite.'

He was finding this difficult. But she wasn't going to help him.

'Then I decided to try and see things from your angle,' he said. 'I started asking myself some questions. Like, What if . . . ?'

She leaned forward. Eager. But still guarded.

'The first question I asked I put to the pathologist. I asked him whether it was possible Bianca had not drowned in the pool but drowned somewhere else.'

'And he said?'

'He said it was possible. That given the circumstances surrounding her death it was unlikely. But not impossible. He hadn't tested for some things called . . .'

'Diatoms,' she supplied.

'Yes well. Then I asked him if it was possible that she had not drowned at all. And again he said he could not rule it out. That it looked as though she had died of heart failure. Which could have been brought on by hitting the water. He called it a—'

'Vaso vagal.'

'He said it was even possible she could have been suffocated.'

261

'And the head injury?'

'Wouldn't have been life threatening or he wouldn't have discounted it. It would have just stunned her.'

Megan nodded.

'I asked him if he could be more precise as to when Bianca had died.'

'And he said?'

'At the earliest Sunday morning. At the latest Sunday night. Late. Up until midnight. So then I began to wonder why Bianca hadn't been seen since the Saturday morning.' Alun was squirming. 'Umm where she could have been. You know. If Bianca wasn't seen after Saturday morning but didn't die until some time on Sunday where was she? Was somebody holding on to her.' He spoke tentatively, almost apologetically, as though he expected her to laugh at the sheer drama of it all.

But she wasn't laughing. She was shivering. Part of her mind was struggling with the concept of Bianca being imprisoned by someone who intended to kill her.

'Did you mention this to Jones-Watson?'

Alun nodded.

'What did he say?'

'He said it was possible. That he couldn't rule it out. She could have been kept prisoner, been suffocated elsewhere. There was plenty of dope inside her. And her body could have been dropped into the pool. He said that circumstances suggested otherwise but that he couldn't rule out the possibility of my theory being correct. It was all down to an index of suspicion. In other words, Meggie,' His eyes held mute apology. 'If we'd alerted him to the fact that there was something suspicious about Bianca's death he could have come out of the postmortem with a different set of findings.'

She was silent.

Alun gave another tentative half-smile. 'Then I asked myself another stupid question. Why would anyone want Bianca dead? Why would they go to all that trouble to kill someone who was so nutty nobody took a blind bit of notice *whatever* she said? In fact if she made allegations against someone we'd be almost sure to give that person a clean bill of health. See what I mean?'

'Did she make allegations?'

'That's the trouble, Meggie. She said things about everyone.' His face was brick red.

'We didn't take any notice.'

Then she knew. 'She said something about Guido, didn't she?'

Alun fixed on a point in the corner of the room.

'That he looked more at boys than girls?'

Alun said nothing.

'Well, that was true.'

He nodded and looked uncomfortable. 'And then I thought about your stupid boxes,' he said next, his eyes drifting around the room. 'I suppose those are them, in the corner of the kitchen. I had a look while you were rinsing your hair.'

'Yes.'

'I remembered the names you'd told me, Meggie. And I decided to run them through the computer with a bit more of an open mind. There's very little similarity between the cases, ages of victims, circumstances surrounding their disappearances, things like that. But the one thing that struck me was that no bodies, no clothes, no clues were found of any of them. There were no real suspects—if you discount a local paedophile who was dragged in any time something happened to a child. There wasn't anything to connect him with Marie Walker's disappearance. And there were no sightings either—of anybody from the four cases. Once they'd gone they really had gone as though they were spirited away in a spaceship.'

She couldn't resist a smile. Alun, the pedantic, literal policeman sharing fanciful ideas with Bianca? It was enough to make her smile, which Alun misinterpreted. 'I wouldn't have thought you'd find it funny Megan,' he said severely.

'I don't, Alun. I promise you, I don't.'

'So you see what I'm saying?'

Spell it out, Alun.

'I think it's possible Bianca did stumble on something accidentally. Goodness knows what or how. And I don't understand what she

264

could have understood when no one else did.'

'It was something to do with having an open mind, Alun.' She struggled to explain it. 'Rational beings hunt for rational explanations. She didn't. And—'

This time it was he who finished the sentence for her. 'She accidentally got too near the truth.'

'I think so.'

'Well. Chance or luck. Bad luck,' he corrected. 'It was certainly bad luck for her.'

'So now you believe in the whole thing?'

Alun looked even more awkward. 'I'm not saying that, Meggie,' he said. 'It's just that I'm not dismissing it out of hand. That's what I'm saying.'

'Why now, Alun? Why are you suddenly prepared to believe in it all when before you dismissed it as rampant wanderings of a nutcase?' She thought she already knew the answer but she wanted to hear from his lips.

'Stefan Parker,' Alun said shortly. 'He isn't at any of his usual haunts. He went everywhere with Mark Pritchard and Ryan Jenkins. Thick as thieves the three of them were. Stefan never got into trouble on his own. He didn't have the guts and he was too small. He needed his two big mates to lead him into mischief and to protect him if he was threatened. We've tried every avenue. He didn't have any money on him. And the family are worried sick. He hasn't rung to say he's all right and he was close to his ma. Stefan hasn't run away, whatever the child experts say. He was intending going to school that morning. I'd swear it. He's been taken. I think he's probably dead.'

'There's some new evidence, isn't there?'

Alun nodded. 'His schoolbag. One of those cheap rucksack affairs. Turned up in someone's garden in Bethesda Street. The straps were ripped off. We had the teacher look at the books inside. He'd done his homework. All of it. There was no need for him to bunk off school.'

The address rang a dull chime in her mind.

'So where do you go from here?'

'Feed all the details onto the Major Incident programme of the National Computer,' he said. 'Talk to my superiors and put the word around that we're reopening all the previous cases of disappearances around Llancloudy.'

She could have flung her arms around him.

CHAPTER TWENTY

The story of the schoolbag broke the next morning and fuelled a fever of speculation in the *Western Mail* and the *Welsh Mirror*. It was displayed by the police on Breakfast TV; a sad, scruffy item, faded red, placed on a table. A blonde WPC held the straps up and the camera zoomed in to show where the stitching had torn, while a burly DI stood in the background and explained that the bag looked as though it had been ripped off the ten-year-old's back.

*   *   *

Even though she believed it was hopeless, Megan braved a biting wind to volunteer and help the search on the following afternoon. But as what light there had been finally faded, nothing more had been found of the missing boy.

He would not be found.

The evening paper was full of speculation. The boy had been kidnapped. The boy had been murdered. He was walking the streets of London selling his body. Someone claimed to have seen him in Swansea, standing on the jetty, staring out to sea, like the French Lieutentant's Woman. Megan cut out all the stories and placed them carefully inside 'Stefan's box'. The police, she noted, were hiding behind bland statements—enquiries were proceeding . . .

And from Alun she heard nothing more.

But life—and death—must go on in some muddled way or other. By Monday morning Mandy Parker was beginning to substitute her son for a supply of Temazepan. It was her way of surviving. Megan listened as she unburdened herself, racing through the entire spectrum of emotions in a few minutes—from denial to acceptance through guilt and anger with some terrible anguish thrown in. It would have been difficult for any doctor to help her through, fatuous to pretend that there was an answer; pharmacological, physical or mental. So Megan felt no responsibility as she wrote out the script and handed it over with the usual warning about not becoming too reliant on the drug. As Mandy's eyes scanned the prescription, Megan studied them and read there a shocking vulnerability. She never had been a well nourished person. Now she looked thin, haggard, old way beyond her years. It brought home to Megan what pain there was in these sterile disappearances.

'Do they have anything to go on?'

Mandy was too choked to even cry. 'They spoke to Mark Pritchard and Ryan Jenkins.' Her voice was flat, lifeless. 'Thick as thieves the three of them were. If Stefan had plans to do anything he would have told them what they were.'

'And?' Megan denied that she was asking through morbid curiosity. She was the woman's doctor. It was right that she should know everything.

'I can't imagine what happened. I *thought* he was going to school. He *looked* as though he was going to school. But he never went near the place he didn't.' The anger burst through.

268

'Deceitful little swine. If he'd gone . . .'

A great flood of tears welled up inside her eyes. 'What's happened to him? I can't sleep. He could be alive—somewhere. He might be dead. He might be with people. He might be on the streets. He might be cold. He might be suffering. All I know is he isn't with me. I don't know he's safe. I don't know he's warm. I don't know he's fed. I wonder sometimes, doctor, if I'll ever know what's happened to him.'

Megan made soothing noises and touched Mandy Parker's arm. A moment later she left the surgery without saying another word and Megan finished her morning's work feeling grey; as though some of Mandy's misery had been left behind in the consulting room.

Even the face of Gericault's mad woman seemed to soften in the presence of such grief.

*　　*　　*

But the encounter spurred Megan into action. As soon as she had seen her last patient she drove to the 'chicken coop' estate. She knew enough about Stefan's buddies to be sure they wouldn't be at school either. They would have some excuse ready to wave in front of any authority who challenged their presence on the streets this afternoon. As she had expected, they were loafing around the bus shelter, sitting full length along the wooden bench, efficiently blocking the seats from being used by an ancient crone holding on to a 'sholley' and a woman so heavily pregnant she looked as though she was expecting triplets today. Megan greeted them both. They were well known to her. The two boys dropped their feet to the floor and eyed her silently and suspiciously when she addressed them. 'Any chance of a word?'

'We're not at school because we've got time off to grieve, see.' Mark Pritchard had learned a new set of lines quickly.

'Grieving for Stefan?'

Both nodded.

'But no one knows what's happened to him.'

The two boys exchanged glances and Megan felt a sudden jump.

Did they know?

Something that unnerved even this tough little pair? Because buried deep beneath the bravado Megan could read change in their faces. She sat down on the bench between them. 'I think you should help find him. He is your friend—after all.'

She wasn't exactly surprised that they scoffed at her suggestion.

'How?'

'If the police can't find him . . .' This was Mark Pritchard—marginally more intelligent than his mate but wearing the same uniform of huge T shirt showing skinny, cold-blued arms, nylon combat trousers bristling with pockets

270

and trainers with soles thick enough to increase his height by a bright orange four inches.

'Yes—but you know something the police don't.' Megan stared at the ground as she spoke. These two were suspicious of everyone and everything. Eye contact was especially suspicious. She kicked a stone across the floor.

So did Ryan. 'We told the police what we know.'

'Oh yeah?'

'Yeah.' Mark again, stroppy this time. 'We did, doc.'

She decided to play her dummy Ace. 'You two think you know what happened, don't you?'

Both lads shot to their feet. And Meggie instantly saw the reason. The police car cruising like a surf watcher, spanking white with fluorescent pink streak. The jam sandwich. The boys didn't wait. They simply legged it.

Alun dropped the window and she crossed the road towards him. He was not alone. Police Constable Jarvis Watkins eyed her with a faintly confused air. She smiled the same smile to both of them.

'What are you up to, Meggie?' Alun's voice almost soft enough to persuade her that this was a personal question. And she had her answer ready. Up her sleeve. 'The boys, Stefan's friends, are off school. They're disturbed by what's happened to their mate. I doubted they'd come to the surgery to see me so I thought I'd seek them out on their own home ground. Make sure they were OK.'

'Liar.' It was said with grudging admiration. 'Well, find out anything?'

'No. I didn't. But . . .' she stared along the road, frowning. 'I think they know something.'

'Well in that case they know more than us. We don't know anything, Megan, except that he isn't around. Anything else is pure speculation.' Alun gave a small smile half to himself. 'I followed up one of your helpful leads.'

'Oh?'

'Bloody mistake. Thought I'd pay a call on Esther Magellan. What a nut.'

It was then that Megan began to realise. Without prejudice and with access she could move in where no one else could. She could communicate with 'nuts'.

'She wasn't helpful, then?'

'Once I'd calmed her down and told her I wasn't going to arrest her she gave me a load of tripe.' He gave Megan a hard stare. 'I'll be honest with you, Meggie. I don't know where I am in this case. It's weird. I'm not even quite sure what we're investigating.'

She gave a non-committal nod. 'But you've looked at all the cases on the police computer?'

'Yes.'

'And Stefan Parker?'

'He could have hopped it down to London—or Brighton—or any one of those places that attract kids who want drugs. A good time. Don't mind how they get either.'

'Except that he didn't.'

He looked straight up at her then, full in the face as though trying to read all that she held in her mind, from her approach to Bianca's death, to the disappearances, to how she really felt about him. She stared back. She had no secrets.

Jarvis Watkins cleared his throat noisily. It was that that broke the spell. Otherwise she and Alun would have stared at each other until they had both confessed where they stood.

And it would have been a mistake.

Alun slid his hands around the wheel, depressed the clutch and slipped the car into gear. 'I'll be seeing you, Meggie.'

She stood on the pavement and watched the pink flash disappear around the corner, then turned back to the bus shelter.

The two boys were instantly back, jeering with a 'Whoah. Fancy him, do you?'

She shrugged.

'He's a rozzer. I wouldn't have nothing to do with him.' How often it was the smaller kid who was the tougher. Megan started to walk towards her car. Before she got there she was surrounded by the two boys. 'You do know something about Stefan, don't you?'

273

'No.' But there was fear in their eyes.

Ryan began to back away.

'Don't you understand,' she said urgently, longing to shake the pair of them, 'it's dangerous. Stefan's gone. You don't want to be next. If you know something tell me. Please tell me.'

Mark's eyes drifted towards the spot where the police car had finally turned the corner.

She knew he was needing reassurance. 'I won't say anything.'

'You can't. You're our doctor.'

Megan smiled to herself. 'I'm only bound by the laws of confidentiality if I learn facts through the fact that I *am* your doctor. But I won't tell, anyway.'

'Look, we don't really know anything.' Ryan was getting cold feet. This was a plea to his friend to stop speaking.

Mark turned on him with a jutting chin and mouth furious enough to intimidate a grown man. 'Stefan's fuckin' gone. And all you think of is chickenin' out. You're pathetic, Ryan. Pathetic. Whatever Stefan did at least he had guts.' He directed the conversation back at Megan. 'Look, we don't know but a couple of times he'd say he was frightened of someone.'

'Who?'

Mark Pritchard simply stared at her.

*　　*　　*

As though she had mounted one of the horses on the carousel it began to spin. The ride had begun. And once spinning it would move faster and faster. There was no getting off until the ride had finished. And the music stopped.

As she drove back towards the surgery for her evening patients her mobile phone rang. She pulled off the road and answered it.

'Doctor Banesto?'

She should have recognised the condescending, supercilious voice with its 'posh' Cardiff accent. He introduced himself.

'Franklin Jones-Watson here. Pathologist. Do you mind if I ask you a question?'

'No.' She was bemused.

'Why wouldn't you issue a death certificate on Mr Geraint Smithson?'

She had forgotten about Smithson. 'Well— I—I didn't know what he'd died of. The sister at Triagwn wondered whether he might have had acute heart failure but I wasn't sure.'

'Did you have any, er, suspicions?'

He sounded a different person from the cocksure doctor who had given evidence with such aplomb at Bianca's inquest and she was curious.

'He'd been difficult to handle lately, very agitated. We'd needed to sedate him fairly heavily. Why are you asking me this? What *did* Mr Smithson die of?'

'I'm not sure. It could have been . . . Unfortunately the bedding was missing. The

275

forensic evidence is tricky. It could have been
. . .'

'What are you talking about?'

'It *could* have been acute heart failure. But the bedding had been washed. The pillow was missing.'

'So?'

'Some fibres were in his nose. And there was a tiny bruise on the inside of his lower lip. As though . . .'

She could work it out for herself. 'Pressure had been applied. You mean?'

'There isn't a lot to go on or even to be sure but I think it's possible that Mr Smithson was smothered. Only possible, mind.'

And all she could think of was two deaths. Two cunning and clever deaths which had hoodwinked the pathologist. And Franklin Jones' arrogance was born out of competence in his job. He was no fool.

Someone clever was behind this. Clever enough to hide bodies where no one could find them. Ever. And the bodies he did leave to find were impossible to attribute as homicide.

'So what are you going to do?'

'I've referred the matter to the police, explained everything. Including the fact that there isn't any concrete evidence. Geraint Smithson was old. It's up to them whether they investigate. I rather think not.'

'So what will you write on his death certificate?'

'Inconclusive.'

As you should have done on Bianca's death certificate. And prevented her burial.

But she said goodbye with a touch of sympathy for the pathologist. Gleaning evidence from corpses was not always so easy.

*   *   *

The search for Stefan continued but Megan sensed the hope of finding him frightened, yet alive, was fading. And there was another death. Two days after she had supplied Mandy Parker with her Temazepam she was summoned to Triagwn again. Old Mr Driver had succumbed to his bronchopneumonia.

Icy rain was sheeting down as she turned up the drive. Winter was beginning in earnest. The cherub spewing water contrived to look cold. And for Mr Driver life was over.

So take him up tenderly
Lift him with care.

Certification of death might seem a significant event. It is, after all, the final act of life. In fact to a doctor it is one of the least dramatic chores in a day's work. The stethoscope placed over the spot where a heart no longer beats, the token shining of a torch into fixed, dilated pupils, the feeling for a pulse you already know you won't find, the folding of a sheet over the face and the filling in of the death certificate.

Sandra Penarth stood over her silently, waiting for her to speak.

'It's going to be a long winter.'

'Yes. Our patients are elderly. And plenty of them have got bad chests.'

Sandra Penarth's face held a strange expression as she stared down at the bed. 'I've known Mr Driver for years, you know. He was friends with my grandfather. They were down the mine together. Awful place.'

Someone stood in the doorway.

'Mervyn.' Someone else Sandra knew well. 'I'm so sorry.'

'Do you know Mr Jones, doctor?'

'No—but you were at Bianca's funeral.'

He was a short man, wiry with a pair of fierce blue eyes. She'd thought of him then as 'the angry man' and named him, Rumpelstiltskin. Even today, in grief, he reminded her of the angry dwarf of the fairy story who stamped his foot when his name was guessed.

'You were a friend of Bianca's?'

Mervyn Jones snorted. 'Not exactly, doctor. I *knew* her, like most of the people in Llancloudy. She was always around.'

Sandra interrupted. 'I suppose you've come to fetch Mr Driver's belongings.'

Jones grunted. 'Such as they are, Sandra.'

She handed over a black carrier bag with a sigh. 'Exactly. Such as they are. He didn't have much in the way of personal possessions. But

278

his watch is nice.'

Jones fished around the carrier bag and drew out a gold watch with a black, leather strap. 'It is a nice watch. Got it when he retired. From the Coal Board. But not so nice when you consider what it cost. Bloody curse of the valleys, doctor, sitting on this stuff. Glad I was when they closed the doors for the last time and stopped the wheels from winding men up and down, up and down.'

Megan nodded. She too had watched men cough up black dust from their lungs then wait years, many dying before they received their compensation. She had watched their widows receive cheques in bitter tears and not known whether it was worth cashing them.

Sandra turned away briskly. 'The Death Certificate Book is down in my office,' she said.

'Mervyn, do you want to stay with your old friend a minute or two longer. Say goodbye?'

Jones' eyes were bright. 'If you don't mind,' he said gruffly.

*   *   *

This time Megan had no hesitation what to write on the Death Certificate. 'Broncho-pneumonia, secondary to penumoconiosis,' she wrote then crossed to the window and picked up the fifties black and white photograph of the smiling couple.

279

'This is your grandfather?'

Sandra nodded. 'Lovely man, he was. Died nearly thirty years ago. Another one destroyed by coal dust.'

As they wandered back towards the front door, Megan broached the subject. 'You must miss Mr Smithson.'

Sandra's reply was tart and predictable. 'We always miss patients when they die, especially people who've been with us for years.'

'He was such a character. So full of stories.'

'He told some mad stories.'

'Just like Bianca.'

The nurse looked genuinely astonished. 'Bianca? What's she got to do with it? She didn't die here.'

'She worked here.'

'You're saying Mr Smithson made up stories like she did?'

'I just thought it was funny that they made up the *same* stories.'

'I don't know what you mean.'

'About children disappearing.'

'They were just stories.'

'But Bianca—'

'Surely, doctor, Bianca *imagined* things.'

'And now Stefan has disappeared.'

Sandra Penarth gave her a strange, frightened look and Megan felt she must say something quickly. 'Nothing.' It was surely nothing. Hot air, stories, illusion. Nothing.

Sandra tugged the front door open and

Megan dived outside to the icy air.

*   *   *

Arwel Smithson was leaning against her car and she knew he had been lying in wait for her. 'Hello, Megan,' he called heartily. 'How are you?'

She replied stiffly. 'Fine, and you?'

'Oh—missing the old man. You know. We were pretty close.' He looked down at his feet and Megan could have sworn he meant what he said. Maybe he really did miss his father.

Smithson's face looked tired. The red veins on his cheek stood out more than before. He wrapped his coat tightly around him. 'Better go then. See you, Megan.'

She left Triagwn House feeling more confused than ever.

*   *   *

Driving home she switched her car radio off. She wanted to think. Two people were dead, almost certainly three. Stefan Parker had been missing now for eight days.

Someone was behind all this. Someone more strange than Esther Magellan and more insane than Bianca.

And the thought that had crossed her mind as she had watched Arwel Smithson stride across the gravel and disappear inside Triagwn was that he was a man who would be capable of putting a sick animal down if it was of no further use. If a sick animal, why not a sick human? Or a sickly one?

CHAPTER TWENTY-ONE

But even major dramas are forgotten. Newspapers move on to other stories. With no new angle and nothing different with which to headline their story the local newspapers began to lose interest. Megan watched Stefan's name move from headlines to sidelines and by the end of November the boy's disappearance had been relegated to one short column on page four. And even that feature was not solid fact but a vague sighting in Blackpool.

And from Alun she had heard nothing. But knowing him as well as she did she knew he would be better left alone. He never had been someone who liked to be pushed. His involvement would be with the official police investigation. He was better deployed there.

Her line must be another one.

*   *   *

She decided to speak to Barbara Watkins again.

It was a Thursday, two days before the end

of the month. It had been eerily quiet in the surgery so Megan had finished by midday with no firm plans for the afternoon. She had no evening surgery. As she left the building, the sun was hidden behind a band of thick grey cloud but across the valley she could see where the cloud ended and blue sky began. It would be a good day to climb the mountain. She drove home impatiently, pulled her hiking boots from the cupboard, cleaned and ready for action, found her fleece and orange kagoul, ran upstairs and slipped into a pair of comfortable, stretch jeans. She caught sight of her face in the mirror and was surprised at how eager she looked.

Eager for what? To find the truth? For a walk? Eager for life?

Whatever. She slicked some lipstick on and drove back down the valley.

She found Barbara in the garden, clearing debris from the drains, deaf and blind to Megan's approach, startling like a jack-in-the-box when she felt a hand on her shoulder.

'I'm sorry,' Megan said, taken aback. 'I didn't mean to surprise you.'

Barbara looked embarrassed. 'Oh, normally I'm not so jumpy but . . .' For the first time ever Megan read fear in the retired schoolmistress' eyes. She who had faced rebellious teenagers and angry parents for years looked anxious.

'It's with you telling me all those stories. It's

set my mind thinking. And now Stefan Parker. Megan,' she appealed, 'what is going on?'

* * *

Megan linked arms with her. 'I thought we might go for a walk,' she said. 'It's easier to talk when you're active, isn't it?'

'All right.' Barbara welcomed the idea. 'Let me just get ready then.'

The initial climb was a steep one and they were puffed out when they reached the ridge. They sat down in a small hollow, out of the wind. Megan took a bottle of water from her rucksack and they both swigged at it in turn. Below them was the town, squashed into the narrow valley, slate roofs in tight lines with a snake of traffic between. There was little noise. The wind up here whistled softly through its teeth and blotted out the town's synthetic sounds.

They both stared around for a while and then Barbara spoke. 'It's hard to believe, isn't it, that anyone could vanish from a place like this. I mean there's only one way out. Down the valley. If you keep going up you simply reach the mountains and they never did build a road straight over.'

Megan knew exactly what she was saying. It was harder for people to disappear from Llancloudy than from another place. In a way it was almost an island, joined only by the narrowest of isthmuses—the width of a road, a narrow river and a railway line. There was one road in and one road out. It wasn't like a city or a town where people could permeate to another place. It was cut off, practically sealed in.

And yet . . . She glanced at Barbara and knew her thoughts were moving in exactly the same trajectory.

'Tell me about the real Bleddyn Hughes. The one you remember.'

Barbara was unsurprised at the question. She thought for a moment, her face screwed up in concentration. 'Quiet, polite and thoughtful.' She closed her eyes. 'The sort of person who bought birthday cards. With flowers on. Gentle. He had very beautiful hands, I remember. Long, slim fingers. And a lovely speaking voice. He was fond of poetry. Would read it aloud to the children.' She opened her eyes with a jerk. 'Especially a Hood poem. Great favourite of his. *The Bridge of Sighs.*'

One more unfortunate
Weary of breath,
Rashly importunate
Gone to her death.

'I can picture him now, reciting it. I thought it a very inappropriate poem for children but there you are. He had a lovely voice. Quite musical it was. Not much of an accent. He was a Swansea man.' She turned and looked at

285

Megan. 'It's funny, isn't it. The papers put a different angle on him; hinted at unsavoury habits, his sexuality. It had made me forget. I liked him. He seemed a decent man. But . . .' She was frowning. 'Perhaps he was not. Perhaps he was a deceiver. Papers distort things but sometimes they put a finger right on the pulse. Sometimes they are very perceptive.'

Megan nodded.

'There was such a lot of gossip when he went. Silly ugly gossip really. Great clumps of people gathered outside the chippie or the Co-op. Lots of rumours must have started there. I expect Bianca would listen. And that's what started her threading bits together. So many tales flew around but even now I don't know whether they were true. Whether any of it was true. No one came forward and said anything definite. Not after he'd gone.' Her face was puckered with concern. 'How do we know what to believe?'

'Perhaps it was easier to believe he was gay and had gone to be with like friends rather than face the truth and the prejudices of Llancloudy.'

'Maybe.' Barbara was getting to her feet. 'Maybe. Perhaps we'll never know what really happened to any of them.'

They carried on with their climb. And the head of the valley came into view, the pen and the huge winding wheel of the mine which still watched over Llancloudy.

286

Derelict buildings scarred the coal yards though the mines were long since shut. However hard they tried to wash the coal away from the soil of South Wales, the scars would always be there, in the irregular line of the hills, in the grassed-over slag heaps, in the pool the locals called the Slaggy Pool. Megan suddenly felt agitated.

'It's in the ground. Underneath our feet.'

Smithson was right. All the old mine workings still existed. The shafts and tunnels were still there, beneath the feet of the twenty first century. And as though she could sense the vanished as she trod over their heads she felt afraid. She was beginning to see too much. She was seeing Llancloudy through Bianca's eyes, the past as vivid as the present, dead souls mingling with the living. A child that chattered, a little girl who probably dropped her chip papers on the floor, a trio of childish vandals separated by ten years.

*   *   *

But the pathologist was prepared to believe that Geraint Smithson had been murdered. And she could believe his son could have 'finished him off'. For expediency? Because his father had become an inconvenience? An embarrassment even? Why *had* Arwel waited for her the last time she had visited Triagwn? Megan knew. He must have known that she had refused to issue the death certificate. He had been gauging her reaction, wondering how much she guessed.

But while she could picture Arwel pressing a pillow to his father's face, could she really believe he had murdered Bianca? She had a vision of Smithson's cottage. Isolated enough to be able to keep someone prisoner for a day and a half. Near to the tumbled gryphon statue whose claw had found its way into Bianca, the collector's, pocket. Had she wandered towards the Woodman's Cottage and said something which had led Arwel to believe she knew something about the disappearances?

*   *   *

'What are you thinking?' Barbara's voice sliced through her thoughts. And well as she knew her old teacher she could not share them all.

'I was wondering,' she said slowly, 'about Stefan.'

Barbara nodded. 'Me too,' she said. 'I think he's gone.'

Megan watched her, surprised.

'Out of the valley?'

'Where else?' Barbara's hand was on her arm. 'Where else *could* he be? Llancloudy isn't that big a place. You know what it's like here. We're all on top of one another. The places that aren't built on are old slag heaps, still sliding down towards the river, or crumbling into derelict mine workings. There isn't anywhere to hide him. And people have looked everywhere. Everywhere.' She took the bottle of water from Megan, swigged at it and wiped her mouth with a rough, brusque action.

'So where is he?'

Involuntarily they both swivelled around to look at the winding wheel. Barbara shivered. 'Not down there,' she said. 'Not down there.'

But it was the only place.

They both gazed around the wide sweep of the valley beneath the rolling clouds which would, later in the night, surely release more icy rain. Maybe even some snow. There was a cruel nip in the air that would bring all the bronchitics to the surgery, needing their antibiotics. Doctors' surgeries reflect the seasons in disease. Summer brings pollen sufferers, the winter the asthmatics, bronchitics and the old, trying to fend off death with a 'flu jab.

*   *   *

There was the distant sound of sheep bleating. Barbara smiled. 'My mam always used to say Welsh sheep sounded as though they were moaning about something. The heat, the cold, the wet, the dry. Always something to complain about she used to say. But me, I don't think they are complaining at all. They're just communicating. Though what they're saying is anybody's guess.' She pointed towards a flattened patch between the sheep and the trees. Paler than the rest with a fire scar at its centre. 'When I was a girl, an old tramp lived in a tin caravan halfway up there. I suppose he was a sort of shepherd. Certainly he had a dog. A lovely black and white Welsh Border collie. Such an intelligent animal it was. Used to round up the sheep in minutes however far they'd strayed. I used to take the dog the bones after the Sunday joint and, for his master, the shepherd cakes my mother had baked. Ginger cake, *Teisen Lap*, Welsh cakes sometimes. He was so grateful. Used to ram them in his mouth as though he was in danger of starving to death. Maybe he was. He was awful thin. Then one day I went and he was lying in his bunk, grey-faced, hardly breathing. I didn't know what to do, Megan. I dropped the bones and the cakes and ran all the way home. I didn't have a clue. I felt so helpless. Terrible thing, ignorance is.' Her eyes were trained to the pale green spot on the side of the hill. 'It was a promise I made to myself that I would not be ignorant again. I enrolled in a First Aid course run by the St John's Ambulance down in Bridgend. You could say Megan,' her eyes were fixed on the side of the mountain, 'that this one event was the reason I became a teacher. So I could prevent other people from being ignorant. The only way out of these valleys is through education.

290

Otherwise you don't get the choice. It's all right for you, Megan. You elected to return and bring your knowledge with you to help the valleys people. You wanted to be the voice of people who had lost theirs. But for some they *have* no option but to stay. And that's one of the reasons people get frustrated and we have problems with our young. Boredom and ignorance are our enemies.'

'And if they want to remain in their ignorant state?' Megan tried to ask the question lightly but she was disturbed by Barbara's words and even more by its unbending underlying attitude. You could not force people to learn. It was not possible. Like pigs in mud, some people preferred to wallow in their ignorance.

Barbara's reply was an angry jerk of her shoulders.

So Megan moved back to her story. 'And the tramp?'

'He'd had a heart attack. Dad came back with me while my mam fetched the doctor. He gave my old friend an injection into his arm and he was sent to the hospital. He was alright—for a year or two anyway. He was an old man, Megan. And old people have to die sometimes.'

Megan straightened. 'But not the young, Barbara. Not the young.'

'I can't think Stefan's dead, Megan.'

'And Rhiann Hughes and Marie Walker, Neil and George?'

291

Barbara had no answer.

'Come on.' She stood up. 'Let's walk. We've still an hour left of daylight.'

They followed the sheep path. Narrow and shorn of grass by the nibbling animals. Now they were forced to walk in single file. It stopped them talking. And Megan was glad. It allowed her to think.

She dreamed of a gentle man with long, slim fingers who had loved the same poem as she and whose disappearance had been explained by ugly rumour. She knew what he looked like from the newspaper photographs; dark, lugubrious eyes, a thin, rather weak mouth suggesting hesitancy and a lack of confidence, hair cut long and in an old fashioned, square, sideburned style. In none of the newspaper pictures had she seen his hands. And she had never heard his voice but she could almost hear it, a soft, Swansea voice reciting . . .

Take her up Tenderly.

They walked in silence for ten, fifteen minutes.

Then Barbara caught up with her, speaking into her face. 'Is it even conceivable that Bianca could have been right?' She frowned. 'Who is mad, Megan, Bianca for imagining such a thing, you and I for wondering whether it's the truth? The police for failing to connect the crimes? Was Bianca the only one with insight?'

Which she communicated with Smithson?

292

And which Smithson believed? Did you need a mind which was not quite normal to understand what lay at the centre of this mystery?

Megan felt inadequate. 'I don't know. I don't know . . . Possibly.' She didn't know what to say.

Lights were being switched on below in the valley. Only the rounded tops of the mountains were still dark. The lampposts formed bright lines, like runways. If she jumped she could fly. And then land.

Daylight was fading. Colours were damped down for the night. Like a coal fire. They threaded their way silently down the hill following yet another of the sheep paths, emerging near the rugby pitch.

*　　　*　　　*

As they reached Barbara's front door she spoke. 'I hope . . . I wish . . .'

Megan knew exactly what she wished. That none of it had happened. That it really had been a figment of Bianca's distorting mind. Maybe it was. It was what she wanted to believe too.

'Come in for a cup of tea,' Barbara said warmly. 'And I've made a *Teisen Lap*. It'll save you cooking when you get home.'

It was this practical streak, Megan reflected, which had made Barbara such a good headmistress. Her practical housekeeping.

The atmosphere inside was homey, organised, still fragrant with lingering baking smells, clean and traditional. They sat and drank tea and skirted round the main issues. Neither of them mentioned Stefan Parker—or Bianca—or anyone else who would have broken the spell. Megan felt lulled into a sense of well-being. All was right with the world. And Llancloudy in particular.

It was what she wanted to believe.

She kissed Barbara goodbye and climbed into her Calibra, still with that warmth pervading.

But it didn't last.

She bought a paper on the way home and read, on page four, that the body of a young boy found floating in the mouth of the Bristol Channel had been ruled out as being the body of the missing boy Stefan Parker. A couple were understood to be travelling down from Yorkshire for purposes of identification.

She tore page four out, folded it up and tossed it in the back of the car.

*   *   *

Halfway home she was suddenly seized with curiosity. Barbara had sparked it off, colouring in the picture she had had of Bleddyn Hughes, breathing life into the man, making her feel as though she knew him—even if only for the

294

reason that they both enjoyed the same poem. She had memorised the address at which he had once lived. And forty-five Bethesda Street was on her way home; an uncompromising row of dirty stone terraced houses probably built at a period just before the First World War, when piety was more important than sanitation and the men trooped home late from the pits to clean themselves in a tin bath in front of the fire. She turned in to the right of the enormous chapel. There was a parking space blocked off with a traffic cone right in front of number forty-five beneath a Neighbourhood Watch sign fixed to a lamppost. She shifted the cone and manoeuvred her car between a fourteen-year-old Fiesta and a blue Toyota Celica with a personalised numberplate. *Cariad,* darling. She locked her car door, threaded round the front and read the numberplate again—only to feel cheated. It didn't read Cariad at all. On closer inspection it was simply a trick. CAR14D. But it was a nice car.

She knocked on the door feeling a silly, vague disappointment at the mild deceit. And knocked again, wondering. Thirty years later would anyone in this street remember the disappearance of a nondescript school teacher? Even in the valleys where memories were so long that elephants appeared amnesiac in comparison.

Grubby net curtains twitched. An old man glared out at her with frank hostility. He was shouting something. Banging at the window. She recognised him straight away. It was the angry man at Bianca's funeral . . . Caspian Driver's visitor . . . Rumpelstiltskin. He must have recognised her but he was scowling. She smiled at him. He glared back at her and shook his fist. She was taken aback.

She took a deep breath and banged on the front door. The face at the window vanished then reappeared as he pulled the door open.

'Mr Jones—'

'That's my bloody parkin' spot you're in. Tight they are in this street.'

She turned around to look. 'Where is your car?'

'Not here at the moment. It's being done at the garage. Some soddin' vandals broke the windscreen. Now, what is it?'

*   *   *

'I wanted to ask you something, about someone who used to live here.'

He looked only vaguely curious, still angry. 'Well, come in then, won't you? No need to stand on the doorstep. I expect you'll have some tea.'

Tea was a delaying tactic Megan usually avoided, but in this case she accepted and waited while he shuffled around in the kitchen, boiling up a kettle and pouring milk painfully slowly into a jug, rattling cups and saucers before shuffling back into the sitting room and placing a tray on an oak dining table which stood at the back. It was a dark, old-fashioned room, stuffy with the musty scent of stale tobacco. The focal point was a beige-tiled fireplace at which burned slowly and without enthusiasm a few lumps of dusty coal.

'So what can I do for you? This isn't one of those elderly health checks they keep offerin' me, is it?' He gave a thin smile.

'No.'

'So?' He sucked a long, greedy sip of tea, his eyes not leaving her face. 'Get to the point.'

'How long have you lived in this house, Mr Jones?'

'All of my life.'

'Do you remember the school teacher? The one who disappeared in the early seventies? Bleddyn Hughes.'

'I do. My wife and I took him in as a lodger when we was first married. It was slack down the pit and we were down to a three day week. My wife didn't earn much doing people's hair and we badly wanted to keep the house. His money helped, you see.'

Megan searched Jones' wrinkled face for some knowledge, some emotion but she would have sworn there was nothing. He stared back at her, the only expression on his face irritation.

'He disappeared.' She hadn't meant it to sound so much like an accusation.

'I know. The police. They came looking for him, turned the house over from top to bottom they did. Couldn't find nothin'. He'd just gone.'

'Where?'

'London, they said.' For the first time she heard doubt in his voice.

'What do you think happened to him?'

'I wasn't sure.'

'I said think, Mr Jones. Think.'

The aggression blazed back. 'I don't know what it's got to do with you. It was years ago. You probably never even knew him. Whatever happened to him it's all dead and forgotten. The papers said—'

'I know what the papers said. What do you say, Mr Jones?'

'I say he was a bad influence. Better that he went. Though he owed us rent and never said he was going I was still glad we was rid of him.'

'Did he have,' Megan hesitated, 'boyfriends?'

'Not here. We would not have tolerated that.'

'But—'

'But nothin'. The man was a rotten apple. And he was busy convertin' others to his ways. Not safe to leave near children. Better he went. He was gettin' . . .'

Megan's interest quickened. 'He was getting what?'

'Noticed. Picked on, a couple of times.' She had a feeling this had not been what he had planned to say but she let Jones plough on. 'Unnerved him something terrible. Came home one night shivering and his nose bleeding.'

'Did you tell the police all this?'

'They didn't want to know,' Jones said simply. 'They'd already made up their minds well before they came here. They *knew*, you see.'

'How do you explain the fact that Hughes has never been found?'

Jones shrugged. 'Don't know and I don't care neither. And neither should you.'

There was a silence.

'*Other* people have gone missing,' Megan said quickly. 'Children.'

He dismissed the vanishings. 'They aren't important. But now there's this other little boy.'

Megan smiled. She wasn't quite sure how Stefan Parker would have reacted to hearing himself described as, 'This other little boy.'

But the phrase sobered her too. For all his illegal tattoos and piercings Stefan was or had been a child of ten years old. If he had been hurt or threatened, his reaction would soon have crumbled from Rambo bravado to a childish terror. Children were children. Only their veneers were different. Cheap copies of designer clothes, earrings, tattoos, foul language and the air of fake sophistication that streetwise kids of the valleys wore like a suit of armour. Put them against the little sweeties from the Howells School in Cardiff or the Llandaff choir school. Underneath they were the same. Children.

'You're a mining engineer, Mr Jones. You must know the place. Could he be lost in the mines?'

'It's possible.'

'And not found by the police?'

'Oh for goodness sake. Have you any idea what's underfoot at Llancloudy? It's a rabbit warren. There's no way you'd be able to explore all that's under the ground of this valley.'

'But the mines were deep. How would you . . . ?'

'There's access points all over the place. Holes for inspection. They have to make sure they aren't flooding. The engineers, we have to go down to inspect. I did—until I retired.'

'But—'

'But nothing.' He stared back at her, defiantly and she was intrigued. He struck her as an intelligent man. Yet he had worked all his life underground. She wondered whether he had trod the path of many here, supporting his family, unable to afford the expensive and unearning luxury of higher education. She wondered what he thought about the vanishings, whether he might know something

300

about Geraint Smithson. He had spent enough time at Triagwn.

'There have been a few accidents or disappearances lately. Bianca drowned.'

'Oh, Bianca,' Jones said contemptuously. 'She was a nutcase. A nuisance. Well rid of her we are.'

A pair of hostile dark eyes stared into her own. 'I can't understand why you're asking all these questions. You're a doctor. What's it got to do with you? Why are you pokin' your nose in?'

She produced the lamest of excuses. 'The well being of the town.'

Jones chortled. 'Don't make a fool of yourself. Leave all this to the police, why don't you? It's *their* job. *Yours* is the health of the citizens of this little place. You've got enough work keeping it healthy, doctor, while the police keep it safe and leave the locals to weed out undesirables.'

Through Neighbourhood Watch.

She stared at him, sensing the misanthropy of a small town Welsh preacher.

She left soon after feeling chastened and reflective. He was right. It was not her place to investigate disappearances. But no one else was. First-hand she was watching the story of Stefan Parker's disappearance trickle away to nothing. As she unlocked her car door she saw Jones watching her through the window. As soon as she had vacated the spot she replaced

301

the traffic cone. A police car slid passed. She couldn't see who was in it. It was too dark.

She wanted to be home, alone. She felt shaky and uncertain as she drove towards the top of the valley. She backed her car into the one available space left outside her own front door. Barely large enough for the Calibra. A sense of relief flooded through her as she closed the door behind her, drew the curtains, switched the lamp on, tossed her shoes in the corner and settled in the chair. Her eyes closed but she could see people.

Bianca as she had looked when she had last met her. Heavily powdered, whitened skin, thickly smeared lipstick, an uncomprehending expression on her face. Megan recalled the way she had submitted to the fortnightly injection given without ceremony into her bottom as Bianca held her knickers down. As Megan's trance deepened, Bianca transformed into the woman in the Gericault. *Madwoman inflicted with envy.* In the painting the woman was clearly envious. But it was not normal envy; it was a distortion of the emotion. She did not know what it was she coveted. Megan breathed deeper. Sane people recognise, understand, analyse their emotions. Mad people, according to Gericault, do not. Cannot. Their emotions merely add to their confusion. They are *inflicted.*

Dreadfully staring...
Thro' muddy impurity

302

As When with the daring
Last look of despairing
Fix'd on futurity
What had Bianca seen when she had 'fix'd on futurity'? What had she heard?

Megan breathed deeply and heard other words.

'A rabbit warren.'

Caspian Driver had been a mining engineer.

Bianca's urgent words.

'Such a sweet little girl. Always chattering.'

'You're not so smart as some that are labelled mad.'

'The little girl was going to buy some chips she was.' Smithson who had babbled indiscriminately.

Rumpelstiltskin dancing his dance of fury.

*   *   *

Her mind flicked from Bianca, Smithson and Jones to Arwel Smithson. He would have been nineteen years old when Bleddyn Hughes had vanished. She could picture him, swaggering, bullying, swearing, a drinker even at that age. And a womaniser too. The very antithesis of Hughes, the English teacher. Cultured, gentle, sensitive.

And what had Geraint Smithson been like thirty years ago? Back to Bianca and the Hood poem, *One more unfortunate.* Or to shift the emphasis, One *more* unfortunate.

Alun with his wife, soon to be doting on the new born baby? She squeezed her eyes shut in sudden pain, struggling to blot out the image of pride, achievement, love.

Barbara's words, *'I hate ignorance.'*

Megan sat up, her eyes wide open. How much had the teacher hated ignorance? Enough to destroy those who refused to learn?

What was the makeup of Llancloudy?

CHAPTER TWENTY-TWO

She posed the question the following day to her two partners and, as she had expected, each had their own perspective. As a rank outsider, Andy viewed Llancloudy in a very objective way. 'I think the people here are friendly but quick to make judgements. Old-fashioned.' His dark eyes fixed on hers with a hint of sadness. 'And they can be very unforgiving.'

'What made you choose here?' she asked curiously.

'I had an uncle in Cardiff,' Andy said. 'He told me the valleys people would make me welcome,' he said. 'He told me they would not even notice my colour.' He gave a great, belly laugh, 'because they were blacker than me—from coal dust.'

She chuckled. 'And is that true?'

304

He looked serious. 'About the coal dust no,' he said, 'but about them not even noticing what colour I am.' He hesitated. 'Yes,' he said finally. 'That is true. They are not prejudiced.'

Phil looked up from the pile of prescriptions he was signing. 'Except against the English,' he said and they laughed.

'So what do you think? How do you find this little place?'

Phil too thought for a moment. 'I think it's hard to be private here. People don't have a lot of space. And that causes problems.' He grinned. 'Sometimes I'm reminded of rats in a cage. If they're denied enough room they start to bite each other's heads off. It's the same here. Didn't Robert Frost make the comment, Good Fences Make Good Neighbours? Here there aren't enough fences.'

There aren't enough fences,' Megan said slowly.

*   *   *

As she left the surgery she pondered over her partners' words. They seemed to have great significance. Somewhere, buried in them, was the answer to it all. She could find it if she searched with her eyes wide open, her consciousness attuned.

She drove to Triagwn. And met Sandra in the hallway. who looked startled to see her. 'We didn't expect you today,' she said. 'Still.

It's nice to see you. Who have you come to see?'

'You,' Megan answered steadily. 'I wanted to see you.'

'Oh?' It was not welcome.

'Can we go into your office?'

Sandra led the way silently, shooting swift glances from side to side. When they reached the office door Megan closed it behind them, crossed to the window and picked up the photograph that stood on the coffee table.

'Can I ask you something?'

'Go ahead.' Sandra looked nervous.

'You didn't like Geraint Smithson, did you?'

'I don't need to *like* my patients, Megan. I simply have to *nurse* them. But since you ask, no, I didn't like him.'

'Why not?'

'Look—what's this got to do with anything?'

'Please—answer the question.'

Sandra stared back at her, vaguely hostile.

'All right,' Megan said, 'I'll answer it for you. Your grandfather. He worked down the mine?'

Sandra took the photograph from her, held it and stared down. 'And it cost him his life. He was barely sixty when he died. And he'd been on oxygen for the last four years of his life. While Smithson lives to be ninety-four. My grandfather had no choices in life. There weren't any other jobs. It was the mine or education in South Wales. Most families couldn't afford to educate more than one

306

youngster. And everyone had to contribute towards their education. In my grandfather's time he went down the pit at fourteen. No. I didn't like Smithson. I couldn't separate him from what he'd done—exploited the people of the Welsh Valleys and got rich.'

Megan eyed her defiantly. 'And what did you think he died of?'

Sandra's answer was guarded. 'I don't know what they've put on the death certificate. Heart failure?'

'The pathologist rang. He . . .' Megan was aware she must tread very carefully. There was no proof Smithson had died of anything other than natural causes. 'The postmortem was inconclusive,' she said finally.

Sandra let out a short breath. 'Well,' she said calmly, 'that's often the way with old people. Difficult to tell what they've died of. Multiple pathology.'

Megan nodded. She could say no more. An accusation without proof would land her up in the courts. And she knew it.

*   *   *

She returned to her evening surgery, her mind tussling furiously with the ever growing questions.

Gwen Owen had decided to drag her long suffering husband along to her Friday evening's consultation. And as usual she had a stream of complaints. Her arthritis, her pain, her headaches, her depression, her tiredness. She couldn't sleep and her stomach was playing her up—again. Her husband sat back, his eyes half closed and Megan wondered how on earth he could put up with her.

*   *   *

Surprisingly Carole Symmonds had been pushed in as an extra, apparently demanding to see her. Megan was prepared for another long list—depression, anxiety—but here she was in for a surprise. Carole winked at her and asked for the 'morning after pill'. Obviously her grief had faded. Her life had picked up again. Megan wrote out the prescription, gave her some further advice and then was struck by another question.

'Who cut your mother's hair?'

Carole looked astonished.

'Mam's hair,' she said. 'I don't know. Years ago it used to be Muriel Jones. But she died two—three years ago. Since then I don't know. But it always looked tidy, didn't it? Apart from the colour. I think she did that herself.'

She grinned and sallied out of the surgery clutching her prescription like a trophy. And now Megan had finished for the weekend. It stretched ahead of her with promise.

She drove home past Bethesda Street and noticed an aged yellow VW Golf pulled up outside Mervyn Jones' house, parked next to the blue Celica, with the *Cariad* numberplate.

She was forced to pull in to let another car thread through as the street had been reduced to one lane by the close parking. A woman came out of a door, descended the steps and unlocked the Toyota.

She was a young woman in her late twenties with long, brown hair and she was heavily pregnant. She turned and waved to someone in the house before climbing into the car and turning over the engine. Megan drove off.

There must be plenty of pregnant women in Llancloudy. The woman who drove the Cariad car was not necessarily Alun's wife.

*   *   *

She'd had plans to go to a concert in Cardiff that night; the Manic Street Preachers were playing in the Millennium Stadium. But there was a message on her answering machine that her friend had the 'flu and she didn't want to go alone. It was a bit late to ring round other friends. She tried two or three, got no answer and gave up. She glanced through the paper but there was nothing she wanted to watch on the TV.

She felt fidgety. She would walk down to the video shop and rent a film.

*   *   *

Ryan and Mark were hanging around outside, both of them dragging away at cigarettes. They eyed her warily.

'Hi,' she said. 'How are you?'

She ignored their fags. This wasn't the time for Health Education. They wouldn't have taken any notice anyway.

'We're all right.'

'No news then, about Stefan?'

Both of them looked at the floor and she knew their friend's disappearance had cut very deep. She also knew that it had frightened them, unnerved them.

'Heard anything from the police?'

They shook their heads in unison. Mark chucked his cigarette away. It fizzed in a puddle.

Megan jerked her head towards the lurid posters in the video shop window. 'Recommend any good films?'

'*Hannibal.*'

'*Texas Chain Saw*—'

'Not my cup of tea. Too gory.'

'But you're dealing with blood all day.'

She laughed. 'Not in the quantities Hollywood use.'

They laughed too. Mark mumbling, 'Anyway, it's just fake.' Ryan gave him a swift glance.

She broke the taboo.

'Did Stefan have a row with anyone?'

Mark looked at her. 'What do you mean?'

'Did someone threaten him? Did he make anyone angry?'

Ryan stared at her with pity. 'We're always annoyin' someone,' he said. 'Someone's always shoutin' at us.' And they scuffed away, down the street, hands deep into their pockets. Megan watched them go with a feeling of frustration.

*　　*　　*

She selected a film, a Merchant Ivory classic but something was niggling at her all the way home. However good the film she would find it hard to concentrate. She was far too agitated. A night's clubbing would be more appropriate than a polite film to blot up all this excess energy. Maybe she should have gone to the concert alone.

The police car had stopped a little way up the road but she knew it was Alun even before she put her key in the door and felt his hand behind her. 'Meggie,' he said.

He followed her inside. She threw the video on the sofa. 'Good to see you, Alun.'

'You too.'

'I—I—'

'I don't know what I'm doing here,' he said awkwardly. 'I should be at home, really.'

She nodded.

'Well—as you're here you may as well sit

311

down.'

He sat opposite her and they smiled awkwardly. 'I worry about you, Meggie.'

She moved then, knelt on the floor and looked up at him. 'I'm all right, Alun. I'll be OK now. It's been a bad year. But now I'm fine.'

'I wish,' he began but she shushed him with a finger on his lips.

'We move on,' she said. 'It's the best way—to move on. Put the past behind us, change. There was a point in time when we were—could have been. But we moved on.'

'Did you love me?'

She nodded and touched the thick, wiry hair. 'I did,' she said. 'Of course I did. Don't you know,' she teased, 'that your first love imprints on your mind so anyone you meet after that is compared to them?'

He had beautiful eyes, dark green-brown, fringed with thick black eyelashes. She still loved those eyes.

'Is that true?'

'Oh yes.'

His arms were around her. 'Then . . .'

She pulled away. 'But you can't lose what you have—a wife, practically two children.'

'But it isn't perfect, Meggie.'

She felt suddenly weary. 'Nothing ever is. If it seems so then we are deceived.'

He drew her hair into a pony-tail, tilted her face up to his. An age-old, well-remembered

312

gesture.

'Do you really think if you dumped your own family what we'd have could be anywhere near perfect?'

He nuzzled her neck and didn't answer.

'Do you really think you could live with your conscience?'

Again he didn't answer.

'Look around you, Alun. How many families stay together in this area? Not so many. Keep yours.'

He was staring at her woodenly, his breath coming in short gasps.

'I mean it,' she said. 'You're walking down Memory Lane. It's too late.'

He tried to pull her back to him but she felt disheartened. The image of the woman in the blue Celica depressed her. She whispered, *'Cariad.'*

'The sun always shines down Memory Lane,' she said bitterly. 'The birds never stop singing, the flowers are brightly coloured and always in bloom. Nothing ever dies down Memory Lane.'

He came to, let go of her hair, sat back in his chair. 'I'm sorry,' he said. 'I couldn't help it. I'll always carry a torch for you, Meggie.'

And I for you.

'But you're right. I have responsibilities. And you did leave me. Besides, I am happy with Sandra.'

She rejected the last part of his statement.

'Anyway I didn't only come to talk to you on a personal basis,' he said. 'I've got a bit of news for you. I don't think any of this is going to be relevant but it's come up on the PNC and I thought you'd want to know.'

She moved away farther. 'What?'

'There had been complaints,' he said, 'about all of them, logged on at some time. Hughes, the teacher, George and Neil and Marie Walker too.'

'What sort of complaints?'

'Oh—general nuisance. Hughes—you know about. A few parents had said they were uncomfortable with the way he dealt with their children. Nothing specific, you understand, otherwise we'd have acted.'

'And what about George and Neil?'

'Vandalism. They'd smashed up a couple of phone boxes, nicked money, and a couple of weeks later they'd broken the glass in the bus shelters. That sort of thing. They'd been cautioned more than once.'

'And Stefan?'

'Him too.'

'The same sort of thing?'

'Yes. You know, shop windows broken, incivilities. Underage drinkin' on the street.'

'Alun,' she said, 'what are you saying?'

'That they weren't wanted here. Llancloudy didn't want them.'

She turned around then with a smile touching her face. 'So are you telling me that

Llancloudy disposed of them?'

He laughed, uncomfortably. 'Don't be silly.'

She reached up then and touched his face, remembering the first, awkward, embarrassed time they had made love. The memory was strong, particularly when she searched his eyes. It had stayed with her, vivid enough to make her want him again.

This time it was she who blushed.

CHAPTER TWENTY-THREE

She knew where to look. Bianca had pointed the way, Geraint Smithson too.

She had buried it deep. But now it was time. Everything was falling into place—the reason why a name on the side of one of the boxes had struck a chord.

It was late when Alun left. She had stood on the doorstep and waited until his car had turned the corner before closing the door behind him. There was a frost. The night was pure and happy. Angels called. The stars glistened far above her. It would soon be Christmas.

And Alun's wife would bear him a second child.

*   *   *

315

Early the next morning she drove to Barbara's house. It had the look of a sleeping home. No lights were on. The curtains were still drawn. The front door was shut. She pulled up on the flattened tip and sat for a moment, savouring the warmth from the car heater, wrapping her fleece around her. But the minute she climbed out she could still sense the chill subterranean breath whisper to her. She locked the car door behind her.

*   *   *

A mist hovered over the rugby pitch, which looked like a stage empty of actors. As she crossed to the far end she was dwarfed by the huge 'H' bars with their thick padding wrapped around the bottom. And suddenly she was a child again, shrunk down like Alice, staring up at the crossbar and wondering how the ball could possibly be kicked over.

But her errand was not here.

Resolutely she continued to the edge and lost herself in the malicious gorse. Her skin was scratched before she'd penetrated even fifty yards. For a swift moment she glanced back at the empty pitch.

'Pass it yer, mun. Take it out to the side. Don't drop the ball, my boy.' She saw the grimace of an ambushed player felled. Not recent. Not Alun but long ago, as a child, when she had sat on her father's shoulders to gain a grandstand view of

316

the police team playing the local pub. The Oddfellows' Arms. 'A friendly.' By then she had grown too big to sit on Daddy's shoulders for the entire match so he had set her down. But she had been plenty big enough to run away and wander through the undergrowth, find a path beneath the gorse, scrabble on hands and knees, lose the people. That had been the day she had found the ventilation shaft which she imagined then must lead right down into the centre of the earth. She had lain on her stomach and peered down the side of the hole. And been terrified by a sudden vision.

Megan stood for a brief moment, turning through ninety degrees, away from the pitch to face the winding wheel at the head of the valley and had a vision of the men, faces blackened with coal dust, singing. And she longed for a return of this togetherness which had been at the heart of the coal industry, dying throughout the second half of the twentieth century, almost dead by the time she had been born.

She re-entered the pictures which were flashing through her mind like a flipchart. Suppressed for years but sparked subliminally into life by Bianca's concerns.

'Little Rhiann is dead. Definitely dead.'

She had felt that too.

She had dropped a pebble and waited for it to land. Her father was reading her a story.

Deep in the bowels of the earth was where

Gollum lived. Gollum of the huge eyes and the blanched skin, of the lisping, whispering voice, wanting his 'pessus'.

Scratching the floor with his long, long fingers. Down there.

She knelt down and peered through the grill into the deep, black hole. That day while her father had been engrossed in a rugby match she had believed that she had found the entrance to Gollum's lair. With her eyes tight shut she had counted to twenty . . . thirty . . . forty believing that when she opened them again he would be peering up at her, blinking at the light with his horrid, pale eyes. She stared at the iron grid, marvelling at how well she had retained the entire memory. She had been a child of ten years old when three-year-old Rhiann Lewis had vanished. Ten was a little old for her parents to worry over a brief absence from the side of a crowded rugby field. But her own parents, like all the other mothers and fathers in Llancloudy, must have been twitched with fear for their own child's safety. And transmitted those fears to her. So that day as soon as they had missed her they had panicked. She could still recall her father's face when she had reappeared from between the gorse bushes, scratched and bleeding. There had been no opportunity for explanation. He had shouted at her, hugged her, cried in front of her, finally bundled her into the car and raced her home.

There her grandmother had made dark reference to Rhiann. And her mother had made her promise she would never never wander off again.

*   *   *

All she knew was that she had been very bad. And in great danger.

*   *   *

But that night Gollum had entered her dreams by climbing up the iron footholes set in the side of the rock. Hand over hand. Slow foot behind foot. Inexorably coming towards the surface. Coming for her. She had tried to run back to her father. But children in dreams can find themselves unable to move. Her feet had been stuck to the floor. And webbed—like his. She had screamed as he had rattled the grid. And then she had woken up, her head against her father's shoulder, his pyjama jacket wet with tears. For weeks Gollum had haunted her, made her too frightened to sleep. She had altered in character then, slept with her light on, developed a terror of the dark, formed other habits she as a doctor would now label obsessional; washing hands, avoiding walking

319

on cracks in paving stones, under ladders, feeling a fear for the entire world outside. And it had all stemmed from the combination of that one book, and this place. And something else which until now she had locked inside her memory because while she had known Gollum was fantasy, something else was not.

*   *   *

Megan sat back on her haunches and forced herself to see that day with clarity. Why had Bianca's reference to 'Little Rhiann' disturbed her? Why had she had such a conviction that she had known something for years about the child's disappearance that no one else shared? And why had that secret knowledge been tinged with sick guilt?

At any time since she had been ten years old she could clearly have visualised every single bar or fragment of rust or the locks that secured this grid and kept her safe from Gollum.

If she had wanted to.

Now she looked again.

And saw. The screw heads that held the grid against the metal flange were rusted. But the grooves were shining silver. Even the grooves would have rusted had they not been touched for years. She ran her fingers over them and they felt sharp.

She touched the grid and remembered

something else, before she had been witched by the vision of Gollum. Her own fingers were reaching through the metal because she too wanted something. Caught on one of the rungs of the ladder was a tiny, red and gold hair elastic. Hair caught in it. Black and curly. Megan rolled back, felt the dampness of the grass, heard the sheep bleating.

Always complaining about something.

Complaining that a child's body lay here and no one cared. Barbara's mother had been right. They did have something to moan about.

*   *   *

She sat back on her haunches, ignored the assault of the gorse. And was oblivious to the soft rustling through the undergrowth.

The wind?

Again she peered down the shaft, and sensed a gasp of fetid air. She could just make out Gollum's iron rungs until they vanished. As they had vanished. Or not vanished. Were they down there? Was Bleddyn Hughes ready to grasp her with his long sensitive fingers and his destroyed reputation? Was he with the two little girls, Marie, still with her bag of chips, and Rhiann, missing her hair elastic. Were the boys waiting to mock her? All of them, George and Neil now joined by Stefan Parker. All of them except Bianca whose body lay in the churchyard of the Bethesda Chapel.

And Geraint Smithson who was the only one of all of them to have had a Christian burial?

The decay wafted up the shaft on a draught of coal-soiled air. And the voice was behind her now, whispering in Gollum's lisping tones.

'Don't you want to go down there, Meggie? Sssssee them all for yourssssself? How elssse are you going to convince the logical people of Llancloudy that they have harboured a killer in their midst for the last thirty years when they never have believed it before?'

*   *   *

The voice was right.

She peered over the edge. The iron rungs were inviting her to take a handhold, a foothold. She must go down.

The voice came from behind her now. *'You are mad. What do you think you will find down there?'*

'I must search for the vanished,' she said.

'And who are the vanished?'

'The people who disappeared without trace.'

'And you think you'll find them down there?' The voice was mocking her.

'I don't know. I can only look.'

'You are sadly deluded.'

'I hope so.'

'Do you think Bianca knew where they were?'

322

'I don't think so. Only that they never had left Llancloudy—any of them.'

'But Bianca was mad. How could she have known anything?'

'Sometimes the mad know more than the sane.'

'And if you find you are wrong?'

'Then I am wrong.'

'But if you are right?'

'I'm not sure.'

*   *   *

She did turn around then and saw nothing but the sun rising behind the high straight line of the hill. No one was there.

CHAPTER TWENTY-FOUR

She reached the car and tugged the door open, the mundane action dragging her back to normality; at the same time strengthening her resolve.

She *would* go down there. If they were there she would find them. The truth would finally be unearthed. And someone would be brought to justice. Not only for the vanishings but for the death of Bianca. The slurs, rumours and questions would stop.

In the back of her car she carried a flashlight—one of the necessary pieces of equipment for out-of-hours visiting. And also a small tool kit, plus a can of WD40. She grabbed them all, locked the car behind her and strode back across the rugby pitch, resolute. The action felt positive.

*   *   *

She was back at the grill in minutes. The screws were stiff. She sprayed them with the lubricant and tried again. And moved all six. But she dropped one down the shaft and heard it land far below. She felt a frisson of fear—and suppressed it.

Fear would not help but hinder her.

She lifted the cover and dropped it to the side, shining the torch downwards. All she could see were the iron rungs, vanishing into the void. She used her belt to secure the flashlight to her and stuck the toolkit in her kagoul pocket. Then she began her descent.

Hand under hand. Foot under foot, a metallic chink as her zip struck the iron. She glanced up and saw the grey winter's day circled above her. The wind felt like ice. She continued the descent.

Into the dank unknown.

About thirty feet down the light had almost

vanished but the air had changed. There was a breeze that came from another direction. Across her face.

She flashed the light to her right and picked out a tunnel, about four feet in diameter. She could guess what it was—an early drift mine, probably worked in the eighteenth century. Later workings had been much much deeper.

If she had wanted to hide a body she might well have chosen here. Accessible, protected by an army of gorse thorns, well away from the rugby pitch. Not part of the main mine workings so not subject to the rigorous search. Few people would remember it was here. At a guess, the police would not have thought to search here.

There was another point in its favour. You could drive a car around the rugby pitch to within fifty yards of this place. And it would be concealed. A small dip in the land plus the thick vegetation ensured that necessary privacy.

*   *   *

She crawled along the tunnel, partly crouching, sometimes on her hands and knees, the beam of the torch shining ahead of her. When she had penetrated maybe six feet she stopped and shone the torch back. Against the opposite side of the mine shaft she could see the palest pool of daylight. Ahead the air was slightly stuffy, the temperature warmer than on the surface. The walls were chillingly damp. She flashed the beam ahead, hesitated. Were they there?

*   *   *

Thirty metres into the tunnel, the torch picked out a rock fall. Either natural or the tunnel had been deliberately collapsed when the last miners had vacated it. But it would be enough to halt her progress.

She must have been wrong. They were not here.

'Bugger,' she said out loud and listened to the walls mock her with an echo.

'Bugger . . . Bugger . . . Bugger . . .'

So had she been wrong?

She flashed her torch up and down the rockfall and realised that a few of the top boulders had tumbled. In fact it was not a blind ending. There was a way over the top.

She strapped her torch to her wrist and clambered over. It was tricky. The rocks were loose and shaley, likely to tumble and she could see nothing ahead. Besides, the air here was not pure. She had a suffocating attack of claustrophobia and tried to use one hand to flash the torch ahead. *If she could only see something she could return to the top, persuade a professional team to search here for Stefan.*

It was a mistake.

She lost her grip on the torch and it slithered down the other side. The light shone uselessly into a corner, illuminating nothing but dark rock.

And someone was coming down the rungs.

Hand under hand. Foot under foot with the familiarity and deliberation of someone who had done this before.

Instinctively she clung to the rocks, tried to scrabble to the other side.

He was coming back.

A voice bounced along the walls towards her.

'Hello . . . Hello . . . Hello . . . ?'

She knew better than to answer.

If only she could reach the torch, switch it off, hide.

Where?

The footsteps stopped. She heard the sound of feet on loose stone. The voice came again. Distorted by its echo. 'Hello . . . hello . . . hello.'

And then a light. Dancing along the sides of the tunnel like a Will o' The Wisp. Searching for her.

She crouched behind the stones.

'I know you're there . . . . *there . . . there . . . I* saw your car . . . *car . . . car.*'

All she could see was a powerful beam. She stretched out, found her own torch, switched it off and fought to control her breathing. The worst thing was she didn't know who it was. Like a child in a lethal game of hide and seek she convinced herself that if she didn't answer he could not be sure she was here.

The light came nearer. 'Don't make things difficult, there's a good girl.'

He was near.

'Come on. What are you frightened of?'

Of Gollum. And a man who makes people disappear. I am frightened of whoever killed Bianca and Geraint Smithson and took Stefan. I am frightened of death. I am frightened of never seeing daylight again.

She backed up the tunnel.

He must have heard her. 'You can't get out along there. It's a blind ending. Look, I know you're there.'

He was near.

She tried to peer beyond the flashlight. But she saw nothing. No one.

'Why did you come?' It was a reasonable voice, distorted only by the confined atmosphere. She grabbed her flashlight and turned it on.

Rumpelstiltstkin blinked into the beam.

'Mr Jones,' she said. 'What are *you* doing here?'

He lowered his torch and blinked at her light. 'More to the point, doctor, what are you doing down here?'

'I thought . . . I wondered.' *She could not tell him what she had thought.*

'When I saw your car I asked myself where on earth you had gone. Maybe up the mountain. But it isn't the day for a walk. I came wandering through the gorse and then I saw you'd taken the grill off. I thought you must have taken leave of your senses to come down here. It's not safe. Why have you come?'

This was the voice of normality. She had been wrong. He was not the killer. It was simply Mervyn Jones, worried for her safety.

She scrabbled back towards him. But again she dropped the flashlight. And this time its beam did not pick out bare wall but something else. A scrap of material. Pointed and striped. The end of a tie. A red and brown tie which had been knotted around a schoolboy's neck.

Then she screamed. And the tunnel filled with horror.

They *were* here. All of them. Bleddyn Hughes with his long fingers, the children.

And Jones was scrabbling over the rocks towards her. She turned the torch back on him. He put his arm up to shield his eyes. 'What's the matter?'

She stared up at him in terror and suddenly his anger exploded.

'You had to come, didn't you? Poke your nose in to things that don't concern you. What *business* is it of yours?'

She gaped at him but her hand holding the torch was steady. His anger was calming her.

She knew now. Behind her were the vanished. Ahead was . . .

She dared not think ahead. She felt a

329

suffocating terror. And the air was fetid. Full of death.

She must get out.

Otherwise . . . She whimpered. *Otherwise . . .*

'I don't understand why,' she said. 'What were they to you?'

'No, you wouldn't understand, would you? They weren't annoying you,' he said. 'You, the doctor, you got the respect.'

'Then tell me why,' she said. 'Start with the beginning. Start with Bleddyn Hughes.'

'Hughes.' He spat out the name. 'This was a good place once. We worked hard all day. And on Sundays we attended chapel. The mines shut and slowly Llancloudy was destroyed, its people weakened by indolence. And who by? People of low moral fibre. Like Hughes. He was a no good. I caught him one day, reading poetry to my Muriel. Trying to woo her, he was. I knew what dirty little games he was playing. Showing up my ignorance. And it wasn't my fault I wasn't *educated* like him. What parents could afford education? Use big words, he would, at the table, just to impress and show off, knowing I would not be able to understand. Oh yes, I knew what sort of a person he was.'

'You let the papers destroy his reputation. You let people think . . .' Her voice trailed away, its echoes no more than a whisper. *'Think . . . think.'*

'I told them a thing or two.' It was said with

smug satisfaction. 'I'm not responsible for what the papers choose to print.'

'You—?'

'Oh, yes. Easy really when you know how.'

She tried to block out the calm complacency in his voice. It chilled her more than his anger.

'But Rhiann? She was only a child. What could she have done to you?'

'Know her family, do you?'

A swift vision of Gwen Owen's endless voice gave her some, tiny insight.

'All make too much noise. The child, Rhiann, she was the same. Always noisy. Never—shut—up. Chattering, singing. They lived in the street behind us. I'd been on nights makin' sure the mines didn't flood. Keepin' the people of this little place safe while *they* slept. But was I allowed to sleep? No. All I asked for was some peace and quiet. I wanted to sleep with my windows open in the fresh, clean air. I tried. For an hour or more I tried to sleep. I put ear plugs in. But the little girl kept on and on makin' a noise. Until I couldn't stand it any more. So I got up and went round the back. Come 'ere, my little darlin', open the door now to your Uncle Merv.'

She could picture it, the little girl, innocently pulling back the bolt. She closed her eyes then slid the beam along the floor. He was blocking the tunnel. She would have to push past him. But he was a small man, and not young. She was strong. She should be able to do it. Her torch wavered. His was shining directly on her. He must have caught some lack of concentration, a wavering of her purpose.

'It's no use your thinkin' you're getting out of here. You won't get past me, *Doctor* Megan Banesto, educated pride of the valleys. Fool of Llancloudy who goes on holiday and marries a waiter who only wants to be with the boys.'

Now she felt angry too. But she concealed it. Later she would use it. Against him.

'Marie—?' she began.

'Thought herself *very* clever. Was fond of baiting me, throwing her filthy chip and sweet papers, coke cans, right into my garden. But I got her. Chuckin' her rubbish away. I got her— in the end.'

The tone was the same; smug satisfaction. Jones was pleased with himself.

'The boys? George and Neil?' She already knew the answer. Some act of mindless vandalism, or rudeness.

'Little bloody vandals. Always up to something. Hated the pair of them. Well, if their parents weren't goin' to do something about them then I was.'

His tone had altered. Now he was the avenging angel.

'But Bianca? She wasn't like that.'

'No-o.' The first sign of hesitation. 'Not like that. She used to come round and ask me to cut her hair after Muriel died. I didn't mind her too much. At first.'

The light from his torch was wavering behind her. She dared not look for fear of what she would see . . .

'But I made a mistake. I talked to her one day about the people who had disappeared. I said this place was the better for some of its inhabitants being under the ground. And then she started with her mad stories of trolls. I heard her one day clacking away to Smithson. 'Mr Jones knows about the trolls too', she said, 'what take people.' Mad sad woman that she was. Only even mad as she was at some point someone was going to listen to her stories about 'flying plates' and people who'd disappeared. And Mr Jones who knew they were underground. I couldn't take that risk. Not any more. I'd had enough of her. But she was so damned easy. I must say. I enjoyed tipping her in that filthy pond.'

'Not alive?'

'What would it matter to you?' The anger was back. 'As it happens, no. I just kept giving her stuff to keep her under. I even tried to be humane. She was no more than an animal after all; not responsible for her actions like the others. But she fell over and banged her head. And I put her under the water in the bath to make sure she was dead then took her up the pool in my car, late on the Sunday night when nobody was around. I must say it was quite exciting being the one to draw everyone's attention to the clothes floating near the

333

surface of the pool. For the first time I could see why people actually *want* the bodies to be found. It is much more rewarding. Of course, it was a bit of a shame it wasn't a murder investigation. That would have livened up Llancloudy. But all the same.'

'Did she know you were the one?'

'Know?' He was shouting. 'Bianca know? She didn't *know* anything.'

'Then what harm . . . ?'

'Maybe none. Maybe some. I couldn't take the risk.'

'Smithson?' she asked faintly.

Again she sensed doubt, maybe even grief. 'I watched my old friend, Caspian, dying of lung disease knowing old Smithson was behind it all. And only two rooms away. Ranting and raving like he was sorry. Sorry . . .'

The words bounced along the sides of the tunnel. 'Sorry . . . sorry . . . sorry . . .'

'He wasn't sorry. He didn't have an ounce of regret in his dirty soul. He was an arrogant heathen, a pig. I stuffed a pillow over his face and rejoiced when he was dead.'

She could guess now about Stefan. The broken windscreen must have finally sealed his fate.

And now there was her fate, hanging in the delicate balance of life and death. And if she died no one would ever know what had happened. She would be another vanishing, turned eventually into a pile of stories in yellowing newspapers in a crazy person's house.

It was as though Mervyn Jones' thoughts had shifted along the same plane. She could sense it, a swift turn of direction, a fumbling in his pocket, the beam of his torch wavering away from her face.

She tasted fear like bile. Fumbled in her pocket for something. A weapon. Something from the toolkit.

But Jones knew.

And the tunnel was too close a space.

He lunged and she felt something small and sharp graze her.

He had a knife.

'Now come here, my lovely,' he said. 'Just come here, to your Uncle Merv.'

She smelt the hatred in his voice.

But she felt it too. She hated him. Who did he think he was? *The avenging angel of Llancloudy? His the right to be judge, jury, executioner?*

It would not be.

He was nearing, his hand outstretched.

She could have touched him.

She remembered a long ago talk, aimed at Health Service employees. Eyes, testicles and drop.

She dropped her torch and jabbed outstretched fingers at his eyes. And felt them connect. He screamed. Then she jerked her knee up. Hard.

And heard him scramble to the floor, the

335

torch beside him, beaming against her feet.

She used them next. Kicking him harder and harder with all the viciousness she could summon up. She kicked him and listened to his screams without pity. The tunnel filled with the sounds. Then she ran, crouching low, towards the bottom of the ladder.

Hand over hand. Foot over foot. Back towards the small, pale light.

CHAPTER TWENTY-FIVE

An hour later and drama was screaming around her. Blue lights flashed, police everywhere, men in white suits, radios. Noise. She sat and shivered in her car feeling as though she would stay cold and frightened for the rest of her life.

They'd roped in cavers and potholers and ex-miners with lights fixed to hard hats, bulky equipment and ropes. A pathologist had been summoned down there too, to carry out his grim examination. At some point a small figure with a blanket flung over his head was bundled into a black Maria and she was told she would need to attend the police station and make a statement.

Again a crowd of voyeurs had gathered. The people of Llancloudy were curious, standing round in whispering clusters, spreading rumours,

336

guessing. Because they did not know the truth. Yet.

Megan sat and shivered, longing to go home, to have a hot bath, to blot this all from her memory. Pretend none of it had happened. That it was nothing but a bad dream. And she would wake soon, feeling refreshed.

The area was ribboned off with official tape. An important looking police officer, resplendent in his uniform disappeared behind the gorse bush only to reappear some while later looking grim and cold.

And then the bodies were brought up, zipped into dark blue vinyl bags. Six of them, some smaller than others, one very tiny. It only took one WPC to cradle this one.

Megan watched.

So Lift them up tenderly
Take them with Care

*　　*　　*

Then Alun arrived and crossed to her and she shot out of the car and clung to him, ignoring the fact that Police Constable Nigel Jenkins was standing at his side, embarrassed and uncomfortable. Alun held her tightly, stroking her hair as though she was a child. Once he pressed his lips to her. But only for a few seconds before his grip on her arm pulled her away. 'What the bloody hell do you think you were doing. He could have killed you, Meggie.

337

And we might never have found you. You utter, stupid, absolute idiot.'

Then her tears came. His anger had finally thawed her.

'I'll take you down the station,' he said finally. 'You'll have to make a statement. Do you want me to run you home first to take a bath?'

She shook her head. 'I'd never get out of it.'

Alun sighed. 'All right then. Leave us your keys and someone'll drop the Calibra back at your place and leave the keys with a neighbour. Come on, girl.'

She wiped her nose and Alun took a handkerchief out of his pocket. 'You do look a sight,' he said reprovingly.

*   *   *

All the way to the station he was reproaching her. 'I don't know what possessed you . . . I don't suppose it would have occurred to you to tell us of your suspicions.'

'But I didn't know. I was only guessing.'

'We'd have searched that damned tunnel even on the strength of a guess. Do you think we don't listen when people tell us things?'

She said nothing, but stared resentfully into the passenger mirror.

*   *   *

338

He had to force a way through the watchers by turning both the light and the siren on. She knew most of the faces that pressed against the car, Carole Symmonds, holding the hand of a youth half her age, Ryan and Mark, grimacing, Gwen Owen. They all saw her and she wondered what the stories flying around Llancloudy would soon be.

That she was the killer?

That she had found the bodies because . . . ?

That she had been arrested . . . for . . .

She smiled. She didn't care any more.

Alun glanced across. 'Now that's my girl,' he said.

She dabbed her face with the hankie a little more and saw his face lighten until he smiled. 'You are such a damned . . .'

She waited.

'Woman.'

And she smiled again.

CHAPTER TWENTY-SIX

Alun called to see her a month later. On a cold day when snow had iced the tops of the mountains, the fires were lit and people were staying indoors. 'I've had my wish,' he said proudly. 'I thought you'd want to know. Another little boy.'

She kissed him on the cheek. 'You'll have

your rugby team soon.'

He nodded.

She knew she must ask the question. 'Your wife?' she said.

'She's fine. Tired but fine.'

That wasn't what she had wanted him to say.

'I'm glad,' she began but she knew Alun had more to say.

'We've had all the results of the postmortems typed up and decent.'

'And?'

'I don't know whether you really want to know this,' he said.

She shrugged.

'Hughes had had his throat cut. The pathologist found knife marks on his jaw. We've had positive ID from dental records and the clothes he was wearing. Marie Walker and Rhiann had been strangled. Manually, we think,' he said. 'No sign of a ligature. But some bone had been broken.'

'The hyoid,' she said automatically. 'And the boys?'

'Strangled too, Stefan—'

'With his tie.' She finished for him.

Alun nodded. 'There's more. We've just had word from Jones' solicitor. Believe it or not he's pleading insanity—or at least balance of mind disturbed—and all that. And we think the CPS will probably accept the plea.'

'Which means?'

'He'll be detained,' Alun said, 'but not in a

340

prison. In an approved institution.'

'For life?'

'Probably.'

She nodded. There was an awkward silence between them. Alun looked across at her, for once sensing something he didn't understand.

'Your wife,' she said.

He looked uncomfortable.

'What colour car does she drive?'

'Blue.'

'I see.'

The word Cariad mocked her.

'What make,' she asked sharply

'A Corsa,' he said. 'A Vauxhall,' and she felt nothing but relief.

'And what was all that about?'

'Nothing,' she said. 'Absolutely bloody nothing.'

*   *   *

Who in the rainbow can draw the line where the violet tint ends and the orange tint begins? Distinctly we see the difference of the color, but where exactly does the first one visibly enter into the other? So with sanity and insanity. In pronounced cases there is no question about them. But in some cases, in various degrees supposedly less pronounced, to draw the line of demarkation few will undertake, though for a fee some professional expert will.

Billy Budd, Herman Melville.

*   *   *

There would be more funerals in the valleys.

We hope you have enjoyed this Large Print book. Other Chivers Press or Thorndike Press Large Print books are available at your library or directly from the publishers.

For more information about current and forthcoming titles, please call or write, without obligation, to:

Chivers Press Limited
Windsor Bridge Road
Bath BA2 3AX
England
Tel. (01225) 335336

OR

Thorndike Press
295 Kennedy Memorial Drive
Waterville
Maine 04901
USA

All our Large Print titles are designed for easy reading, and all our books are made to last.